Wish Pendant

A Wish Pendant is a powerful accessory worn by a Star Darling. On Wishworld, it helps her identify her Wisher and store the ever-important wish energy.

Power Crystal

Once a Star Darling has granted her first wish and returns to Starland, she receives a very special treasure—a beautiful Power Crystal.

DRUMS

Instrument

Each girl in the Star Darlings band has a unique musical talent that helps her light up the stage.

Scarlet Discovers True Strength

ALSO BY SHANA MULDOON ZAPPA AND AHMET ZAPPA

Sage and the Journey to Wishworld

Libby and the Class Election

Leona's Unlucky Mission

Vega and the Fashion Disaster

ALSO BY AHMET ZAPPA

Because I'm Your Dad

The Monstrous Memoirs of a Mighty McFearless

DON'T MISS

A Wisher's Guide to Starland

COMING SOON

Cassie Comes Through

Scarlet Discovers True Strength

Shana Muldoon Zappa and Ahmet Zappa
with Zelda Rose

Disney Press
Los Angeles • New York

For information address Disney Press,
1101 Flower Street, Glendale, California 91201.

Printed in the United States of America
Reinforced Binding
First Paperback Edition, January 2016
1 3 5 7 9 10 8 6 4 2

FAC-029261-15324

Library of Congress Control Number: 2015946377
ISBN 978-1-4847-1424-9

For more Disney Press fun, visit www.disneybooks.com

To our beautiful, sweet treasure,
Halo Violetta Zappa. You are pure light and joy
and our greatest inspiration. We love you soooo much.

May every step upon your path be blessed with positivity and the understanding that you have the power within you to manifest the most fulfilling life you can possibly imagine and more. May you always remember that being different and true to your highest self makes your inner star shine brighter.

Remember that you have the power of choice. . . . Choose thoughts that feel good. Choose love and friendship that feed your spirit. Choose actions for peace and nourishment. Choose boundaries for the same. Choose what speaks to your creativity and unique inner voice . . . what truly makes you happy. And always know that no matter what you choose, you are unconditionally loved.

Look up to the stars and know you are never alone.
When in doubt, go within . . . the answers are all there.
Smiles light the world and laughter is the best medicine.
And NEVER EVER stop making wishes. . . .

Glow for it. . . .
Mommy and Daddy

And to everyone else here on "Wishworld":

May you realize that no matter where you are in life, no matter what you look like or where you were born, you, too, have the power within you to create the life of your dreams. Through celebrating your own uniqueness, thinking positively, and taking action, you can make your wishes come true.

Smile. The Star Darlings have your back.
We know how startastic you truly are.

Glow for it. . . .
Your friends,
Shana and Ahmet

Student Reports

NAME: Clover
BRIGHT DAY: January 5
FAVORITE COLOR: Purple
INTERESTS: Music, painting, studying
WISH: To be the best songwriter and DJ on Starland
WHY CHOSEN: Clover has great self-discipline, patience, and willpower. She is creative, responsible, dependable, and extremely loyal.
WATCH OUT FOR: Clover can be hard to read and she is reserved with those she doesn't know. She's afraid to take risks and can be a wisecracker at times.
SCHOOL YEAR: Second
POWER CRYSTAL: Panthera
WISH PENDANT: Barrette

NAME: Adora
BRIGHT DAY: February 14
FAVORITE COLOR: Sky blue
INTERESTS: Science, thinking about the future and how she can make it better
WISH: To be the top fashion designer on Starland
WHY CHOSEN: Adora is clever and popular and cares about the world around her. She's a deep thinker.
WATCH OUT FOR: Adora can have her head in the clouds and be thinking about other things.
SCHOOL YEAR: Third
POWER CRYSTAL: Azurica
WISH PENDANT: Watch

NAME: Piper
BRIGHT DAY: March 4
FAVORITE COLOR: Seafoam green
INTERESTS: Composing poetry and writing in her dream journal
WISH: To become the best version of herself she can possibly be and to share that by writing books
WHY CHOSEN: Piper is giving, kind, and sensitive. She is very intuitive and aware.
WATCH OUT FOR: Piper can be dreamy, absentminded, and wishy-washy. She can also be moody and easily swayed by the opinions of others.
SCHOOL YEAR: Second
POWER CRYSTAL: Dreamalite
WISH PENDANT: Bracelets

Starling Academy

NAME: Astra
BRIGHT DAY: April 9
FAVORITE COLOR: Red
INTERESTS: Individual sports
WISH: To be the best athlete on Starland—to win!
WHY CHOSEN: Astra is energetic, brave, clever, and confident. She has boundless energy and is always direct and to the point.
WATCH OUT FOR: Astra is sometimes cocky, self-centered, condescending, and brash.
SCHOOL YEAR: Second
POWER CRYSTAL: Quarrelite
WISH PENDANT: Wristbands

NAME: Tessa
BRIGHT DAY: May 18
FAVORITE COLOR: Emerald green
INTERESTS: Food, flowers, love
WISH: To be successful enough that she can enjoy a life of luxury
WHY CHOSEN: Tessa is warm, charming, affectionate, trustworthy, and dependable. She has incredible drive and commitment.
WATCH OUT FOR: Tessa does not like to be rushed. She can be quite stubborn and often says no. She does not deal well with change and is prone to exaggeration. She can be easily sidetracked.
SCHOOL YEAR: Third
POWER CRYSTAL: Gossamer
WISH PENDANT: Brooch

NAME: Gemma
BRIGHT DAY: June 2
FAVORITE COLOR: Orange
INTERESTS: Sharing her thoughts about almost anything
WISH: To be valued for her opinions on everything
WHY CHOSEN: Gemma is friendly, easygoing, funny, extroverted, and social. She knows a little bit about everything.
WATCH OUT FOR: Gemma talks—a lot—and can be a little too honest sometimes and offend others. She can have a short attention span and can be superficial.
SCHOOL YEAR: First
POWER CRYSTAL: Scatterite
WISH PENDANT: Earrings

Student Reports

NAME: Cassie
BRIGHT DAY: July 6
FAVORITE COLOR: White
INTERESTS: Reading, crafting
WISH: To be more independent and confident and less fearful
WHY CHOSEN: Cassie is extremely imaginative and artistic. She is a voracious reader and is loyal, caring, and a good friend. She is very intuitive.
WATCH OUT FOR: Cassie can be distrustful, jealous, moody, and brooding.
SCHOOL YEAR: First
POWER CRYSTAL: Lunalite
WISH PENDANT: Glasses

NAME: Leona
BRIGHT DAY: August 16
FAVORITE COLOR: Gold
INTERESTS: Acting, performing, dressing up
WISH: To be the most famous pop star on Starland
WHY CHOSEN: Leona is confident, hardworking, generous, open-minded, optimistic, caring, and a strong leader.
WATCH OUT FOR: Leona can be vain, opinionated, selfish, bossy, dramatic, and stubborn and is prone to losing her temper.
SCHOOL YEAR: Third
POWER CRYSTAL: Glisten paw
WISH PENDANT: Cuff

NAME: Vega
BRIGHT DAY: September 1
FAVORITE COLOR: Blue
INTERESTS: Exercising, analyzing, cleaning, solving puzzles
WISH: To be the top student at Starling Academy
WHY CHOSEN: Vega is reliable, observant, organized, and very focused.
WATCH OUT FOR: Vega can be opinionated about everything, and she can be fussy, uptight, critical, arrogant, and easily embarrassed.
SCHOOL YEAR: Second
POWER CRYSTAL: Queezle
WISH PENDANT: Belt

Starling Academy

NAME: Libby
BRIGHT DAY: October 12
FAVORITE COLOR: Pink
INTERESTS: Helping others, interior design, art, dancing
WISH: To give everyone what they need—both on Starland and through wish granting on Wishworld
WHY CHOSEN: Libby is generous, articulate, gracious, diplomatic, and kind.
WATCH OUT FOR: Libby can be indecisive and may try too hard to please everyone.
SCHOOL YEAR: First
POWER CRYSTAL: Charmelite
WISH PENDANT: Necklace

NAME: Scarlet
BRIGHT DAY: November 3
FAVORITE COLOR: Black
INTERESTS: Crystal climbing (and other extreme sports), magic, thrill seeking
WISH: To live on Wishworld
WHY CHOSEN: Scarlet is confident, intense, passionate, magnetic, curious, and very brave.
WATCH OUT FOR: Scarlet is a loner and can alienate others by being secretive, arrogant, stubborn, and jealous.
SCHOOL YEAR: Third
POWER CRYSTAL: Ravenstone
WISH PENDANT: Boots

NAME: Sage
BRIGHT DAY: December 1
FAVORITE COLOR: Lavender
INTERESTS: Travel, adventure, telling stories, nature, and philosophy
WISH: To become the best Wish-Granter Starland has ever seen
WHY CHOSEN: Sage is honest, adventurous, curious, optimistic, friendly, and relaxed.
WATCH OUT FOR: Sage has a quick temper! She can also be restless, irresponsible, and too trusting of others' opinions. She may jump to conclusions.
SCHOOL YEAR: First
POWER CRYSTAL: Lavenderite
WISH PENDANT: Necklace

Introduction

You take a deep breath, about to blow out the candles on your birthday cake. Clutching a coin in your fist, you get ready to toss it into the dancing waters of a fountain. You stare at your little brother as you each hold an end of a dried wishbone, about to pull. But what do you do first?

You make a wish, of course!

Ever wonder what happens right after you make that wish? *Not much*, you may be thinking.

Well, you'd be wrong.

Because something quite unexpected happens next. Each and every wish that is made becomes a glowing Wish Orb, invisible to the human eye. This undetectable orb zips through the air and into the heavens, on a one-way trip to the brightest star in the sky—a magnificent place called Starland. Starland is inhabited by Starlings, who look a lot like you and me, except they have a sparkly glow to their skin, and glittery hair in unique colors. And they have one more thing: magical powers. The Starlings use these powers to make good wishes come true, for when good wishes are granted, it results in positive energy. And the Starlings of Starland need this energy to keep their world running.

In case you are wondering, there are three kinds of Wish Orbs:

1) GOOD WISH ORBS. These wishes are positive and helpful and come from the heart. They are pretty and sparkly and are nurtured in climate-controlled Wish-Houses. They bloom into fantastical glowing orbs. When the time is right, they are presented to the appropriate Starling for wish fulfillment.
2) BAD WISH ORBS. These are for selfish, mean-spirited, or negative things. They don't sparkle

at all. They are immediately transported to a special containment center, as they are very dangerous and must not be granted.

3) IMPOSSIBLE WISH ORBS. These wishes are for things, like world peace and disease cures, that simply can't be granted by Starlings. These sparkle with an almost impossibly bright light and are taken to a special area of the Wish-House with tinted windows to contain the glare they produce. The hope is that one day they can be turned into good wishes the Starlings can help grant.

Starlings take their wish granting very seriously. There is a special school, called Starling Academy, that accepts only the best and brightest young Starling girls. They study hard for four years, and when they graduate, they are ready to start traveling to Wishworld to help grant wishes. For as long as anyone can remember, only graduates of wish-granting schools have ever been allowed to travel to Wishworld. But things have changed in a very big way.

Read on for the rest of the story. . . .

Prologue

"So you're saying Vega heard from her?"

"Cross my stars. A holo-text. She got it last night."

"Well, what did it say? Where has she been this whole time? Is she in Starland City? Did she run away?"

Scarlet recognized the Star Darlings' voices outside her window immediately. She didn't have to peer down, but she did. She could also tell right away that they were talking about her. *How dare they?* was all she could think.

Scarlet was perched up in the loft of her dorm room—her *new* dorm room—a place that, these stardays, she seldom left. It had all happened so fast it still felt like yesterday: Lady Stella's informing her that her being assigned to the Star Darlings was all a "starmendous and most unfortunate" mistake, and that, as a result, she would need to be reassigned to a new dorm room so her replacement—some meek-looking orange-haired first-year student—could move into hers. At first, Scarlet had looked at that, at least, as the silver lining, since she and her roommate, Leona, had been bickering. But it didn't take long for her to realize that there would never, in a moonium staryears, be any silver linings to the cloud she had found herself in.

"It didn't say where Scarlet's been, unfortunately." That tinkly voice belonged to Cassie. Scarlet gazed down at the top of the first-year student's silver-white pigtailed head. She and her roommate, Sage, were walking along the path between their Little Dipper Dorm building and the Big Dipper Dorm, where third and fourth years, like Scarlet, lived. Scarlet couldn't help smiling as she thought how clueless they were; she was right there, just two floors above them, and they had no idea. "All the holo-text said," Cassie went on, "was for Vega to meet her in the hedge maze . . . which makes me wonder if Scarlet's still here at school. . . ."

Sage tossed her long lavender hair dramatically from one shoulder to the other, a habit that had always made Scarlet roll her eyes. "I don't know," Sage said. "If Scarlet was at school, don't you think she'd go to classes? I mean, she's already been kicked out of the Star Darlings. Does she want to get kicked out of school, too?"

Kicked out! She nearly leaned out to yell, "I was not *kicked out*!"

"She wasn't kicked out . . ." said Cassie.

Thank you! thought Scarlet. Cassie always had seemed a little smarter than the rest.

". . . exactly. I mean, she didn't do anything wrong."

"Mistakes happen, I guess," Sage said. She shrugged and re-tossed her hair.

Mistakes . . . thought Scarlet. *Mistakes?* Accidently using your roommate's toothlight was a *mistake*. Being told that you, in fact, weren't Star Darlings material? That wasn't a *mistake*. It was just plain wrong!

"I don't know. . . ." Below, Cassie slowed to a stop, pulling Sage with her. Their arms were linked, as Starling arms usually were when they walked together.

"What?" said Sage.

"It's just . . . so many strange things are going on. There's poor Leona . . . ruining her Wish Pendant and not getting a Power Crystal when her mission was otherwise such a success."

"Well, wasn't that her fault? She never used her special powers."

"I know . . . but to ruin your Wish Pendant?" Cassie shook her head.

Above, Scarlet nodded sympathetically. Leona's ruined Wish Pendant didn't come close, of course, to Scarlet's losing her place as a Star Darling, but it had to hurt.

"And then, of course, there are those flowers," Cassie went on. "Have you noticed, by the way, that we aren't fighting anymore?"

"Oh, Cassie!" A laugh bubbled out of Sage as she started to pull Cassie forward. "You and your conspiracy theories. You are too cute! Really, you are."

CHAPTER 1

"Hellooooo?"

Scarlet turned from the window at the sound of a reedy, shrill voice calling from below. She slid from the window seat and peered down the stairs. "Who's there?" she said cautiously, not sure she wanted to know.

As she started down the curving ladder, a Starling came into view. It was a woman—an old woman, Scarlet could tell immediately—grinning and bent over a crystal-tipped cane.

"Hello?" Scarlet said. Her eyes swept the room uneasily for a glimpse of her roommate, Mira. "Er, excuse me," she said, not finding her, "but how did you get in?" Usually, Scarlet was the one sneaking up on people, not the other way around. Plus, as far as she knew, the only way to open the door was by using the palm scanner outside. Then it had to approve you. So how did the woman get in? "Er . . . can I help you?"

The little old Starling craned her neck to peer up at Scarlet. "Why, hello, and star salutations, dearie," she said sweetly. Her voice cracked with age. Wire-rimmed star-shaped glasses rested halfway down her nose, and silvery lilac curls framed her pinched but pleasant face. "As a matter of fact, you can. I'm looking for my granddaughter, Mira. The Bot-Bot guard at the front told me this was her room?"

"Oh . . ." That made a little more sense. Scarlet guessed family members' hands must work on the palm scanners, too. Not that she would know. After two and a half staryears at Starling Academy, her own family had still never visited her, not once. The only time Scarlet saw her parents was when she met them on tour. They were classical musicians and composers, famous throughout Starland for their otherworldly sounds and scores. Scarlet's mother played the halo-harp, her father the violin, and they traveled staryear-round throughout Starland, recording holo-albums and selling out the most prestigious concert halls. Even when they played in

Starland City, Starland's capital and the home of Starling Academy, rehearsals and interviews kept them so busy that Scarlet always had to go to them. Their schedules were simply too full to fit in a visit to the school.

Growing up, Scarlet had toured Starland with her parents, living out of suitcases, staying in five-star hotels. In between shows, her mother or father—depending on whose turn it was—would tutor her backstage as they tuned their precious instruments. By the time she had reached the Age of Fulfillment, Scarlet had met every dignitary on Starland—but not many other kids.

Scarlet's parents were naturally proud and not surprised when she showed an interest in music. They were astonished, however, when she chose to play the *drums* and began to wear a lot of black. At first, she'd just wanted to shock and annoy them and rebel against their stodgy ways. And she succeeded—particularly when she started adding black streaks to her hot-pink hair. Soon, though, she found herself loving the drums and her adopted color, too. Both made her feel strong. Both let her show her feelings without having to say a single word.

Still, Scarlet needed more. She needed a life that was truly her own, which was why she had applied to Starling Academy. She was stunned when she got in and sure she would struggle in her classes, but she found they were easy for her. The only things that were hard were fitting in and making friends.

"What's the matter, dearie?" The elder Starling chuckled. "Glowfur got your tongue?"

"Oh . . . star apologies," Scarlet said quickly. She was suddenly aware that she probably seemed rude. "Uh, yes. Yes, this is Mira's room. But, well . . ." She looked around and shrugged. "She's not here."

"Oh, what a pity!" The woman's face folded into a pained expression, like one of those comedy/tragedy masks that hung over Mira's bed. She sighed and shook her head slowly. "Well. I suppose I'll just wait for her, then. I should have told her I was coming. Hopefully she won't be long." She shuffled across the room, smiling sweetly and looking ever so slightly confused. "Please do forgive me for surprising you. I didn't realize she had a roommate, you see. I could have sworn the last time she wrote to me she said she lived alone."

"She did," said Scarlet. "I just moved in." She tried to sound less bitter than she felt.

"Ah, good!" said the old woman. "Glad to know I wasn't wrong." She tapped her head just above her ear. "Two thousand and three and still sharp as a prism. So what's your name, my dear?"

"It's, um, Scarlet."

"Scarlet! How lovely! We had a glowsow on the farm with that name when I was a girl. So!" She crossed the star-trimmed corners of her shawl. "Just moved in, you say. Does that mean you're new?"

"No, ma'am . . ." Scarlet shook her head and turned back to her loft, longing to climb back up. She was usually so glad her new roommate, Mira, was always at "play rehearsal," or whatever that drama stuff she loved so much was. For once, though, Scarlet wished she would hurry back to their room so her grandmother would have someone else to talk to.

The old woman, meanwhile, settled onto the bench in front of Mira's dressing table with a frail yet eager sigh. She took a moment to catch her breath and take in Scarlet's side of the wide, softly lit room. Her eyes lingered on the hot-pink drum set perched on a raised platform across from Scarlet's black-and-fuschia-covered bed. Scarlet's things had been moved for her the same starday Lady Stella had broken the news. When her Star-Zap finally led her to her newly assigned room on the other side of the Big Dipper Dorm, it wasn't clear who was more put out: Mira, who'd been quite content having a single, or Scarlet herself.

"Are those drums?" asked the old woman, pointing.

Scarlet nodded. What else would they be?

"Ooh! What fun! Can I try them?" She was already out of her seat. She hobbled over to the platform, raised her cane, and gave the cymbal a powerful smack.

CRASHHH!

"Don't! *Stop!*" Scarlet cried, hurrying over. "I mean, I'd rather you didn't, um, please." Scarlet didn't want to be rude, but nobody—not even a little old Starling—was touching her precious drums. "Maybe you'd be more comfortable waiting for Mira in the Luminous Library. I'm sure a Bot-Bot guide could show you the way."

"Oh, starry nights, no." The old woman grinned and set her cane back on the polished star-studded floor. "I'm just as comfortable as can be. Where is my lovely granddaughter, though, do you know? I'm just as eager to see her as I can be."

Scarlet didn't know, though she wanted to be helpful. If Mira had ever said anything to her about where she was going, Scarlet was too focused on her Star Darlings problem to care. Besides, Scarlet preferred for other Starlings to keep their noses out of her business, so she tried to set an example by keeping her nose to herself, too.

"I'm not sure . . . maybe play rehearsal?"

"Oh, yes, you're right, I'm sure!" crowed the old woman. "That Mira is quite an actor! Destined for stardom! Don't you think?"

"Is she? I don't know," Scarlet confessed. "I've never seen her act." Since leaving her parents to attend Starling Academy, she'd tried to steer clear of theaters and auditoriums. Quite frankly, she also had yet to see the appeal in running around, dressed up like a fool, pretending to be somebody else.

"Moon and stars!" Mira's grandmother gasped. "Never? What a shame. Oh, but surely you've seen her act *sometime*. . . ."

Scarlet shook her head. "Star apologies. No."

"Never?" The old woman leaned forward, twisting slightly. The corners of her mouth twitched, one at a time. A bluish star-shaped freckle on her cheek began to sparkle. Scarlet watched it closely, the familiarity clicking at last. How hadn't she noticed it before?

"All right, I'll admit it." Scarlet sighed to hold back a groan. "I saw her once."

"Really? You did see her? When?"

"The Time of Shadows production. Our first year at school."

"Oh, that was a good one!"

Scarlet stifled a smile as she clicked her tongue and slowly shook her head.

"It wasn't?" The woman's blue eyes grew round. "You really don't think so? Why not?"

"Well, some parts were good . . . like the scenery. . . . And the props could have been worse."

"What about the acting?" croaked the old woman.

Scarlet looked down and smiled.

"*Well?*" Mira's "grandmother" waited, tapping her cane against the floor, sending sparks into the air. "Wasn't it good? Of course it was! We got a standing ovation at the end!"

"*We?*" Scarlet glanced back up, raising one eyebrow in a sharp arch.

The old woman threw back her head. "*Starf!* You knew it was me!" she groaned. Then she laughed and tossed off her shawl so it dangled behind her. "Tell me I had you going there for a while, though," Mira said as she pulled off her wig. Her long indigo hair spilled down her back in shimmering waves. Beneath a thick layer of stage makeup, a whole galaxy of bright blue freckles flashed like sunlight on a lake.

"For a starmin," muttered Scarlet. She did have to live with her, after all.

"Really? Is that all?" Mira sighed. "Sunspots. I guess that's why you're not in that remedial group anymore." She grinned at Scarlet—then blanched in the heat of Scarlet's simmering glare. "No offense!" she said quickly. Like everyone at Starling Academy, it seemed, Mira assumed the special class the Star Darlings went to last period was for extra help so they didn't fail out of school. "Star apologies. I just thought . . . you know . . . since it was a mistake and all . . ."

"It was a mistake, all right," hissed Scarlet.

"Are you mad?"

Am I mad? thought Scarlet. Did a glowfur eat green globules? She was mad, all right. Madder than Leona when she'd had to try out for her own band!

Suddenly, Scarlet's Star-Zap beeped. A holo-text was coming in.

She read it: IN THE HEDGE MAZE. R U STILL COMING?

It was Vega, waiting to meet.

"Forget about it. I'll be fine," Scarlet snapped as she climbed off her bed.

She'd be perfectly *startacular* . . . just as soon as she set everything straight again.

CHAPTER 2

Scarlet burst out of the Big Dipper Dorm and hopped onto the Cosmic transporter. She passed the dancing fountain as she headed to the hedge maze, ignoring the water's friendly wave. She knew all too well that once encouraged, the fountain would only work harder to try to keep a Starling there.

The campus was quiet, as it often was after dinner, when most students flocked to the Lightning Lounge. That was a place, though, that Scarlet usually avoided. Everyone was far too sociable and eager to hang out and chat. One couldn't even lie back and gaze at the stars from underneath the retractable roof without some shiny Starling leaning over and saying, "Ooh! Aren't they pretty?" or "Do you think they look the same from Wishworld?" Scarlet's jaw ached from holding back rude responses, like "*No*, they look like globerbeems from Wishworld. What a startacularly silly question! Of course they look the same!"

Scarlet didn't care much for the hedge maze, either—for a different reason. The hedge maze drove her crazy, the way its pattern constantly changed. No sooner would she think she'd found a way out than a path would turn, a wall would shift, or a leafy new hedge would suddenly appear. Where the fun in *that* was, Scarlet had no idea. She thanked her stars for the single red blossom in every hedge wall that would open a door when plucked. She plucked one every time. Vega, on the other hand, would never have dreamed of doing such a thing. She loved the maze and spent more time there than all the other Star Darlings combined, so it was the best place Scarlet could think of to get a few words with her—alone.

Even before she spotted Vega, Scarlet saw her sapphire aura. The constantly changing maze, however, made actually reaching her hard.

"Vega!" Scarlet finally shouted through the glittery hedge wall. "I'm over here! Come! Hurry up!"

Vega was beside her in a starsec, only slightly out of breath.

"How did you get here so fast?" asked Scarlet as a new wall of hedge popped up behind Vega.

"Easy," Vega said. "I waited for the hedge to shift left, then ran south ten degrees, then doubled back through the—"

Scarlet held up her hands. "That's all right. Never mind. I don't care." At the same time, though, it was exactly this love of puzzle solving that gave Scarlet hope that Vega could help.

"So what did you want to talk about—*finally*? It's good to see you, by the way. Where in the universe have you *been*? We've been worried about you for star-days. So . . . did you want to hear about my mission?" Vega smiled proudly, ignoring Scarlet's immediate sneer. "You'll be happy to know that—unlike Leona's . . ." Vega sighed. "Poor thing. Anyway, unlike Leona's mission, mine was a *great* success. Another Power Crystal collected! Not that I didn't have a little issue—but everyone does, it seems. I found my Wisher fairly easily. It's the wish *identifying* that's so tricky. I know they always tell us that, but you don't really know until you try. Luckily, Clover came down and helped me figure it out in plenty of time. It was actually quite an interesting wish. . . ." She paused, finally noticing Scarlet's pained expression.

"Really, Vega? Do you truly think I wanted to meet to hear all about a Star Darlings mission when I can't go on one anymore?" Scarlet shook her head and her black hair swung back and forth across her eyes. "I thought you were smarter than that. That's about the *last* thing I want to talk about."

"Of course!" said Vega. "What was I thinking? Star apologies." She reached out to pat Scarlet's shoulder, but Scarlet shrank away. "So then . . . what is it? Oh!" Vega nodded. "It's the *band*! You want to come back. That's startastic!" She clapped. "We need you! We really do! Clover was filling in, but she couldn't take Leona anymore. Not that *you* should worry about her. Yes, she's mad that you dropped out, but she also knows what a starmendous drummer you are."

"Freakin' fireballs," Scarlet groaned. "The band is the *second*-to-last thing on my mind!" Sure, she missed the band—well, she missed playing the drums—but she definitely wasn't ready to go back to it, and she wasn't sure she ever would be. Of course Vega, who played the bass, was fine. And Sage and Libby were okay, too. Sage wasn't the best guitarist, but she had good instincts and worked to improve. Libby tried way too hard to make everyone happy, in Scarlet's opinion, but she was startastic on the keytar. It was Leona who drove everyone crazy by bossing them around. Frankly, Scarlet was surprised she didn't try to play every instrument herself.

"Then *what*?" said Vega. Under her bangs her forehead wrinkled. For Vega, the only feeling worse than having the incorrect answer was not having an answer at all.

"Something's wrong. Very wrong," said Scarlet.

"Ah." Vega nodded. "I see. I know. You're right. It's so unfair. It really is. And I'd feel exactly the same if I were you, I'm sure."

"What? *No!*" Scarlet scooted out from under Vega's hand again. "I mean, yes. It's unfair. Of course. But it's unfair because it's a huge mistake. That new girl—Ophelia, or whatever her name is—should never have been picked to take my place!"

"You don't think so?"

"I do not!"

Vega sighed and crossed her arms. "Truth be told, you could be right. I've been wondering about her myself."

"You have?"

Vega nodded. "She's so far behind in Star Darlings class—which made sense in the beginning. No one expected her to know anything yet. But she's just not catching up. Do you know she still can't manipulate a watt of energy? Not a single watt! Ooh!" She suddenly jumped as a branch reached out to tickle her ribs. "Come on, we should keep moving," she told Scarlet. "The maze doesn't like it when you stop."

Vega moved to link her arm with Scarlet's. But Scarlet had never been the touchy-feely, arm-linking, hand-holding type. Instead, she put her hands behind her back as they moved along the ever-twisting starlit path.

"You know," said Vega, sensing Scarlet's impatience with their route, "if you just focus and look for a pattern, you have a much better chance of making it out. It's when you try to fight it that you end up feeling trapped."

"Whatever," said Scarlet. "Just get me out of here."

So Vega linked arms with Scarlet (despite her protests) and they quickly made their way out of the maze.

"Star apologies," said Scarlet, "but I just can't play peekaboo with a bush and think at the same time. You're good at solving puzzles, Vega. I've never had patience for them. So think: why would someone so new and totally unprepared to grant wishes be picked to take my place when my wish-granting potential's so starmendously high?"

"You're right. I do like puzzles . . ." said Vega. "At the same time, though, this was Lady Stella's decision, and we have to trust her, don't you think? Still . . ." She paused. "It is strange." Scarlet could sense that an idea was being born in Vega's mind. "And if you talked to Cassie, she'd tell you that's not the only strange thing going on."

"I know," said Scarlet.

"You do?"

Scarlet shrugged and scowled. "I might have . . . overheard her . . . talking about me, and Leona's Wish Pendant."

"And the whole flower thing?" Vega's bright blue eyebrows shot up.

"She did say something about flowers . . . but I didn't actually get that part. What flowers was she talking about?"

"The bouquets," said Vega. "You know. The ones we all—all the Star Darlings, I mean—had delivered to our rooms?"

"Oh, those." Scarlet nodded. She did remember, though she hadn't thought it strange at the time. "So you still don't know who they're from?"

"No," Vega said, "but that's not even it. Cassie has this crazy idea that they were making us fight with each other over the littlest things. In fact, she's so sure, she took my bouquet to the botany lab to be evaluated. She'd already thrown hers and Sage's away."

"What do *you* think?" Scarlet asked. "Do you think Cassie might be right?"

Vega smoothed her hair back. "No, I don't. In fact, we made a bet. If I was right, she would do a puzzle with me every day for a double starweek."

"And if she was right?"

"I'd help her study for her Astral Accounting test."

Scarlet frowned.

Vega winked. "I know. Win-win. But I'm not too concerned about helping her study. Piper's still annoying me as much as ever. She makes these sounds when she's meditating. . . ." Vega closed her eyes and cringed. "Ugh! I can hear them all the way from upstairs in her part of the room. It sounds like a Bot-Bot on the fritz. Like this high, whiny *ohmmmm*." She winced. "How about you and Leona?" she asked Scarlet. "How were you getting along? Before you switched rooms, I mean."

"Oh, I don't know. Leona and I had our testy moments. . . ." Scarlet shrugged. "But I'm sure we would have anyway. So what did the botany lab say?"

"Nothing . . . *yet*. But we should probably hear soon."

"Promise to tell me when you do."

Vega drew an X over her heart. "Cross my stars—and moons. But . . . how? I mean, when will I see you again? Where have you been all this time?"

"I've been . . . around," said Scarlet vaguely. "They gave me a new roommate. Her name's Mira."

"I don't know her," said Vega.

"Neither did I."

"Is she nice?"

"She's fine," said Scarlet. "We don't really know each other yet. She isn't around that much, and I pretty much stay in my loft all the time, so maybe we never will. . . ."

"Have you been to any classes since . . ."

"No," said Scarlet bitterly.

"Don't you think you should?" Vega gently asked. "I mean, I can understand dropping out of Leona's band. No one—well, except Leona maybe—blames you for that. But even if you're not in the Star Darlings anymore, you're still a student at the school, and you can still go to Wishworld and grant wishes one day . . . but only if you graduate, of course."

Scarlet looked over her shoulder, past the hedge maze, toward the majestic Crystal Mountains, which glimmered across Luminous Lake. Vega was right, she guessed. Not that Scarlet was worried about falling behind in any subjects. Her classes seemed to get easier for her every year. But hiding from everyone and everything, while it made life simpler right then, wasn't helping her solve her problem, either.

"You can't hide forever," Vega went on, almost as if she'd peeked into Scarlet's mind. "How about I make you a deal like I made with Cassie?"

"I don't make deals," muttered Scarlet. "But what?"

"You start going to your classes, and I'll do whatever I can to help you get to the bottom of what went wrong."

CHAPTER 3

The next day, Scarlet went through the motions of going to morning assembly, classes, meals . . . all the things she was *supposed* to do. But the more she tried to act like everything was normal, the surer she was that everything was wrong.

She didn't even try to move all the desks in Wishful Thinking class, and yet with a single eyebrow raise she did exactly that. She was just as surprised as everyone else when it happened but was determined as always not to let her emotions show.

Even Professor Dolores Raye's mouth fell open. "Who did that?" she gasped.

In the far corner of the room, Scarlet slowly raised her hand.

"Oh, my stars!" said Professor Raye. "I didn't even see you back there, Scarlet. Welcome back to class, by the way. I must say, I've never seen such control in a third year. Those are very special powers. Er . . . now, if you don't mind, would you be so kind as to move the desks back to where they were?"

This only confirmed something Scarlet had already begun to sense: somehow, instead of feeling less special since leaving the Star Darlings, she felt as if her wish energy powers were stronger than ever before.

At lunch, Scarlet managed to sit by herself: no small feat in the Celestial Café. The tables were large and round and designed to encourage Starlings to linger and talk for starhours. Scarlet sequestered herself at an empty corner table, where she promptly spilled her mug of Zing. "Forget it," she told the Bot-Bot waiter who appeared instantly with another as the puddle disappeared. Instead, she ordered a steaming bowl of stewed garble greens—the smell of which was guaranteed to keep other Starlings far away.

Rather than eating, though—she *hated* garble greens—Scarlet observed the Star Darlings from afar. They sat together, as they had since they'd been summoned, at the middle table near the window overlooking Luminous Lake. Astra was dressed in her neon-trimmed fiery-red star ball uniform. It could have been a game day or not. With her, you never knew. Cassie was nose-deep in a holo-book, and Gemma was giggling and prattling away. Listening to Gemma was one thing Scarlet did not miss in the least.

Vega noticed her and waved so that the others couldn't see. She flashed Scarlet a sparkly smile of friendly encouragement, which Scarlet accepted reluctantly.

As she watched them all, Scarlet couldn't help remembering what Vega had told her in the maze about roommates bickering. And, indeed, they were. If they weren't barking at or arguing with each other, they were sitting far enough apart that they didn't have to talk. Cassie and Sage were the only roommates who appeared to be enjoying each other's company—and Leona and Ophelia, who were sharing a glimmerberry shake.

What a dud, thought Scarlet as she studied Ophelia. There was nothing at all best or brightest or star-charmed about her—at least from what Scarlet could see. While the Starlings around her radiated confidence, brilliance, and power, Ophelia gave off an awkward, muddled aura of confusion and fear.

So why was she there instead of Scarlet? Instead of *anyone*, really . . . but especially Scarlet.

Scarlet remembered the explanation Lady Stella had given when the headmistress had delivered the shocking news.

"I'm truly sorry, Scarlet. Star apologies don't begin to express how I feel. But accidents happen, even on Starland, and I'm afraid one has occurred here. As you know, I chose the twelve Star Darlings myself, using an intricate algorithm comprising numerous factors, including grades and test scores and energy records."

"Yes?" Scarlet had said. She could tell something grave was coming, but she had no idea what on Starland it could be.

"Naturally, great care was taken with the data, and yet . . . somehow, somewhere, a glitch occurred along the way . . . and your name, most unfortunately, was given to me in error."

"I don't understand . . ." Scarlet had whispered with what little breath she could find in her chest.

"I must say, I don't, either. And yet the holo-records Lady Cordial has shown me are as clear as the night sky. Your scores and those of another Starling, Ophelia, were mixed up in the holo-files. Therefore, *she* is the rightful twelfth Star Darling—something you, Scarlet, were never truly meant to be."

Naturally, Scarlet had argued—vehemently. But the energy had been spent in vain. She left Lady Stella's office stinging, as if a hive of angry glitterbees had attacked her, and the feeling still hadn't gone away. The black hole Scarlet had felt in her stomach at that moment was still there, just as deep. In fact, sitting in the Celestial Café, watching Ophelia in her place among the other Star Darlings, only made the feeling worse. Scarlet knew her grades and scores were strong, so the whole thing already made no sense. But in what crazy parallel universe could a starling such as Ophelia have one score higher than Scarlet's, let alone a whole file's worth?

Scarlet blinked and slid her now cold bowl of garble greens across the table before standing up and leaving the café. She had Lighterature next period, but she didn't care. The thought of sitting in a class full of happy, care-free Starlings made her want to zap something. Besides, they were reading a tragedy by Shakestar that she had read hydrongs of times—*Romea and Jupiter*. The whole star-crossed romance thing made her want to hurl. So when she left the Celestial Café, she turned away from Halo Hall and headed across the Star Quad, straight back to the Big Dipper Dorm.

The building was empty except for the Bot-Bot guard inside the front door. "Star greetings, Scarlet," it welcomed her.

"Star greetings," she muttered back.

Scarlet stepped onto the Cosmic Transporter as it rolled through the halls.

Outside her door, Scarlet placed her hand on the palm scanner. The door opened with a gentle *whoosh.* As she walked in, the door slid smoothly closed. Scarlet scrunched her eyes to dim the lights and gazed around the room. Her eyes fell on her drum kit on its platform. *Yes!* That was just what she needed to do! Bang out a few dark and angry riffs . . . or maybe a few hydrong.

Scarlet hadn't played the drums much at all since she'd left the Star Darlings. Before that, she'd played hours every day—either with Leona's band or in their old room while Leona sang. They found it was the one thing they could do together without getting on each other's nerves. As soon as Lady Stella told her she was out of the Star Darlings, however, Scarlet stopped going to band practice, too. Every other member was still a Star Darling, and the last thing she needed was to hear them talk about their missions—or deal with their pity or, worse, their phony good cheer. The only place she could play was her room, but lately the inspiration just hadn't been there.

That day, she felt different, though. The drums seemed to be calling to her. She grabbed her sticks and climbed the platform and sat down. She waited a moogle for the stool to adjust itself beneath her, then gave her bass drum pedal three fierce stomps: *BAM! BAM! BAM!* The energy in the room flickered and rolled away from the star-shaped drum pad in powerful glittery waves. Scarlet smiled and whacked the cymbals—*CRASH! BANG!*—one at a time. She did it again . . . and again . . . and again . . . and again. *CRASH! BANG! CRASH! BANG-A-DEE-BANG! CRASH! BANG! CRASH! BANG-A-DEE! BANG-A-DEE! BOOM!*

With her eyes closed, she let her arms fly in a series of rolls and riffs, wherever they wanted to go. If her eyes had been open, she would have seen the energy aura surrounding her glow brighter and brighter pink. But the light grew so blinding she would have soon had to close them again.

Scarlet had never played her drums so hard before or felt so energized. All her frustration, her bitterness, her confusion dissolved with every beat. Finally, after what felt like a moogle but could have been a staryear, Scarlet had to stop. Exhausted, she let go of her drumsticks and let them twirl in the air above the tom-tom while her head fell back. As her eyes opened, she let out a gasp at the dazzling sight of pure sparkling energy pulsing throughout the room.

Did I do that? Scarlet wondered. There was no other source she could see.

Gradually, the energy faded, but Scarlet's clarity did not. From the beginning, she had suspected there was something not right about Ophelia's replacing her. Now she was sure. And if *she* didn't get to the bottom of it, who else on Starland would? Maybe Vega could help her. But maybe not. Who knew? *And why wait to see,* Scarlet thought as her eyes fell on her roommate's jam-packed costume closet, *when I have all I need to do it on my own?*

CHAPTER
4

The door to Scarlet's dorm room slid open and a small, distinguished-looking man stepped into the hall. He wore a long silver topcoat with a wide forest-green collar and half-moon-shaped buttons as big as ears. His own ears were covered by a burnt-orange fedora tilted so far forward it concealed his face. The only feature not hidden, in fact, was the very tip of his emerald beard. Pausing, he stroked the bright green whiskers as his head swiveled right and left. Satisfied that the hall was empty, he raised a star-studded shiny black combat boot and boarded the Cosmic Transporter as it rolled past him.

Scarlet hoped her disguise (courtesy of her roommate's closet) was convincing. The first test was the Bot-Bot guard at the front door.

She brushed past it, keeping her head down and her velvet collar up.

"Star greetings, Scarlet," the Bot-Bot guard said cheerfully.

Scarlet sighed. "Star greetings," she mumbled without turning. Bot-Bot guards were a useless gauge, she guessed. They could read an aura a floozel away. Hopefully, the Starling adults where she was going would be easier to trick.

Once outside, Scarlet headed directly for the enormous star-shaped building between the hedge maze and the Celestial Café. Although it wasn't geographically at the center of campus, it was the hub in every other way. Halo Hall, as it was called, housed all the Starling Academy classrooms, as well as the Astral Auditorium, where assemblies and performances were held. In the hall, too, were various offices, including that of Lady Stella, the headmistress. Its most spectacular feature was the gleaming lone white tower attached to the Wish-House. At the very top sat the Wishworld Surveillance Deck, the platform where Starlings could observe

Wishworld and its Wishlings through telescopes and where they waited to catch a shooting star when their day for a Wish Mission came at last.

Normally, a Starling walked up the white starmarble stairs and entered through the front doors. Since this starday was far from normal, however, Scarlet hurried around the Bot-Bot guard at the front and made her way into Halo Hall through the back. After all, she wasn't going to some old class in Stellation four or five. She was on a mission to right what was wrong.

If only she knew exactly where she needed to go.

As far as offices went, Scarlet was familiar with only two: that of the perky guidance counselor, Lady Solara, who had made it her mission to "light Scarlet up," and Lady Stella's. Both were offices Scarlet hoped to stay well clear of, since she didn't want to see either administrator just then. Fortunately, they were clustered with other faculty offices in Stellation one and she was fairly certain that the office she was looking for was in Stellation two . . . or maybe three.

She decided to try the second wing first, since it was closest. Like every hall, its walls and floor were made of gleaming rainbow-hued starmarble. In that wing, they gave off a pink-tinged glow. Up near the ceiling ran a series of windows, letting light from outside shine in.

Scarlet hurried down the hall, passing door after door. As she did, she lifted her hat brim ever so slightly to read the holo-signs outside of each.

SUPPLY ROOM, read one star-shaped plaque. STAR-ZAP REPAIR AND MAINTENANCE, announced the next, followed by TECHNOLOGY, SWIFT-TRANSPORTATION SERVICES, and WISH ENERGY MANAGEMENT. Then Scarlet read the holo-sign by the door at the end: BOT-BOT SECURITY.

Freakin' fireballs, she thought. *Security! Time to turn around!*

Heart thumping, she scurried back down the hall and rounded the corner into the safety, she hoped, of Stellation three. *Please let me find what I'm looking for here,* she wished.

That hall looked basically the same, except the glow given off by the marble walls was a bit aquamarine. These doors, too, had holo-signs, and Scarlet read the first one on her right: ADMISSIONS. Lady Cordial's office. Of course. Scarlet remembered it now from her own Time of Applying, when she had first visited the school. She'd come alone, since her parents had been on tour and unable to take the time off. Lady Cordial, the head of admissions, had been pleasant in their interview but not as welcoming as one might have hoped—especially one with test scores such as Scarlet's, which were practically off the charts.

But that was Lady Cordial, Scarlet now realized: stiff and skittish and often at a loss for words. Scarlet had eventually learned, like every Starling Academy student, not to take things too personally with her.

On the other hand, Scarlet's next interview with Lady Stella had been one of the best starhours of her whole life. There was something about the headmistress that made every Starling feel as if she'd known her for staryears. Scarlet had already *thought* she wanted to go to Starling Academy, but meeting Lady Stella had sealed the deal. The headmistress didn't care if Scarlet didn't like rainbows as much as rain clouds or loved the most unloved of Starling colors—black. She seemed to know, too, that Scarlet wasn't half as interested in learning to grant wishes as she was in living on her own. And yet she welcomed Scarlet into Starling Academy with warm and open arms. Lady Stella had always seen Scarlet for who she was and admired her for being herself, which only made Scarlet feel worse about having to leave the Star Darlings—and more determined to get back in.

With that in mind, she moved on, shifting her hat to continue reading each star-shaped sign.

ATTENDANCE, ACCOUNTING, ALUMNI RELATIONS, STUDENT LIFE, FACULTY LOUNGE . . .

"'Faculty lounge'?" *Hmmm.* Scarlet paused. So *this*

was where their professors hung out when they weren't teaching the finer points of Wishful Thinking or giving a pop quiz on wish identification. She could only imagine what they did in there. Compare lesson plans? Share grading tips? Complain about students, such as Scarlet, who liked to bark out answers instead of politely raising their hands? She pictured them gathered around a table, sharing sighs and cups of Zing.

"Are you going in?"

Scarlet froze.

The person behind her spoke again. "Star apologies. I don't mean to rush you." A hand reached over Scarlet's shoulder to cover the scanner in the middle of the door. "It's just, well, my class ran a few moogles over and I'm late for my massage."

The scanner glowed bright blue. "Welcome, Professor Nicola Cecelia," a Bot-Bot voice greeted the teacher—her Astral Accounting teacher, Scarlet realized—as the door to the faculty lounge opened wide.

Starf! thought Scarlet as her eyes took in the scene. She was careful to keep her hat low, but she could still make out much of the room—everything from the frozen cocomoon yogurt bar to the manicure/pedicure stations to the hot tub *and* swimming pool! Most classes were still in session, so the lounge was far from full.

Nevertheless, there were plenty of teachers already enjoying themselves. Professor Elara Ursa, the Wishers 101 teacher, was having her hair done by a Bot-Bot stylist as she read a holo-magazine. Professor Eugenia Bright, meanwhile, was playing a rather intense spark-filled game of star-pong with Professor Dolores Raye. Giggles spilled out of a holo–photo booth, but Scarlet couldn't see who was inside. She sniffed. Was that zoomberry trifle she smelled? She sniffed again. *Mmm* . . . yes, it was . . . and glorange meringue pie, as well. Scarlet's mouth was already watering by the time her eyes found the buffet.

"Come on in!" By now, Professor Nicola Cecelia had slipped around Scarlet and stood inside. Reaching up, she pulled a silver-star-topped comb out of each side of her tight plum-colored bun. With a shake, she let her hair tumble down loose over her shoulders, and it stopped well below her waist. "Don't be shy. Substitutes are welcome. More than welcome, in fact!" She flashed a smile far sunnier than Scarlet had ever seen on her normally dour face. "You could probably use a break the most. These students are bright, but give them half a chance and they'll wear your glow away. Whose class did you have, by the way? I didn't realize anyone was out. I hope you didn't wear that hat and coat all day. You know, there are Bot-Bot valets to see to things like that."

For a moogle, Scarlet was actually tempted to play along and follow her teacher inside. Before, she had thought that the students' Lightning Lounge had everything a Starling could ever desire. But its cozy fireplaces, pillows, and walls of holo-screens were nothing compared with the faculty's giant lounge. The only problem was Scarlet knew that as soon as she took her hat off, she would give herself away. Frankly, she was surprised—*star*tled, even—that Professor Nicola Cecelia hadn't raised a single violet eyebrow at her beard, which was steadily shifting sideways.

"*Ahem.*" Scarlet cleared her throat as deeply as she could. "Star salutations," she said gruffly. She gave the brim of her hat a dapper tap, the way she'd seen her father do. "But, *ahem*, I'm looking for another, *ahem*, room. *Ahem.*"

"Oh." The teacher's grin faded. "I see. And what room is that?"

"*Ahem.* Er, holo-records."

"You mean the holo-records room right there?" Professor Nicola Cecelia pointed a delicate sparkly purple-polished fingernail at the next door down the hall.

Scarlet turned and squinted to read the sign. STUDENT HOLO-RECORDS. There it was!

"Star salutations!" Scarlet said—too quickly, she

feared. But then Professor Nicola Cecelia's head suddenly snapped around. Her Bot-Bot masseuse was summoning her, rather impatiently by then.

"*Starf!* Got to go. So there it is. Glad I could help. Oh! And so you know, Lunadays we always play astro-poker in the lounge. I almost always win, but still, keep it in mind."

Scarlet let out a long sigh as the door slid shut between them. She hadn't even realized she'd been holding her breath. She checked to make sure no other teachers were coming. They weren't. She sighed again.

It took just a starmin to reach the door of the holo-records room. Then the only question left was, how was she going to get inside?

CHAPTER 5

Scarlet knew better than to try the hand scanner. That would only give her away. There were other ways to get into a room, though, especially now that Professor Nicola Cecelia had confirmed the strength of her disguise.

Scarlet checked her reflection in the mirrorlike surface of the polished marble wall. She slid her beard back to the center and gave it a fluff. She tugged her hat down even farther and propped her collar higher. Satisfied, she raised her fist and rapped on the door . . . once . . . twice . . . three times.

While she waited for the door to open, she went over the story she'd already rehearsed a hydrong times in her mind:

"Hello, my name is Sir Copernicus, and I am here on behalf of Sir Andromedus and Lady Melodia, the famous musicians, as I'm sure you're well aware. Apparently, they've sent numerous holo-requests for their daughter's records, none of which has received a reply. You can imagine what an eclipse they're having. One would think a school like this would have all its stars in a straighter row. But since they're clearly not, the family has sent me to retrieve Scarlet's records, as they're on an extended tour across the Star-Belt region and so could not do it themselves. It's crystal clear, of course, that you're very busy, so I wouldn't dream of taking up your valuable time. Rather, if you'll just point me in the direction of the third-year holo-files . . . Star salutations for understanding. I'll take it from here, if you don't mind."

Scarlet would be free to compare all her scores to Ophelia's—and anyone else's she chose. Leona's, for one . . . Gemma's maybe, too . . . Then she would at least understand why *they* were all Star Darlings and she suddenly was not.

It had to work. It just had to. Otherwise, Scarlet didn't know how she was going to go on. She couldn't keep avoiding everyone and everything forever. Her grades would suffer, and so would she. But until she had some real answers, she would never, in a hydrong star-years, be able to relax.

The only problem was the door wasn't opening. So Scarlet took another breath and knocked again. She tapped the toe of her thick-soled boot. Sparks bounced up from the floor. Did she have to *keep* knocking? She raised her fist. She guessed she did. That was when she noticed, for the first time, the hand scanner—or not the scanner, but what it said.

Scarlet groaned.

She should have looked at it sooner, but she'd been too focused on the door. Instead of displaying a hand outline along with the unnecessary PALM HERE message, the scanner scrolled a series of words: OFFICE HOURS: SUNRISE TO APEX. PLEASE COME BACK. STATUS: CLOSED.

On the way back to the dorm Scarlet shed her disguise behind a lumilac bush about halfway to the building. Classes had ended and Starlings were wandering about, and if one more student had pleasantly waved and called, "Star greetings! Welcome to Starling Academy!" Scarlet would have exploded into a moonium bitter, red-hot stars right there in front of them. When she wasn't in disguise, the other students knew better than to try to talk to her or even share a smile. After Scarlet's more than two staryears at Starling Academy, her reliably antisocial reputation preceded her.

Thankfully, Scarlet made it back to her room before Mira, so she had time to put everything away. The floppy orange hat went back on the hat rack, and the coat went into Mira's costume closet, along with the itchy beard. Scarlet had just sat down at her drums and picked up her drumsticks when the door slid open and Mira breezed in.

"There you are!" Mira pointed one long glittery finger at Scarlet. The other hand perched on her hip. She was dressed as a regular Starling student for a change, even if she had a cobalt blue scarf the size of a bedsheet around her neck. "*Starf!*" she exclaimed. "*So* many Starlings have been asking me about you! Especially all those remedial Starlings, like Leona and Adora—and Ophelia now. 'Where's Scarlet?' 'Have you seen her?' 'Could you please give her a holo-message for me?' I'm like, 'Send her your own holo-message.' And they're like, 'We do, but she won't reply.'" Mira cocked her head and frowned. "Did you lose your Star-Zap or something? We could literally find it in a moogle with my Zap-locate app, you know."

"I didn't lose it," mumbled Scarlet. "I've just been busy."

"Oh." Mira's eyes skimmed Scarlet's drum kit. "Right. Okay. I see. Well, don't let me stop you." She shrugged and tossed a long triangle of scarf over her shoulder. It took three tries before it stayed. "I'm zipping right back out again, anyway. I just popped in to get my holo-script before rehearsal. Now . . . where did I leave it do you think . . . ?"

"Why don't you just memorize your lines overnight?" asked Scarlet. Wasn't that what sleep and headphones were for, after all? So Starlings could play back and absorb class lectures and textbooks and anything else they needed to learn?

Mira sighed. "You don't know anything about acting, do you?" She tossed her head to show that *she* did.

Scarlet lowered her own head to hide the smile she couldn't keep from springing up. Oh, after her day, she knew about acting. . . . Too bad Mira hadn't seen her. She would have been impressed.

"A script," Mira went on, "is just the beginning. Like a supernova!" She held her fists out and flashed open her fingers. "It's merely the raw matter from which superstars are born. In rehearsal, we're taking notes constantly and making changes. It's not just memorizing a hydrong lines," she said, scoffing. "It's a *process*. A *journey*. You know?"

Scarlet nodded, hoping to satisfy Mira, though she'd stopped listening at "beginning."

"Is that your script?" Scarlet pointed to a holo-book near the edge of Mira's makeup-crowded table, behind a long sparkly teal wig on a tall silver stand.

"Is it?" Mira picked up the holo-book and brought it close enough to read. "Star salutations! It is! Okay, I'm off. Again." She paused then, leaning toward Scarlet. "Are you sure you're okay? You know, you look a little green. . . ."

"I do?"

"Mmm-hmm. Around here." Mira stroked her cheeks and chin.

The beard! Scarlet realized. Quickly, she rubbed her face to brush off whatever green glitter was stuck to it. "I'm fine," she said. "Don't worry about me. Just go do your script journey . . . process . . . whatever you call it."

Scarlet had lowered the window shades and blinked off the lights by the time Mira returned. The room had a soft, dreamy violet glow. Dinner was over, as was star-gazing hour, though lights-down had yet to come. Except for the secret Star Caves, of course, no place ever got truly dark on Starland, the way places on Wishworld did. In fact, it actually got brighter as the sun went down and all the wish energy stored in every atom on Starland approached its maximum glow potential.

Scarlet "acted" again, this time as if she was sleeping, in case Mira had more questions to ask her or, worse, offered unwanted advice. She lay as quiet and still as a moonbeam and waited for Mira to take her nightly sparkle shower and slip into bed herself. Actually falling asleep, however, was impossible. The thoughts whizzing through Scarlet's mind simply would not let her rest.

At last, Scarlet had no choice but to get out of bed. She couldn't lie there for a moogle more. Mira was fast asleep, though restlessly muttering something like "Wait! Where's my mark? Somebody moved it from stage left!"

Scarlet slid out from her silky black sheets and scooped her combat boots off the floor. As light as a flutterfocus, she tiptoed past Mira, blinked open the door, and, still wearing her pink-and-black polka-starred pajamas, slipped out into the hall.

To save energy, the hallway Cosmic Transporter ceased flowing after lights-down, but Scarlet was happy to walk. She left her feet bare on the off chance that some other wakeful Starling might hear the *clomp-clomp* of her boots through their chamber doors. Starlings slept exceptionally soundly . . . still, "better safe than lost in space," as Scarlet's father sometimes said.

It wasn't Scarlet's first venture out after lights-down. She'd been taking walks on restless nights since the beginning of the year, when she'd literally stumbled upon the entrance to the mysterious Star Caves. That was before Lady Stella had taken the Star Darlings there, via a secret door in her office, to show them the Wish Cavern she'd had built in the deepest chamber for them and them alone. It was there that the headmistress kept their Wish Orbs. Scarlet knew she had looked as awed and surprised by the caves as everyone else at the time. That was yet another example of her acting talents, she supposed, since she had already discovered the caves herself more than a starweek earlier.

She had arrived at school, as usual, stardays before everyone else. She'd had quite enough of her parents and living out of a suitcase for one Time of Lumiere break. She had checked out her room and was aimlessly riding the Cosmic Transporter around the dorm when she noticed the neon sign on the door in front of her. STARLING ACADEMY STAFF ONLY, it temptingly flashed.

Naturally, she got off and opened it (after peeking over each of her shoulders to make sure she was alone). But it was just a plain old supply closet full of baskets of star-pong balls, sparkle-shower gel, and stuff like that. Because nothing on Starland ever got truly dirty, there were no cleaning supplies, of course. There were, however, a few dust mops and feather dusters for adding an extra layer of stardust to anything that might need shining up. Scarlet had never actually used one, since Bot-Bot maids were always there to shine her hotel rooms. Curious, she took a step into the closet to pull a duster down and see exactly how it worked. "Freakin' fireballs!" she exclaimed as the toe of her boot caught on something and sent her stumbling into a wall of shelves. The next thing she knew, glo-pong balls were raining down on her head like the Perseid meteor shower.

Scarlet looked down as the balls bounced and flashed around her, and that was when she saw the trapdoor. A rogue glo-pong paddle had kept it from closing completely, and that was what had tripped her up. Without thinking twice, she raised the panel and waited as a bunch of glo-pong balls spilled through the hole. She listened to them bounce down a long winding set of metal stairs for several moogles, until they hit a distant floor . . . then, flipping her Star-Zap to flashlight mode, she climbed in to see for herself exactly what was down there.

Since then, not counting her trips with the Star Darlings, Scarlet had been down to explore the Star

Caves more than a dozen times. She'd covered only a tiny fraction, she knew, but on each visit she tried to delve a little deeper than before. This night, without really thinking, she headed due north, down a wide winding tunnel, roughly in the direction of Halo Hall.

As ever, the cave air was cool, like at the top of the Crystal Mountains, but also damp and slightly musty, like her boots before they dried out after a day in Starland snow. The air clung to Scarlet as she moved. Without a doubt, the energy was different down there. What Scarlet liked best of all about the caves was the light that came from glowing rocks set in the walls. It gave her the feeling of being in outer space, where the only light came from distant twinkling stars. Every now and then, as Scarlet walked, a big cold drop of water would splash somewhere on her hair or face. One time, she'd caught one on her tongue. She couldn't say it had much taste.

Suddenly, she heard a high *squeak*, followed by the rustling of wings, and sensed a bitbat swooping down. Scarlet lifted her arm and held out her hand. A starsec later, a silvery-white creature the size of a glowfur settled onto her finger and dangled upside down.

"Star greetings," said Scarlet.

The bitbat blinked its wide fluorescent green eyes

and squeaked twice more, as if in reply. Why bitbats made the other Star Darlings nervous, Scarlet would never know. They were as gentle as any flutterfocus, she thought, just not as hyperactive and ostentatious. Unlike every creature that lived on the surface of Starland, Star Cave creatures did not show off.

The creatures were her second favorite thing about the caves. She envied their solitude, their privacy, their freedom to be themselves and to be alone.

As quickly as it had appeared, the bitbat took off again. Scarlet watched it fly deeper into the cave.

"What's down there?" she called out, following it.

She tried to keep up, but the bitbat was too fast. By the time she rounded a tight corner, Scarlet had lost it in the darkness.

But she had found something else. . . .

CHAPTER 6

Scarlet was dressed and out of her room the next morning before Mira was even awake. Scarlet hadn't slept a wink. She'd spent most of the night in the room at the top of the stairs she'd discovered in the Star Caves, after losing sight of the bitbat. Was it luck that those stairs had led to a trapdoor into the Office of Student Holo-Records? Or was it somehow fate?

Halo Hall would not open officially for another hour but she couldn't see waiting around. She raced across campus to the entrance and begged the Bot-Bot guard to let her in.

"I have to see Lady Stella!" she said. "It's urgent! It can't wait!"

"Star apologies, Scarlet," the Bot-Bot guard replied

mechanically. "Halo Hall is not open, nor is Lady Stella in. Would you like to make an appointment? I can help you with that, if you wish. Lady Stella's office hours are eleven to thirteen starhours. She has another meeting scheduled from twelve to twelve-eighty. What time do you request?"

Scarlet's energy sizzled. That was exactly the problem with thickheaded Bot-Bots. They didn't *understand.* She didn't need an *appointment.* She needed to see the headmistress right *then*!

"Sc-sc-scarlet! Er, st-st-star greetings."

Scarlet turned to see the head of admissions, Lady Cordial, walking briskly toward the door with a stack of files and a mug of Zing.

"Star greetings, Lady Cordial," said Scarlet, bowing.

"You're up early. Feeling better?" She stood before Scarlet, smiling in an awkward but sweet way. Scarlet realized she hadn't seen the head of admissions since learning that her being a Star Darling was a mistake.

"I know what *happened* . . ." Lady Cordial paused and cut her eyes to the Bot-Bot guard, who, like everyone else, knew nothing about the top secret group. "If you don't mind, I'm going to turn off your hearing for a starsec," she told it.

"Yes, Lady Cordial. As you wish."

Lady Cordial fixed her eyes on its head and narrowed them. "Can you hear me now?" she asked.

She waited.

"Very good. So, er, I was s-saying . . ." She turned back to Scarlet. "I know this mix-up with Ophelia was, well, quite a . . . quite a blow, I'm s-s-sure. Of course, I take full responsibility for everything." She lowered her head and shook it. "How it happened, I'll never know."

"But that's why I'm here! I don't think it *did* happen!"

Lady Cordial's head rose slowly, as Starland's sun was doing just then. "St-st-star excuse me? You don't think *what* happened?"

"I don't think there's been a mix-up!" blurted Scarlet. "I mean, yes, there's been a mix-up—but it's the mix-up that's a mistake! I looked at my holo-records and there's no way in the Milky Way that the scores recorded in them are mine! On the other hand, Ophelia, whose records I also checked, has exactly the scores that I should have. And that's why I'm here—to tell Lady Stella that our scores were switched somehow!"

"*What?*" Lady Cordial gasped. Her cup of Zing slipped out of her hand. Scarlet jumped back and used her energy to catch the cup in midair, but not without hot liquid splashing over her tights and boots.

Of course, it all disappeared in a starsec, as spills on Starland always did.

"St-st-star apologies," said Lady Cordial. She blinked her cup back into her hand and clutched both it and her folders to her chest. "Clearly, you've taken me by star-prise here. Moon and st-st-stars . . ." She took a breath. "If this is true, why . . . er . . . we have more problems than we thought. . . . I must look into this immediately. And inform Lady St-st-stella, of course."

"I'll go with you!" Scarlet told her.

"No, no. St-st-star s-s-salutations, but you've done your part—and more." Lady Cordial's smile slowly returned. "Please, Sc-sc-scarlet, let me take this from here. It's, er, the least I can do."

Scarlet was so excited she couldn't eat breakfast. And no way could she go to class. How could she sit through another lecture on energy manipulation when her whole life was about to change? About to get back on track, at last!

She had to find some way to pass the time, though, while she waited for Lady Cordial to set everything straight. She flipped open her Star-Zap, tapped Vega's icon, and dictated a holo-text.

MYSTERY SOLVED! MEET ME IN THE ORCHARD.

Within a starmin another message came through: NO WAY! ★MENDOUS NEWS!

When Vega arrived, she was not alone to Scarlet's surprise. Cassie, with her pinkish white pigtail buns and her star-shaped glasses, was arm in arm with her.

Scarlet knew Cassie, of course, from the Star Darlings class but not very well beyond that. The first-year Starling had become particularly close to Scarlet's old roommate, Leona—something Scarlet could never understand, since Leona was, without a doubt, the most self-centered, self-absorbed Starling Scarlet had ever met.

Still, besides that, Scarlet had to admit that what she did know of Cassie, she admired. Cassie was never too loud or bubbly or bossy, and it was clear that behind her glasses, a very intelligent mind was hard at work.

"You don't mind that I brought Cassie, do you?" said Vega. Something about Scarlet's expression must have prompted her to ask. "I promised her I'd tell her the next time we met. I told her about your . . . theories, and of course—"

"I think you're right!" Cassie cut in. She leaned forward and pushed up her glasses. Her normally soft pink glow flashed bright, almost blindingly white. "I don't care what Leona says. There is no way in the galaxy that Ophelia could grant a wish. Tell us everything!" she said. "What have you found out?"

So Scarlet told them everything. . . .

"Moon and stars!" Cassie gasped at the end. "So when will you hear back from Lady Cordial?"

"Soon," Scarlet said. "I'm sure."

"Oh, I hope it's all a mistake, the way you say!"

"Does that mean you'll come back to the band?" Vega asked. "You know, there was just an announcement this morning—did you hear?—that this year for Starshine Day there's going to be a battle of the bands. We could win with you playing, Scarlet. I really think we could. In fact . . . maybe you should come back, no matter what, even if it turns out no mistake was made."

"First of all"—Scarlet's eyes narrowed—"there *was* a mistake. A starmendous one. That's just a fact. Second, as I've said a hydrong times now, the band is about the last thing on my mind."

Vega and Cassie lowered their eyes and traded glances.

"Star apologies," said Vega. "Of course. We can talk about the band later. One thing at a time. So . . . if there was a mistake . . . how in the stars did it happen? How did your and Ophelia's scores get switched?"

Scarlet shook her head. "That's what I don't know." Her eyes flashed and flickered between Vega and Cassie. "You're the puzzle solvers. Any thoughts?"

"These things happen, I suppose," said Vega.

Cassie frowned. "Not here. Not at Starling Academy. All these 'mistakes,' 'coincidences,' 'mysteries'—they don't just *happen* here."

Vega nodded reluctantly. "Agreed."

"So do you think somebody switched our records?" said Scarlet. "On purpose? But those things don't happen here, either . . . do they?"

The three Starlings traded worried looks. They were all thinking the same thing, but no one was quite ready to put such a dark thought into words. Then, suddenly, Cassie's lacy silver sweater pocket beeped. She pulled out her Star-Zap and read the holo-text. Behind her glasses her eyes grew big and round.

"It's the botany lab!" she exclaimed. "They've finished testing the flowers and have the results!"

"Well? What did they find?" asked Vega.

"They don't say. They just say to come."

"That's one connection I still don't see," Vega told her. "And it's not just because I want to win our bet. I was hoping Piper and I would get along better when the flowers were out of our room. . . ."

"And did you?"

"No. Nothing changed. In fact, you should have heard how she went on about my letting you take them to the lab to be studied. You would have thought I'd stolen her bed."

"Really . . ." Cassie's nearly translucent eyebrows slid together as she frowned.

"But then suddenly yesterday," Vega went on, "she gave me this sweet holo-poem she'd written . . . and this morning we meditated together." She smiled at Cassie's and Scarlet's dumbfounded expressions. "Cross my stars! I know!"

"There might still be a connection . . ." said Cassie.

Vega shrugged. "There's only one way to find out." She slipped one arm through Cassie's, then the other through Scarlet's.

"You want me to come, too?" Scarlet eyed Vega's elbow and gingerly unhooked her arm.

"Of course," said Vega. "Right, Cassie?" She tried not to look too hurt by Scarlet's initial response.

"Moon and stars, yes," said Cassie, smiling warmly. "We're in this together now."

CHAPTER 7

The botany lab was in Halo Hall in the science stellation, where the Starlings' Wishology and Astrophysics classes—among dozens of others—were held. Those labs, though, were on the lower floors. The botany lab took up most of the top floor and had a ceiling made of glass so the hydrongs of plants and flowers growing there had all the sunlight or starlight or moonlight they could want.

Naturally, there were specimens from all over Starland: featherjabbers, mellomallows, even nomadic druderwomps—shrublike knots of glittery branches that were constantly uprooting themselves and lazily rolling around the lab until they got bored and decided to stop and spread their roots, inevitably tripping someone up.

The lab was best known, though, for its extensive collection of flora samples from Wishworld. It was the largest collection on Starland, in fact. Generations of Wish-Granters had brought back everything from Spanish moss to buttercups to fragrant evergreen trees. Scientists were still working to get those to bloom ornaments the way they did on Wishworld . . . but so far, they'd had no luck. Scarlet's personal favorites were the dandelions, which were like two flowers in one, the second better than the first: a starburst of yellow petals followed by tickly cloud-white fluff. And best of all Wishers used them to make wishes! Plus they didn't overwhelm you with that cloying flower smell, which was always such overkill, Scarlet thought.

The three Starlings—Scarlet, Vega, and Cassie—entered and were met by a pair of turquoise-haired technicians in sturdy star-covered overalls under long shimmery white lab coats.

"Ah! Star greetings, Cassie," said one, a short woman with a blue holo–name tag reading GLADIOLUS ROSE. "Oh, my stars, you got here quickly! You must have ridden a laser beam!"

She clasped her hands and bowed, as was Starland custom. Her partner did the same. He was taller by a moonstone and wore a hard-to-miss star-shaped bandage on his nose.

Cassie bowed in return, as did Vega and Scarlet.

"We couldn't wait to hear the results of your tests!" Cassie told the lab technicians. She nodded to the man. "What happened to you, by the way?"

"What? Oh, this?" The man patted his bandaged nose, then turned to his flickering silver-tinged partner, who guiltily sucked in her cheeks. "Flying flowerpot . . . Funny story . . ." He sighed. "Or at least it will be, I hope, one starday."

"Why don't we show them those flowers?" said his partner.

He nodded. "Good idea."

"After you. Please." She waved him past.

"Star salutations, but please, no, after you."

They went on like that, back and forth, until Scarlet couldn't take one more exchange.

"Why don't you show us *together*?"

"Great idea!" they said in unison. "To the back of the lab. This way."

The Starlings followed them down a winding aisle between empty workstations.

"Where is everyone?" Vega asked.

Gladiolus Rose picked up an uprooted kaleidoscope

tree sapling and set it on a counter between a broken beaker and an upside-down microscope. "Most of the botanists decided to go home early yesterday. We stayed to finish this job. The energy in the air was rather . . . *tense*, you might say. Lots of name-calling, flowerpot flinging, energy sapping, I'm afraid."

"Not much work getting done," said her partner. "Not safely, anyway."

Scarlet gazed around at the mess and couldn't help cracking a smile. She could only imagine the scene that must have made it.

"That sounds like Piper and me," said Vega. "Until yesterday afternoon." Suddenly, her expression began to change. "When exactly did your fighting stop?"

"Almost as soon as we put them behind glass," Gladiolus Rose answered. "When was that?" She turned to her partner. "In the afternoon?"

"Indeed, it was."

Cassie's eyes grew round, and so did Vega's. Scarlet's jaw dropped slightly, too.

"Are you saying you think the flowers made you bicker and fight?" asked Vega.

"I'm afraid so," the techs said together. "Star apologies!" They bowed and laughed.

"As you can see," said Gladiolus Rose, "arguing is

not in our nature. So as soon as it started, we knew that something was starmendously wrong."

"The moment we put them behind glass, however," the man said, "the fiery tempers cooled."

He pointed to a glass case at the end of the lab. Inside, the Starlings could see Vega and Piper's lavish coral-colored bouquet.

Scarlet instantly remembered the flowers, though she'd given them little thought when they showed up in her room. Not surprisingly, Leona had claimed them for her half of the room almost immediately, so Scarlet paid even less attention to them after that.

"You were absolutely correct in suspecting those flowers of negative energy," Gladiolus Rose told Cassie as they moved toward the case. "The things are full of it, in fact. The measurements we recorded were frankly *floozels* off the charts. It's as if each and every flower was grown in negative-energy-infused soil."

Scarlet scowled and spoke up. "But isn't that impossible? Every Bad Wish Orb is destroyed immediately. That's one of the first things we learn when we get to this school."

"Moon and stars! We didn't think negative energy even *existed* on Starland," said Cassie with a gulp.

Scarlet hadn't thought Cassie could look any paler—and yet, somehow, she did.

Gladiolus Rose shook her head. "It doesn't. Technically," she said.

"What do you mean?" Vega asked.

The two lab technicians exchanged grim glances.

The tall one cleared his throat. "There have been leaks in the past . . . from the Bad Wish Containment Center."

"*But* that was *hydrongs* of staryears ago," his partner assured the Starlings. "There have been mix-ups, too . . . bad wishes mistaken for good ones at first. . . . But such a thing is exceedingly rare, and by the time the mistake is corrected, almost all the potential negative energy has yet to be released."

"'Almost'?" Vega said.

"Almost." The woman nodded. "So, yes, it's not beyond the spectrum of possibility for there to be a microjoule in the air. But nowhere near enough to account for the concentrations we're seeing here. It's unprecedented, frankly." She turned to peer into the case. "Never before, at least in this lab, have we seen negative plant life half as powerful—or *negative*—as this."

"So . . . what you're saying, then," said Scarlet, "is

that this mystery still isn't solved. You don't know where the flowers came from."

"Not yet. No. But our tests aren't finished. There are a few more we can do. Hopefully, we can identify the exact source of the negative energy and even pinpoint where the flowers were grown."

"How long will it take, do you think?" asked Vega.

"I'd say a starday . . . maybe two . . . three at most." Gladiolus Rose shrugged. "It's difficult to say until the rest of the staff returns to work."

Her partner gazed around the overturned lab. "We were also hoping to straighten things up a little first. That's one thing about this Wishworld dirt . . . it doesn't seem to clean itself up. It just sits there when it's spilled."

"Well, we can help you with *that*," said Vega matter-of-factly. She looked down at the loose Wishworld dirt scattered across the floor. Her eyes narrowed as she focused her energy on gathering the dirt into a pile. As soon as she collected it all, Vega flicked her wrist and lifted it in a steady stream, using her finger to steer it into the nearest flowerpot.

Scarlet looked over to see Cassie starting to use her energy, as well. One by one, on the counter in front of Cassie, overturned plants were popping upright.

"Star salutations!" said the lab technicians.

Vega beamed. "It's the least we can do! Scarlet . . . ? What are you waiting for over there? The faster we clean up this lab, the faster they can run more tests."

"Why don't we just zap up some Bot-Bot maids?" said Scarlet, looking bleakly around the room. She would rather have linked arms with Leona than do that job, even with the help of her energy manipulation.

"And where would be the fun in that?" asked Vega brightly, adjusting a trayful of laser-bean seedlings just so.

Suddenly, she jumped, and so did Cassie. Both Starlings pulled out their Star-Zaps.

"Moon and stars!" gasped Cassie. She looked at Vega, who was just closing her device and slipping it back into her fitted coat.

"What is it?" asked Scarlet.

Cassie hurried over to Scarlet and whispered so the lab technicians wouldn't hear: "Another Wish Orb's been identified." Only a few faculty besides Lady Stella and Lady Cordial knew of the existence of the Star Darlings, and it was imperative it stay that way. "We have to go to Lady Stella's office. Immediately. To find out whose wish this will be."

"I'm coming, too!" Scarlet moved toward the lab door.

"Did your Star-Zap go off?" Cassie asked.

Scarlet stopped and put her hand on the pocket of her hooded vest. She hadn't felt any vibration. She looked, but she knew the answer was no before she saw the screen. "I'm going anyway."

"I don't know. . . ." Cassie shook her head. "Lady Stella knows best, and if she didn't summon you, I don't think that you *can* go."

"But I'm a Star Darling!"

"*Shhh!*" Cassie quickly glanced over her shoulder. Luckily, the lab technicians were in the far corner, straightening some crooked holo-screens.

"But I *am* a Star Darling!" Scarlet hissed. "If there's a wish assignment, I should be there!"

Vega had come over, too. Both she and Cassie took Scarlet's hands. "Patience, Scarlet. If you truly are a Star Darling—and I certainly don't doubt it—then the stars will realign for you, all in due time," Vega said.

Scarlet yanked her hands away and squeezed her lips together tightly. She was close to saying something she just might regret.

"We'll let you know what happens," Cassie assured her.

"Whatever." Scarlet raised her chin and looked away.

She would have liked to see how much patience Vega or Cassie or any other Star Darling would have were she to trade places with one of them.

High above, over the ceiling skylight, a pink cloud the shape of a galliope's head slowly drifted past. She closed her eyes and thought of Wishworld, somewhere beyond it, orbiting through space full of wishes.

"Keep your stars up," said Vega. She reached out and gave Scarlet's arm a squeeze. "If we see Lady Cordial, we'll ask her about your reports. . . . I'm sure we'll have some good news for you by the time you're done helping here!"

"*Well?*"

"*Starf!*"

"*Scarlet!* Moon and *stars*!"

"You scared the light out of us!" Vega gasped.

"Star apologies." Scarlet stepped all the way around the column she'd been standing behind and pulled her hood back from her face. They were in the hall outside Lady Stella's office, where Scarlet had been lurking for a starhour, or quite possibly longer. She could have waited for Vega and Cassie to holo-call or text her, but waiting had never been Scarlet's style.

"Why were you hiding?" asked Cassie.

"I wasn't *hiding*. I was just trying to stay out of sight . . ." Scarlet explained.

Cassie and Vega wrinkled their glittery foreheads.

"Anyway," Scarlet went on. "What happened? Who got the mission? And what did Lady Stella have to say about *me*? I didn't see Ophelia come out. Have they already told her about the mistake?"

Vega's cheeks flashed ever so faintly. Cassie's lip slid beneath her teeth. Scarlet couldn't tell if they looked more like they'd eaten too much zoomberry cake or like someone had stolen cake from them.

"What's wrong?"

Vega's and Cassie's eyes met and something passed between them. Scarlet felt her glow dim as it did.

"Tell me."

Vega took a deep breath. "The Wish Orb was Ophelia's."

"The Wish Orb . . . the Wish Orb was *what*?"

"The Wish Orb was Ophelia's," Vega said again, letting her breath out as she did.

"Wait . . . so what are you saying?"

"The Wish Orb was Ophelia's," Cassie patiently repeated.

Scarlet's glow returned in a flash, this time hot pink. "I get that," she muttered. "But are you saying . . . Are you saying a *Star Darling* Wish Orb chose Ophelia? Are you saying the next Star Darling mission is *hers*? Are you saying . . ." Scarlet closed her eyes and opened them slowly. "Are you saying Ophelia is going to go to Wishworld to grant a wish instead of *me*?"

Vega nodded.

"Or at least almost there," Cassie said.

"Star apologies, Scarlet. For what it's worth, we believed you . . . but you were wrong, I guess." Vega reached out to touch Scarlet's shoulder, but Scarlet stepped away.

"I wasn't *wrong*," she snapped. "There was nothing to be wrong about. Scores are scores. I saw what I saw. Tell me . . . Lady Cordial . . . what did she have to say?"

Vega and Cassie responded with shrugs.

"Not much," said Vega, "as usual. She just wished Ophelia lucky stars."

"That's all? She didn't mention the holo-records? Did she at least look starprised?"

"*Everyone* looked starprised," said Vega.

"Especially Ophelia," Cassie agreed.

"Actually, Lady Cordial probably looked the least

starprised," added Vega. "Maybe she'd already looked into your theory, Scarlet, and all the holo-records, and didn't see what you think you saw."

"No one's saying you're lying, Scarlet—or that we were happy to see you go. . . . And we're definitely not saying there aren't weird things going on. . . ."

"But I don't think your leaving the Star Darlings is one," added Vega.

"You can still help us get to the bottom of the flower mystery!" said Cassie brightly.

"*Flowers?* Are you shooting my stars? I don't give a crater about your flower mystery," Scarlet fired back. "I hope whoever sent them sends you a hydrong more, in fact!"

CHAPTER 8

The rest of the day passed in a haze of bitter disappointment for Scarlet. She skipped lunch in the Celestial Café and filled her stomach with cocomoons and gloranges from the Starling Academy orchard instead. Since Starland fruit grew back, full and ripe, as soon as it was picked, Scarlet didn't have to worry about taking too much—or getting in trouble for it.

Skipping class was another story. That wasn't as easy to do. So Scarlet sat through hers, hood pulled down, in the farthest back corner of each room. She barely listened to the lessons, though, since what did they matter to her now? Did she even want to go to Wishworld to grant wishes? The more she thought about it . . . who *cared*?

So as Professor Andromedus Galapas droned on about the Enlightenment and the lighterature of the day, Scarlet drafted a holo-message to her parents, begging them to take her . . . *somewhere*, since they didn't exactly have a home.

Dear Mom and Dad,
Wherever you are, please come and get me. As soon as you possibly can. Or if you're too busy, feel free to send a Starcar and I will come to you. It's taken me almost three staryears, but I finally see that I was wrong and you were right. I was lucky to be able to travel all around Starland with you, having tutors instead of teachers who think they're so shiny and bright at some silly snooty school full of Starlings who act like they're the center of the whole universe. I made a starmendous mistake applying to Starling Academy. I wasn't meant to grant Wishling wishes. Never mind what I said about hating the idea of a family trio. I was wrong. Take me back, please, so I can play the drums with you.

Love and stars,
Scarlet

She read it over . . . raised her finger . . .
She sighed and hit DELETE.

"You'd like to go, Scarlet?"

"Huh?" Scarlet heard her name and looked up.

Professor Galapas was staring at her. So was the rest of the class. Open holo-books hovered in front of everyone but Scarlet, their text projected into the air.

"You raised your hand? You'd like to read aloud next?"

"What? No, sir. I mean, I didn't mean to." Scarlet looked at her finger, which was still in the air, then back at the teacher in the front of the room.

His bald head gleamed like the ice-covered summit of the Crystal Mountains. His face was as round as a star ball and just as bright. When he wore dark robes, as he usually did, it was almost as if the moon was up there teaching the class.

"'*Mean* to.' A mere technicality. Some things are written in the stars. Please, Scarlet, *enlighten* us. Just pick up where Leona concluded, if you don't mind."

Scarlet panicked slightly, and her eyes cut to her old roommate, whose seat was always front and center in every room, like she was a curly-haired sun for the world to orbit.

"Um . . ." She opened her holo-book and projected a page. She had no idea if it was the *right* one. Before she could read, though, and know for certain, the image in front of her blinked. The page changed, and Scarlet sensed Leona looking at her with a half smile on her bright gold-flecked face.

"You owe me."

Scarlet had barely escaped from Constellation Classroom 315 when a voice behind her made her stop.

"What?" She knew the voice before she turned. Still, she hadn't expected Leona's expression, which was somewhere between "Please, don't leave me" and "Gotcha!"

"You owe me," Leona repeated.

"Uh . . . star salutations . . . ?" Scarlet said. Leona had been unexpectedly generous in giving Scarlet the correct page number, she supposed. She bowed and reluctantly worked to soften her permanent frown.

But Leona shook her head. "I don't want your salutations."

"Then what do you want?"

Leona crossed her tawny, sparkling arms over her gold mesh tunic. "I want you to come back to the band."

"Oh." Scarlet jammed her hands in the pockets of her hoodie. "Star apologies. No can do. Besides, have you happened to notice you have a new roommate? *Ophelia?*" She could feel her cheeks glowing hotter and hotter. "I'm not a Star Darling anymore."

Leona shrugged. "Who said you had to be one?"

"Uh, you did, I'm pretty sure."

"Did I?" Leona squeezed one eye shut, trying to remember. "Well, if I did, then I changed my mind."

"Great. Then find one of the other hydrongs of students here to be your drummer, because I'm not interested," Scarlet said.

"Oh, come *on*," Leona groaned. "Stop *pouting* already and just come *back*. At least until Starshine Day, so we can win the battle of the bands."

Scarlet laughed. "You're hystarical, you know that, Leona?" She shook her head in disbelief. "Do you honestly think I care one proton about some Starling Academy battle of the bands? Or if the Star Darlings win? *Especially* after the way you wrote me off the moogle you found out I wasn't a Star Darling anymore? How about I put this in your own words, the ones you said when I came to you then: 'I don't give a star.' How's that? Hmmm? Now you know how it feels."

Leona stood there, her glow visibly faded. She clearly didn't know what to say. Scarlet would have been happy with a simple "star apologies," but that was a lot to ask, she guessed.

Or was it?

Leona's golden lips slowly opened and a word began to form.

Beep!

She jumped at the sudden sound of her Star-Zap and quickly pulled it out. Whatever the holo-text said, it made her eyes pop, and whatever word she'd had primed disappeared.

"Gotta fly!"

"What happened?" asked Scarlet.

Leona paused. "It's Ophelia . . ." she began. Then she checked herself and turned away.

"What about her?" Scarlet went on.

But by then, Leona was gone.

If Leona had any idea Scarlet was following her, she didn't let on. When it was clear that she was heading to Lady Stella's office, Scarlet hung back a little more. She hugged the cool marble wall at the end of the corridor and watched Leona and the other Star Darlings file over the threshold. . . . Then, just as the door started closing, Scarlet silently slipped through.

The Star Darlings were all so excited no one took notice of the pink-tinged shadow making its way to the back of the room. Scarlet slid into the corner, behind a potted boingtree. The branches were far enough apart for Scarlet to peek through but full enough of bright color-changing leaves to serve as an excellent screen.

She looked for Lady Stella but couldn't see her. The Star Darlings seemed starprised by her absence, as well, and stood chattering anxiously instead of taking seats around the large full moon–shaped table in the center of the room, as they'd normally do.

When Lady Stella finally entered through the hidden door in the back of her office, which led to the Star Darlings' secret Star Caves, her face wore uncharacteristic lines. She paused to consider every Star Darling, gazing deeply into each pair of eyes.

"What's up?" Gemma blurted.

"*Gemma!*" Her sister, Tessa, elbowed her in the ribs.

"I'm afraid," Lady Stella began, "that something quite troublesome is up. There are problems with this latest mission."

"What kind of problems?" Sage asked with a flash. "The same kind of problems we've had before?"

"I'm afraid not," said Lady Stella. "These are far graver. . . . Ophelia's Wish Orb has gone black."

A unified gasp whooshed through the room, as if every air molecule was sucked out. From the shadows, Scarlet watched the stunned Star Darlings grab and squeeze one another's hands. A black Wish Orb meant not only a failing mission but the potential loss of a Starling, as well.

"So . . . what do we *do*?" said Leona. "Someone has to *help* her!"

"Yes, someone does," Lady Stella agreed.

"I'll go!" said Leona. "I'm ready right now. I can do it this time! Send me!" She moved toward Lady Stella, but the headmistress motioned her back.

"Star salutations, Leona, for your generous offer, but—"

"But what? I can't go because I failed my mission? But I thought you said that wasn't my fault!"

"No, it's not that, Leona," Lady Stella assured her. Calmly she waved away the sparks that were sputtering out of Leona's ears. "I'm afraid only a Wish Orb can pick who goes, as on every other mission when help is required. This situation, of course, is far more dire. But the same procedure is required." Then Lady Stella reached into the folds of the long silver robe she wore. In her hand sat Ophelia's Wish Orb. Each time before, when Lady Stella had gathered them to see who the Wish Orb would choose to help grant the wish, the orb had lost some of its glow. But this orb smoldered dully like a lump of crater coal. It was the ugliest thing Scarlet, or any other Starling, had ever seen in her life.

Lady Stella spread her fingers and let the orb rise and hover between her and the Star Darlings. After a moogle, it began to move . . . slowly drifting past each glittery, worried face in search of the one it would choose.

"Where is it going?" asked Vega as it floated up to her last, then swerved. "It's not choosing any of us? It's flying away. It's trying to get out of the room."

"No . . . it's not," said Cassie, pointing. "Look. It's heading into the corner over there, toward that kaleidoscope tree."

Sure enough, it was. Scarlet watched it approach, just as confused as everyone else. As it reached the tree and stopped, however, she understood at once.

"It chose me!"

Scarlet stepped out from behind the tree, beaming. It was the first smile she'd worn in stardays. She'd almost forgotten how smiling felt. In her palm rested the Wish Orb, which had firmly settled there as soon as she had held her hand out.

"*What the stars?*" exclaimed Gemma.

Tessa was too shocked to respond to her sister with her usual reproach.

"That's impossible!" said Leona. "She's not a Star Darling anymore!"

"And yet . . ." Lady Stella glided toward Scarlet, wearing an expression of not unhappy starprise. "Scarlet, I do not know how you got here, but Ophelia's Wish Orb has indeed chosen you. And it is you who must go help Ophelia—and hopefully make the wish come true."

CHAPTER 9

By the time Scarlet's shooting star delivered her to Wishworld, she had fully transformed from a Starling into as convincing a Wishling as a Starling could be. Her skin was flat and freckled, without a hint of sparkle or a tinge of pink. Her eyes were brown instead of rose-colored. She had even toned down her hair so it was black with a single streak of bright pink.

Scarlet was pretty sure, too, that the outfit she'd ultimately chosen would convince any Wishling she might encounter that she'd lived there all her life. First she'd picked those pants Wishlings adored—according to Professor Margaret Dumarre, who knew the ways of Wishlings inside and out. Dungarees, she called them, though most Starlings who'd been to Wishworld seemed to refer to them as jeans. Scarlet also wore a deep burgundy hoodie made of a dense, rather stiff Wishling fabric, with a puffy black vest over that. Finally, on her feet were brand-new boots from Lady Stella, which would be her Wish Pendant from then on. One day, on her own mission, the rows of star-shaped energy-absorbing jewel buckles would light up when she met her Wisher and absorb all the wish energy produced when that Wisher's wish came true. For now, however, Scarlet was careful to pull her jeans down to cover as many of the jewels as she could.

Scarlet stood where she'd landed, in a Wishworld meadow filled with green grass and yellow flowers, canopied by a bright blue sky. In the distance, she could see a sharp steeple and the starkly angled rooftops of what looked like a small town.

So strange . . . she thought as she looked around. *And so . . . uncomfortable, as well.*

She sensed it first on her back . . . then on the top of her head, under her hood: a deep, inescapable feeling unlike any other she'd ever had. It didn't take away from the excitement of being on Wishworld at last . . . it just distracted her a bit.

Scarlet pulled down her hood and that helped a little, especially when a light breeze swept through her hair.

But the uncomfortable feeling soon returned, stronger than before. Scarlet slipped off her vest and began to fan herself. That made a big difference, she discovered with relief.

Curious, she checked her Star-Zap to see what the temperature was. *Solar flare!* she thought as she realized how much warmer it was there than on Starland. Quickly, she reactivated her Wishworld Outfit Selector and dialed up a tank top.

Ah, much better, she thought.

She wasn't there to worry about her comfort, though, Scarlet reminded herself. She was there to do a job—and, even more important, to prove what she could do! She needed to fix whatever mess Ophelia had made and get a wish granted and wish energy collected as soon as Starlingly possible. Ophelia had already squandered half the time the Wish Orb gave her, so there wasn't a moogle left to waste.

Quickly, she folded up her star and slipped it into her pocket. Then she switched her Star-Zap to locator mode.

"Take me to Ophelia!" she told it, and directions appeared instantly.

To Scarlet's starprise, the directions led her away from the town and into a vast field. It appeared to be full of some kind of crop, from what Scarlet had learned of Wishling ways of growing food. The plants stood in straight rows and were tall—much taller than she—with long, pointy, floppy green leaves. Near each stalk bloomed tight tubelike flowers nearly the size of Scarlet's arm, each with dark silky threads spilling from its top.

They gave off a distinct sweetish scent, too, which made Scarlet's nose begin to twitch. . . .

She stepped forward and bumped right into something. "*Starf!*" she said, stepping back. She stepped forward again. Same thing. As she reached out into the air in front of her, Scarlet's hand encountered a smooth surface. Aha! A smile spread across her face. It was the smooth surface of an invisible tent!

"Ophelia?"

Scarlet knelt down and cautiously parted the flaps of the glitter-covered tent—Ophelia's glitter-covered invisibility-cloaked tent, to be exact. As she did, a glittery, wide-eyed, freckled face peered out with a tiny panicked squeal.

"*Eeh!* Oh! *Oh*, thank *stars* you're here!" Ophelia gasped, bursting out of the tent and into Scarlet's arms.

Scarlet fell backward onto the star-studded back pockets of her jeans.

"Star apologies!" said Ophelia, clambering off her.

"It's just so good to see a friendly—oh . . . um . . . to see a familiar face, at least."

Indeed, Scarlet's face was far from friendly then. She could feel the irritation hot beneath her sneer. "What in the stars are you doing in your tent, Ophelia? And please tell me you've changed your appearance and you don't still look like *that* to everyone here. . . ." Scarlet knew Starlings always looked glittery to each other, no matter where they were or what form they assumed. Something, though, about the way Ophelia was flashing and hiding made Scarlet think she just might look glittery to Wishlings, too.

Ophelia looked down at her shimmering skin and wrung her hands, which only amplified their glow. "Those answers go together, I guess." She looked up miserably and gulped.

"You were supposed to change your appearance and find your Wisher!" Scarlet said, disgusted. "Did you try to do *either* of those things?"

Ophelia nodded meekly. "I tried. But I don't know . . . nothing seemed to work. . . ." She pulled out her Star-Zap and showed it to Scarlet. "This was supposed to help me change my appearance, right?"

Scarlet nodded.

"Well, nothing happened. . . ."

"What do you mean 'nothing'? It's so easy. . . . No Wishworld Outfit Selector, either?"

Ophelia shook her head. "And when I asked it to take me to my Wisher . . ."

"What? What did it say?"

"It said, 'Reply hazy. Ask again.'"

"So did you?"

"Only a hydrong times," Ophelia groaned. "Finally, I just tried to go and find her in that little town on my own."

"Like *that*?" Scarlet asked, looking Ophelia up and down.

"Well . . . what else could I do?" she said meekly. "But I didn't try for very long. Everyone was staring and asking me questions like 'Is there a circus in town?' and 'Are you a clown?' What's a circus and what's a clown, anyway?"

"Um, they're like royalty," Scarlet guessed, since she didn't know.

"Oh." Ophelia nodded. "So, anyway, I gave up because of that. And because of this thing, too." She held her hand out toward Scarlet. On her wrist was a thick yellow bracelet studded with star-shaped jewels.

"Is that your Wish Pendant?"

Ophelia nodded. "Pretty, isn't it?" She sighed.

"Did it ever glow?"

Ophelia shook her head. "Not even a little," she replied. "I thought it was because I couldn't find my Wisher, but now I'm not so sure that it's not broken, too. . . . But anyway, that's why I'm here." She gazed at the field around her tent. "I didn't know where else to go, and at least my Star-Zap could do this. I really wanted to make this mission succeed. Truly, Scarlet, I did." She sniffed. "I didn't mean to fail." Her glittery orange eyelashes fluttered as glittery orange tears welled in her eyes. "I'm just so happy to see you, Scarlet! Truly, I am! How in the stars did you know to come?" She paused as another question suddenly popped into her head. "But why . . . how is it *you*, Scarlet? I thought . . ." She stopped and bit her thumb.

"It's okay. Go ahead and say it," said Scarlet. "You thought I'd been kicked out of the group for good? You're right. I was. But I never should have been. It was all a big mistake."

"So you're back in?" exclaimed Ophelia. She wiped her tears and began to grin. "That's starmendous! I'm so happy for you! And so relieved . . ." She sighed. "So. Shall I wait here while you go find the Wisher and grant her wish so we can go home?"

"I wish," Scarlet muttered.

Ophelia looked confused.

"It's still your wish," Scarlet told her. She shrugged as Ophelia's smile of relief collapsed. "Hey, don't blame me. I don't make the rules. According to Lady Stella, I'm here to help. That's all."

Ophelia gestured toward her Starling garments, then to her fluorescent-orange pigtails.

"Here." Scarlet dialed up APPEARANCE TRANSFORMATION on her Star-Zap and placed it in Ophelia's hand. "Try mine and see what happens."

Ophelia clutched it tightly, holding her breath.

"Recite the mantra!" Scarlet reminded her. "And put one hand on your bracelet!"

"Oh, right . . . Star light, star bright, first star I . . ."

"See tonight."

"See tonight. I wish I may, I wish I might, have this wish I . . ."

"Wish!"

"Wish . . . tonight."

Scarlet watched with more irritation than relief as the sparkle finally drained from Ophelia's skin and hair like sand through an hourglass.

She noticed a bit of loose glitter clinging to her arms and the frizzy ends of her dull orange pigtails.

"Shake," Scarlet told Ophelia.

She did.

"How do I look?" Ophelia asked, rubbing her newly green eyes and inspecting her pale pink fingernails.

"Dull," Scarlet replied approvingly. "Now dial up the Wishworld Outfit Selector and let's get out of here. See that?" She pointed to the steadily counting-down timer in the Star-Zap's upper left corner. "That's how much time we have left to grant this wish. One moogle longer and the mission fails."

Ophelia gasped. "But . . . isn't that less than a Wishworld week?"

Scarlet shook her head. "More like less than a Wishworld day."

"Oh, I hope we can grant it," said Ophelia. "It will be so hard to go back if we don't. . . ."

Scarlet laughed. She couldn't help it. Ophelia had so much still to learn.

"What's so funny?"

"Don't be silly," said Scarlet. "You'll just use your star." Scarlet sighed. This was way worse than she had imagined.

"My star?" Before, Ophelia had looked anxious. Now she simply looked confused.

"Your star," said Scarlet. "The one that you came on.

The one you have folded up in your backpack . . . Wait. What? No! Don't tell me you don't!"

Ophelia shook her head slowly—once in each direction. Her mouth trembled, but no sound came out.

"Well, where is it? What did you do with it?" asked Scarlet. She groaned. "Oh, don't tell me you let it fizzle out!"

"I didn't mean to . . ." said Ophelia, sniffling back tears. "Nobody told me about folding it up. . . ."

CHAPTER 10

No working Star-Zap . . . No shooting star . . . Was it even possible for Ophelia to get back to Starland, Scarlet wondered, even if they found Ophelia's Wisher and somehow she granted her wish in time? They could use Scarlet's Star-Zap to lead them in the right direction, at least, which Scarlet quickly had them do. But how, if every other Star Darling so far had collected less energy than she'd hoped to on her mission, could an incompetent Starling like Ophelia ever collect enough to enable Scarlet's star and Star-Zap to take them both home?

The answer, Scarlet realized, was that it wasn't her problem! And she couldn't help smiling as she thought about it more. Sure, it would be too bad if a wish didn't get granted. Scarlet valued the energy wishes produced as much as anyone else. And yet . . . if it meant Ophelia was stuck on Wishworld and out of the cosmos at least for a little while, that would also mean Scarlet's Star Darling status would return and her reputation would undoubtedly be redeemed. And Scarlet would just make up for the energy loss on her own mission, when the next Wish Orb chose her!

The thought burned so brightly in Scarlet's mind she couldn't think about anything else, including the quaint, quiet Wishworld town she and Ophelia soon found themselves in.

"Moon and stars . . ." Ophelia murmured as she hung close by Scarlet's side. She'd tried to link arms with Scarlet but had instantly sensed her mistake. "Wishworld is so much different than Starland City. Somehow, I thought they'd be more alike."

"This *town* is different," Scarlet agreed as she, too, took in the scene. Unlike the gleaming high-rise-filled Starland capital that went on for floozels—not including the suburbs, which stretched beyond that for floozels more—the Wishworld town appeared to be built around a single two-way street lined with tidy little stores. Scarlet read some of the signs in the windows and above the rectangular glass doors: LEE'S HARDWARE, GRANNY'S TOYS AND GAMES, MARVIN'S LUNCHEONETTE, ANNIE'S FUDGE

AND ICE CREAM SHOPPE. She wasn't sure what every word meant, but she felt like she got the idea.

A few dull yet cheerful adult Wishlings strolled along the sidewalks, greeting one another as they passed. "Hey, there," a man said warmly to Scarlet and Ophelia. He was pushing a cart full of folded papers and rectangular packages. Those were covered with paper, too. He stopped at the corner by a large blue boxy container with a slightly dented rounded lid. The Starlings watched him reach into the pocket of his short blue pants and pull out a key on a cord. He used it to open a door in the side of the box, where he found *more* paper.

"He's one of the Wishlings who asked me about the circus," whispered Ophelia. But he didn't seem too curious about her anymore. If he or any of the Wishlings in the town thought Ophelia or Scarlet looked out of place, they were not letting on.

"This seems like a small town," Scarlet told Ophelia. "I don't think all cities on Wishworld are this size. Just like on Starland, there are all different kinds. Have you ever been to Solar Springs?"

"Solar Springs?"

"You know, where Gemma and Tessa are from?"

Ophelia shook her head.

Scarlet shrugged. "You're not missing much. It's a lot

like this place. So where *have* you been?" she asked.

Ophelia tapped her fingers together. "Nowhere," she replied. "I've never been outside of Starland City before. I mean, until now."

"Not even Old Prism?" Old Prism was the original Starland settlement and the most popular tourist destination on Starland. Nearly every family took at least one vacation there.

But not Ophelia's family, evidently. She looked down and shook her head in reply.

"I didn't mean to make you feel bad," Scarlet assured her. "Star apologies. I'm just starprised. You know, you're lucky you don't have parents like mine who dragged you all over Starland with them."

"Do you really think? I think you're lucky to *have* parents," said Ophelia. She added, "I never actually got to know mine."

Scarlet caught a breath and swallowed it. Those were not words she'd expected to hear. She instantly wished she could take her own words back. But it was too late. *Now what?* she thought. How was she supposed to respond to something like that? *So you're an orphan? You need parents? Feel free to take mine!* Scarlet had never been good at finding the right thing to say. That kind of stuff was hard.

Luckily, she didn't have to say anything, because Ophelia said something first.

"Stars! Look! Palm scanners!" Ophelia pointed across the street at a square yellow box set on top of a pole. Inside, a big red hand flashed on and off. There was another one, they noticed, on their own corner, high above their heads. And they did resemble palm scanners—in some ways, Scarlet thought—but something about them wasn't quite right. First of all, yes, they were much, much too high for a Wishling palm to reach. Plus, there were no doors to be opened that Scarlet could see.

"I wonder how you reach them," said Ophelia. She stood on her toes and stretched her hand as far up to the one on their corner as it would go. Still, there was more than an arm's length between her hand and the red one, even when she jumped.

"Let's figure that out later," said Scarlet, "when we have to."

"Right," said Ophelia. "Of course."

Just then, a large yellow Wishling vehicle rolled past them on those round black things that Wishlings called . . . whorls? Wools? Whirls?

"That's a school bus!" said Scarlet. "And look! Here come some more."

"What's a school bus?" asked Ophelia.

"Are you serious?" said Scarlet.

She was.

"They're like starbuses, but they roll along on the ground instead of hovering above it. They take Wishling students to school when they don't already live there."

"Oh! So we're getting close to a school?"

"Very close," said Scarlet. She looked down the street at a large tan building with a tall gray pole planted in front of it.

"Look, Scarlet! Stars!" said Ophelia, pointing to the flag up at the top.

There wasn't enough breeze to keep the tricolored banner flying, but now and then it caught a gust. Scarlet saw the stars and instantly counted half a hydrong.

"So is that a school?" Ophelia asked as they watched the first yellow bus and several more exactly like it turn in and pull to a stop in front of the building.

Scarlet nodded and checked her Star-Zap. It was precisely where their directions led.

"It's so quiet. Where are all the Wishlings?" said Ophelia.

That was when they heard the bell. It came from inside the school, but even from that far away the ringing hurt their ears.

"What was that?" Ophelia asked Scarlet just as the doors to the school burst open and a flood of young Wishlings came pouring out.

Scarlet and Ophelia stood and watched lines form beside each school bus while other Wishlings simply walked away. . . .

"Oh, stars! Did we miss the school day?" Ophelia said with a gasp. "Is everyone going home? What are we going to do? I'll never find my Wishling now!"

"Not if you stand here like that, you won't," muttered Scarlet, grabbing her by the arm. She dragged Ophelia toward the school and pointed to her bracelet. "Keep an eye on your Wish Pendant!" she reminded her, sure that she'd forget. "We'll know we've found your Wishling as soon as it starts to glow."

Scarlet eyed Ophelia's bracelet, too, as they hurried past each bus. The lines outside the vehicles had all but disappeared. Engines were revving and drivers were calling, "All right! Find a seat and sit in it back there!"

"Superstar! There it goes!" said Scarlet as the bracelet blinked. "Your Wisher must be on this bus!" A moogle later she sighed. "Oh . . . no . . . The sun just caught a facet. It isn't glowing. Never mind."

She turned as a group of girls brushed past them, then paused by the closest bus. One girl was quite tall by Wishling standards, with laser-straight rows of tight black braids. The others were of average Wishling height. One had straight fair hair that hung smoothly down her back. The other's hair was dark and thick and curly and seemed to defy the basic rules of Wishworld gravity that Scarlet had learned in school.

"So you're sure you can't come home with us?" that girl was saying.

"Sorry. I really am," the tall girl said. "I have . . . all these chores to do today."

The fair-haired girl sighed heavily.

"You know this project is due on Friday," the first girl said. "And we're *all* supposed to contribute. This is a big part of our grade."

"Yeah. A *big* part." The other girl flipped her pale hair back with a toss of her head. "And we're doing *all* the work. I mean, I wish you'd said something about all these doctors' appointments and your piano recital—and today's chores—when we started on this."

"I . . . I . . ."

"If it's just chores, can't you do them later?" said the curly-haired girl. "Won't your mom understand if you just explain?"

The tall girl chewed on either side of her bottom lip.

"Well, you see . . . it's my *step*mom . . . and, well, she's, like, *soooo* mean."

"Oh . . ."

"Sorry . . ."

The two girls nodded sympathetically.

The tall girl heaved a heavy sigh, as if that was the story of her life.

"So what about *tomorrow*?" The girl with the fair hair asked more gently. "Can you at least come home with us then? If the chrysalises start hatching today, like I think they will, we'll have our butterflies and that'll be it."

"Oh, I hope they hatch today!" said the curly-haired girl.

"I know, right? I can't *wait*!" Her blond friend clapped quickly, as if beating a snare drum. "*Ooh!* You know what we should do? We should have a big butterfly party and celebrate!"

"Yes!"

The two traded *aha* grins while the third girl looked down at her shoes.

"Your stepmom would let you do that, wouldn't she?" the blond girl asked.

The tall girl shrugged. "I don't know. . . . She's so mean, like I said. . . ."

"All aboard!" the bus driver called down through the door just then. Both girls looked up and waved.

"Coming." The curly-haired girl turned back to the tall girl. "See you tomorrow, I guess, Arden."

"See you tomorrow, Chloe. Bye, Sydney."

"If the butterflies hatch, we'll text you."

"Great. Yes, definitely do."

"Um . . . sorry . . . about your stepmom and all. . . ."

"Thanks . . ." the girl murmured. "It's kind of hard."

"It's her!" Scarlet leaned over and hissed to Ophelia, more into her pigtail than her ear.

"Do you really think so? How do you know?" Ophelia turned to her. "Are you sure?"

Scarlet twisted her mouth in irritation. "Check your Wish Pendant and you'll see. I'll bet my stars it's that *stepmother*." Her eyes narrowed at the thought. "It's a classic Wishworld wish! She's probably been wishing to get rid of her . . . once and for all. But that's an impossible wish. *Well?*" She nodded toward Ophelia's wrist. "What are you waiting for? Check your bracelet!" Why she was so eager for Ophelia to find her Wisher, Scarlet didn't know. Just a few moogles earlier, she had wanted desperately for Ophelia to fail—but now, oddly, not so much.

She was as sure as a sundial the bracelet would be glowing like a fiery flare. But no . . . the star-shaped jewels on the bracelet were as lifeless as they had been before.

"I thought we'd found her. Didn't you?" Scarlet looked over her shoulder at the tall girl, still so close to them, watching her friends' bus pull away.

"Maybe she is my Wisher," said Ophelia. "Maybe, just like my Star-Zap, my Wish Pendant is powerless, too. . . ." She looked down at her wrist in frustration. Then, suddenly, her head bent farther down. "Did you bring a glowworm here with you from Starland?" she asked, pointing toward the ground.

"What?"

"You're glowing. There, on your ankle. Under your . . . what do you call those again?"

"Jeans," said Scarlet, distracted, as she followed Ophelia's eyes. Her ankle *was* glowing . . . even through the heavy pants!

She yanked up her cuff to discover the hot-pink star-buckles on her own Wish Pendant boots shining like quasars on her feet.

She looked up at Ophelia. "It's not a glowworm, it's my Wish Pendant."

Ophelia's eyes were as round as moons. "Why is *your* Wish Pendant glowing?"

"Don't ask *me*! *How should I know?*"

CHAPTER 11

The next thing Scarlet knew, her Wish Pendant faded from twinkling star to flat pink stone.

"What happened?" gasped Ophelia.

"I don't know. . . ." Could it have been some sort of false alarm? Then she looked up to see the tall girl had moved and was walking down the street. The Wisher just wasn't close. That was how Wish Pendants behaved.

"Come on. You've got to catch her!" Scarlet snapped at Ophelia as she hurried to follow the girl.

"Star greetings, Wishling."

The tall girl stopped midstride on the chalky gray sidewalk. "Excuse me?" she said, slowly turning, with a stiff note of dread in her voice.

Ophelia, who'd offered the greeting, covered her mouth with one hand. "Sorry! Forgot!" she whispered to Scarlet.

"*Hi.*" Scarlet looked back up and smiled at the Wishling. "Sorry." She pointed her thumb toward Ophelia. "My friend here thinks she's so funny when she says weird things like that."

The girl's eyes skipped back and forth between Scarlet and Ophelia. "Sorry, but do I know you? Do you go to this school?"

"No," said Ophelia innocently before Scarlet could stop her.

Scarlet smiled as she gritted her teeth. Had they been on Starland, sparks would have been shooting straight out of her ears.

"What she means is no, this isn't our regular school," Scarlet explained hurriedly. "But *temporarily*, yes, we go here." She checked to make sure Ophelia was listening carefully. "We're *exchange* students, you see."

"Really? That's so cool. Where are you from?" the girl asked.

"Where are we from?" *Good question*, thought Scarlet as her mind suddenly went blank. She tried to remember some of the names of places she'd learned in Wishworld Relations, names she'd imagined using on missions just like this hydrongs and hydrong of times. . . .

"Orion!" Ophelia blurted, lifting her chin and looking proud.

"Orion? Where is that?" asked the girl.

"It's just up there in the—"

Scarlet pulled Ophelia's arm down from above her head and put her other hand over Ophelia's startled mouth. "Did you think she said *Orion*? She said *Ohio*!" Scarlet laughed.

"Oh." The girl nodded, then grinned with a friendly shrug. "Well, welcome to Florida, I guess. I'm Arden. Nice to meet you."

"Hi. I'm Scarlet, and this is Ophelia. Nice to meet you, too," Scarlet replied before Ophelia could speak. She wasn't quite sure how Ophelia would have answered that introduction. She only knew somehow it would have been wrong.

"If you like, I could show you around," Arden offered.

"Really? That would be startastic!" exclaimed Ophelia.

Scarlet swallowed a groan and closed her eyes.

"Would you excuse us for just a minute?" Scarlet asked the girl, who shrugged.

Scarlet dragged Ophelia away from Arden by her backpack. "Ophelia!" she muttered. "You have to stop saying things like 'startastic' and 'star greetings.' Those are Starland phrases. Wishlings say things like 'awesome' and 'sick.' It's one of the first things we learned. Remember? Back in Wishers 101. What have you been learning at Starling Academy, anyway?"

"Star apologies . . ." mumbled Ophelia. "I guess I just forgot."

"Well, start remembering!" hissed Scarlet. "Or better yet, don't say anything else. Just let me do the talking. Okay? You worry about focusing all your energy on granting Arden's wish." She quickly checked her Star-Zap. "This clock is counting down very fast!"

"Yes. Okay." Ophelia nodded, and Scarlet hoped she understood. Scarlet wasn't sure how she'd gone from thinking it might be all right if Ophelia failed to being determined to see her succeed. It was almost as if she had no choice but to make the mission work.

"Is everything okay?" Arden asked when Scarlet and Ophelia returned.

"Everything is great."

"So, what do you think? Do you want to hang out? Do you want me to show you around? What haven't you seen yet?" asked Arden. "I know it's a pretty small town, but we have a really nice park. It's kind of famous for its butterfly attraction . . . er, um . . . but we can skip that part. It's not really all that great."

"Thanks," said Scarlet. "That sounds really nice. Really, it does. But . . ."

"But what?" Arden asked.

Scarlet tried to assume the expression she'd seen the other girls give Arden before—the one that seemed to say, "I feel so sorry for you, poor girl."

"You probably have to go straight home," said Scarlet.

"No," said Arden. "Not really." She smiled and shook her head. "I mean, I have to go home eventually, but later on—by dinnertime—not, like, right away."

Scarlet was confused and could tell that her face showed it. "Are you *sure*? I'd hate for you to get in trouble with your stepmother."

"How did you know I have a stepmother?"

"Er . . . I guessed, I guess?"

"Wow. Good guess," said Arden, who looked surprised but not upset.

"You probably wish you didn't have one," Scarlet went on, nodding. "Or at least that she wasn't so mean." She snuck a wink at Ophelia, then watched as Arden's expression slowly changed.

"No, my stepmother's great. She's not at all mean. In

fact—don't tell my mom this—but she's nicer than her sometimes."

Now it was Scarlet's turn to flip expressions. "But doesn't she make you stay home? And do all the chores? You know, and work all day and night?"

Arden's nose wrinkled and she started to giggle. "What are you talking about?" She looked down at her red ruffled skirt and sleeveless yellow tee. "Do I look like Cinderella? The only chores my stepmom makes me do are the dishes, sometimes, and make my bed . . . not that I ever do."

"But . . ."

Arden waited for Scarlet to finish, but Scarlet wasn't sure how to go on. Why had this Wishling told those others that she had a mean stepmother if she didn't? And most important, what was her wish, then? To have a *mean* stepmother? No, of course not. Why would any Wishling want that?

So then what could it be? Scarlet tried to think. She glanced at Ophelia, who was blank-faced, clearly trying to catch up. She wasn't going to be much help in figuring this out; Scarlet could tell from her frown. Then something else that Scarlet had heard before suddenly popped into her head—something about doctors' appointments. . . .

Of course! That had to be it!

There were no doctors on Starland, of course. There simply was no need. All the positive wish energy on Starland kept Starlings healthy throughout their Cycle of Life, until they began their afterglow. But Scarlet had learned in school about Wishworld doctors and all they did for Wishlings whenever they got sick. She'd also learned about the kinds of wishes that Wishlings often made when doctors couldn't help. Of course, those were impossible wishes, and maybe that was why Ophelia was having so much trouble. But Scarlet was sure they could help her make a more appropriate one.

"You're not well, are you?"

"Excuse me?"

"You're sick. Well, don't worry. We'll find a way . . ."

"But I'm *not* sick. I'm fine. Really. Why?" the girl asked, touching her cheeks. "Do I look bad or something?"

"No, no. You look good. It's not that," Scarlet said. What could she say now? If the Wisher wasn't sick and her stepmother wasn't mean, what wishes were left? Had she also said something about a piano recital?

Or . . . could it be that she wasn't their Wisher at all?

What a starmendous waste of time!

Scarlet looked down to check her Wish Pendant. It

was still glowing . . . which was odd. But it wasn't like this was *her* mission, so maybe it didn't mean anything.

"Omigosh," the girl said suddenly, as if a holo-text had just come through. "I get it." She turned to Ophelia. "You must have heard me talking to Chloe and Sydney."

Ophelia's cheeks filled like balloons as she worked to keep the words in.

"Yeah," Arden went on, not needing a reply. "Some of those things I said back there . . . they weren't exactly true."

"But *why*?" Ophelia blurted. "It sounded like they needed your help."

That was actually a good question, Scarlet thought, so that time she let it go.

"Oh . . . it's complicated," said Arden. She sighed and looked away.

"They're mean girls," said Scarlet knowingly. It was a common basis for wishes, unfortunately, but those weren't too hard to grant.

"No," said Arden. "They're fine. They're really nice and fun. And I want to be their friend. That's why I *wanted* to be in their lab group for this science project."

"Oh," Scarlet said, confused. Was this something Wishlings often did, she wondered—fail to make any sense?

"I didn't know they'd want to study butterflies. . . ." As she said that, Arden winced.

"What's wrong with butterflies?" said Scarlet.

"Are you afraid of them?" Ophelia asked.

Scarlet turned to Ophelia and did all she could not to roll her eyes. "Of course she's not afraid of *butterflies*!" she muttered. Could a Starling be more dim?

"I know," said Arden. "It's ridiculous, isn't it? But I can't help it. Do you know, I can't even look at pictures of butterflies without wanting to throw up? I tried to suggest other topics, but they were so into the idea. And they'd already ordered the caterpillar kit and everything. There was nothing I could say or do. Their minds were totally set."

"Did you tell them you were scared?" asked Scarlet. That seemed easy enough to do.

Arden nodded. "I tried to. But they thought it was a joke. They just laughed and said stuff like 'Can you imagine? Afraid of butterflies!' "

"So . . . they *are* mean," said Scarlet.

"No, they weren't being mean at all. They thought I was being funny. They thought it had to be a joke." Arden kicked a rock and sent it bouncing off the curb and into the street. "I guess I could have told them I was serious . . . except then, instead of laughing at the idea, they would have laughed at me."

"So what are you going to do?" Scarlet asked. She reached for Ophelia and pulled her near. She could sense a wish a breath away and wanted to make sure Ophelia heard it.

"What I've been doing, I guess: making up excuses to stay away. So I'll get an F on the project and Chloe and Sydney will never talk to me again. But what else *can* I do? I *wish* I wasn't afraid of butterflies . . . but we all know wishing doesn't help." She took a few steps away to kick another rock while Scarlet hung back and pumped her fist.

Yes! she thought as a sharp but not unpleasant jolt ran up and down her spine.

Scarlet turned to wink at Ophelia, but Ophelia's eyes were on the ground.

"Ophelia!" Scarlet nudged her with an elbow. "Your Wisher just voiced her wish! She doesn't want to be afraid of butterflies!" she hissed.

"Really? Oh! Sorry," Ophelia said. She glanced over her shoulder at Arden. "What do I do now? Oh . . . and what are butterflies? Are they, like, wings or something you can put on toasted Wishling bread?"

CHAPTER 12

After a quick explanation of what butterflies were ("They're basically like flutterfocuses, only they don't change color or light up."), Scarlet told Ophelia her plan.

"It's easy. We learned about these kinds of fear wishes in Wish Fulfillment, remember? No? Right. Of course you don't. Never mind. Basically, we have to get her to talk more about her fear and where it comes from. Then we have to reassure her that butterflies mean her no harm. Then we need to introduce her to butterflies. It's supposed to be little by little . . . but of course we don't have a lot of time. Luckily, there's that butterfly attraction she talked about—which is perfect! We just take her there! *Zap!* Done!"

"Talk, reassure, introduce," said Ophelia. She nodded

so her pigtails bounced like springs. "Star salutations, Scarlet. I'll try. I really will." Ophelia's chin was trembling, but she managed a smile. And somehow, before Scarlet could help herself, she was returning a grin.

Scarlet could feel it inside her. . . . *Ew!* Something was warming up and softening, like stars melting into thick molten glass. Scarlet tried to will it all back into sharp jagged crystals, but no—it was too late.

It was easy to be mad at Ophelia for taking her place, and even easier to scold her for making so many mistakes. And yet this whole situation wasn't Ophelia's fault any more than it was Scarlet's. The most important thing, whether Scarlet liked it or not, was to help Ophelia as much as she could to make Arden's wish come true.

"No," Scarlet told Ophelia sternly. "You're a Star Darling. You need to do more than try. You need to grant this wish. So go!" She pointed to Arden, who was walking away. "What are you waiting for?"

They caught up to Arden at the corner. She grinned at them warily. "So now you know my secret. You probably think I'm super weird."

"What are you talking about?" said Scarlet. "Everyone's scared of something. Take Ophelia here." She shot a quick nod at her partner.

"Me? Oh, yes! *Me!* I'm afraid of everything!" Ophelia

said. "Black holes . . . asteroids . . . gamma radiation . . . and even those energy bunnies that collect under the bed."

Scarlet and Arden both stared at her, speechless.

"Anyway," Scarlet said. "Being scared is nothing to be ashamed of. But it is something you can try to change."

"How?"

"Why don't we go to that park you were talking about," said Scarlet, "and talk about it there?"

The park was a short walk from the school, away from downtown. A dark metal arch marked the entrance at a corner where two roads crossed.

"Wait!" Arden grabbed Scarlet's and Ophelia's arms as they reached the corner across from it, just before they stepped off the curb. She pointed to the palm scanner across the street and the big bright red hand that was flashing at them.

"Right. The palm scanners," said Ophelia. "But I couldn't reach it. Can you?"

She started to jump as she'd done before in town, to reach the box above them. Scarlet almost joined her. But then she saw Arden laughing—not meanly, just as if they were all in on a joke. Clearly, Ophelia was way off. That wasn't a palm scanner at all. But if Ophelia was helping lift Arden's mood, why not play along?

"*Very* funny," said Scarlet. She chuckled and grabbed for Ophelia's arm. Just then, the hand stopped blinking and began to glow a steady red. As it did, a car whizzed past them, followed by another and more after that.

Scarlet watched Arden press a button on the side of the post on their corner, then read the small sign next to it: PUSH BUTTON TO WALK. A moogle later, the hand disappeared and was replaced by a white symbol of a walking man.

"Are you coming?" said Arden as she stepped off the sidewalk and into the street. "The light's going to change back if we don't hurry up."

"So . . . it's not a palm scanner?" Ophelia whispered to Scarlet as they followed. "I'm sorry. I messed up again."

"Hey, she's smiling," said Scarlet, nodding ahead. "I think you might actually have done something right."

"So this is our park," Arden said as they walked through the arch. She lifted her arms and stretched them out to her sides, turning slightly left and right. "It's small, but it's pretty nice."

It *was* nice, Scarlet had to agree, in an overly green Wishworld way. It was strange, and almost refreshing, to see grass so singular in color—and such straight paths that refused to move. It was actually nice to get away from all the glitter and sparkle of Starland and appreciate not just how colorful and brilliant things were but other qualities, as well. Like how the little brown creature on the branch high above them sounded, whistling its curious tune.

And the way the grass smelled. Scarlet took a deep whiff, which Arden noticed. She nodded as if she understood.

"They must have just mowed."

Ah, thought Scarlet. So that was what that sharp tangy scent was. Scarlet didn't even know how the grass on Starland smelled, she realized, or if it smelled at all. Starland grass always stayed the perfect length, so it never had to be cut.

Ophelia, meanwhile, was pointing at a large dull but colorful, oddly shaped structure behind a green metal fence. At the center was an elevated platform sheltered by a yellow roof. Along with a ladder, there appeared to be several other means by which to reach the platform: a winding blue ramp; a slick yellow pole; a thick knotted rope; and, last but not least, a long sloping red tube, out of which a small Wishling boy abruptly popped.

"What's that?" Ophelia asked.

"What's what?" Arden replied. Her eyes darted from

pole to ramp to tube, not quite sure what Ophelia could mean.

Scarlet pulled Ophelia close. "It's a playground. A *Wishling* playground," she clarified. She had seen them before from the Wishworld Surveillance Deck, but Ophelia obviously had not. If she had, she would have known that Wishling playgrounds were nothing like those on Starland, with their gyro-seesaws and anti-gravity slides and energy trampolines. There was one apparatus Starland and Wishworld shared, however, and Scarlet pointed it out to Ophelia. "See?"

Ophelia's eyes followed Scarlet's away from the platform, along a track of evenly spaced metal bars to a triangular frame from which hung three rubber slings on chunky black chains.

"Lucky stars! *Swings!*" Ophelia exclaimed. "Can we?" She turned to Arden first, then Scarlet. "I love swings so much!"

"*Now?*" Scarlet said. "*Really?* We came here to *talk*, Ophelia, remember? *Not* play."

"Star a—So sorry. Yes. Of course."

"We could do both," Arden said, shrugging. "I mean, why not? I haven't been on a swing in years." She grinned, suddenly looking happier than she had since they had met. "No one else is using them. It'll be fun.

C'mon! Let's go!" She left Ophelia and Scarlet to follow as she headed toward the playground gate.

"Star apologies. Truly," Ophelia murmured to Scarlet. She scrunched her freckled nose. "I didn't mean to delay the mission further. Don't worry. I won't do it again."

Ophelia dropped her backpack next to Arden's just inside the fence.

"Oh, no . . ." said Scarlet, eyeing it.

"What now?" Ophelia moaned. "What did I do?"

"You lost your key chain. I don't know what it's for. But I'm sure we'll find out now." Each Star Darling had received a glittery stuffed star attached to her backpack. Wishers called them "key chains."

"What key chain?" said Ophelia. "I don't know what you mean."

"Didn't you get one right before takeoff?"

"Nooo . . ." Ophelia said slowly. "No," she repeated, more surely.

"Oh . . ." said Scarlet. "Good," she declared. One less thing to worry about, at least.

They turned to watch Arden skip up to the middle swing and fall into the hard rubber seat with a smile.

"Well," Scarlet whispered to Ophelia with the barest of smiles, "what are you waiting for? Let's go."

By the time they joined Arden, the Wishling was flying back and forth, her feet nearly extending past the bar overhead.

Excited, Ophelia took the swing on Arden's right, gripping the chains extra tight in each hand. "*Wheeee!*" she cried as she leaned her head back and eagerly kicked out her feet. After a moogle, however, she sat back up. "Aw . . . mine's broken," she said.

"Mine, too," said Scarlet. It hadn't moved a shortsnip since she'd sat down. She raised her feet once more, just to be extra sure . . . but no, it did not want to move.

Between them, Arden slowed until her own swing was barely swaying. "What do you mean they're broken?" She gave Scarlet's chain a little tug, then peered behind her at the seat. "It looks okay to me."

"Oh, that part's fine, yes. It's the swinger," explained Scarlet. "It's not working." She lifted her feet again. "See? It doesn't fly like yours. It just sits here. Whatever." She shrugged. "It's no big . . . what do they say . . . deal?"

"You know, you have to *pump* to swing," said Arden. "You know . . . like this. . . ."

Scarlet watched Arden lean back and kick her legs out, exactly as Ophelia had done. But unlike Ophelia, Arden didn't stop there. That was only the first step, it seemed. Arden next swung her body forward and sharply bent her knees. Scarlet watched the swing respond by gliding backward, at which point Arden leaned back again. As she kept going like that, whipping herself back and forth, she made her swing fly higher . . . and higher . . . and higher still!

Who would have ever thought that Wishlings had to power their own swings? thought Scarlet.

Fortunately, this "pumping" wasn't half as difficult as it looked. Even Ophelia was successful almost immediately, much to her delight. Scarlet could have used a push to start, but after a few rough kicks and bends, she quickly began to catch up.

They all stopped at just about the same time but for different reasons: Ophelia because her Star-Zap fell out of her pocket when she practically flew upside down; Arden because she saw it fall and wanted to stop and help; Scarlet because as soon as she saw Arden reach for the Star-Zap, she knew she had to grab it—fast!

"Cool phone!" said Arden, who was already out of her swing and running her finger along the Star-Zap. Instantly, the top flipped up.

Scarlet's heart nearly stopped as she stared at it, terrified that a holo-something would suddenly appear. Only after a moogle did she remember that it had no energy. *Lucky stars!* she thought with a sigh of relief.

"It's actually a Star-Z—" Ophelia started to correct her.

"A Star-Zee?" Scarlet cut in, laughing. "Honestly, Ophelia. You make up the funniest names." She took the Star-Zap from Arden and handed it to Ophelia with a tight, open-eyed smile. "Here you go. Maybe put that in your backpack, why don't you. And keep it there. You'd hate for your *phone* here to break."

"Right . . ." said Ophelia. "Right! My *phone*!" She ran over to her backpack and dropped it in. She returned to the swing set, out of breath. "Better?" she asked with a grin.

Scarlet nodded. "Much better. Now." She sighed. "I think it's time we *talked*, don't you?" She turned to Arden and put her hands on her shoulders. "Here," she said. "Have a seat." Gently, she guided her back into her swing, then sank into her own. She didn't have to look at the Countdown Clock on her Star-Zap to know that there wasn't much time left in their mission. She could see the sun drifting steadily down toward the treetops. That meant there wasn't a moogle to waste.

"We're going to help you get over this fear of yours," she told Arden. "But first you need to talk."

"Talk about what?"

"Your fear," said Scarlet. "When it started. Where it

came from. All that good stuff. So go ahead. Fire away."

Arden's face, which had been so warm and open, seemed all of a sudden to hang a CLOSED sign. "My fear of butterflies . . . oh, no . . . I don't want to. It's too hard to talk about. I just can't."

"But . . ." Scarlet paused to check the sun again. "But you *have* to talk about it," she blurted.

Scarlet could feel her own face getting hot and probably red—especially when Ophelia spoke up from the next swing: "That's okay. We understand."

"Thanks." Arden twisted her swing toward Ophelia.

"I know what it's like not to want to talk about something," Ophelia continued. "You probably do, too, Scarlet. Right?"

"No." Scarlet frowned impatiently. "Well . . . okay . . . yes, maybe. Sometimes."

"It's just so embarrassing," said Arden.

Ophelia nodded. "You don't want to be reminded of it. I know."

"It was literally the worst day of my life," said Arden.

"I can only imagine," said Ophelia gently as she rocked her swing from side to side.

Scarlet's eyes, meanwhile, flashed from Ophelia to Arden, as she observed their exchange of trusting smiles.

Arden was actually about to talk, Scarlet realized—thanks to Ophelia, no less!

"I was at my grandparents' house—they live on a big farm. And I was little. I'd only just turned five. It was before dinner. I was playing hide-and-seek with my older cousins out in the fields around the barn. We used to do that all the time. So I see this big tree out at the edge of the meadow, and I decide to go hide behind that. The trunk was literally *this* thick." Arden held her arms out wide. "I mean *huge*. Big enough to hide three or four kids . . . I don't know, maybe more. And so tall that when you stood under it and looked up, you couldn't see the top at all. My grandmother says it was a big tree even when she was a kid, so you can imagine how old it must be now.

"Anyway, I ran up and stood there, hiding behind it—all by myself—while my cousin Jason ran around with no idea, busy finding everyone else. And then . . . I started hearing this kind of *rustling* sound all around me . . . kind of like a cat purring, only *really* loud. And the next thing I knew I was covered, I mean literally *covered*, in all these"—Arden shuddered—"all these *butterflies*! Evidently, they were roosting there—thousands of them—on their way to Mexico for the winter. My grandmother says they migrate through her farm every year. Which is why I refuse to go back there, by the way."

"But the butterflies aren't there all the time, are they?" asked Scarlet.

"No. Just the fall, when they're flying south. But just the thought of being there . . ." She winced and shivered again. "I love my grandparents . . . but it's just too hard. I get nauseous just thinking about it."

"So what did you do when the flutterfo—I mean butterflies landed on you?" asked Ophelia.

"I screamed. Like crazy," Arden said. "I mean, I was five and all alone. Sure, I realized pretty quickly that they were butterflies, but I still thought they were going to eat me alive. I couldn't get them off. It was like they were stuck to me with pins. They wouldn't let go with their little"—she cringed—"*feet.* I tried to brush them and shake them and knock them off, but they were in my hair, my clothes, everything, refusing to let go. Then, finally, I tried to run. But of course I couldn't see. So I tripped . . . and fell . . . and landed on the ground, on, like, a hundred of them." She paused to take a breath. "Basically killing them all. So there I am, lying on all these dead butterflies, covered with hundreds more. All by myself. Screaming. Crying. Oh—and I wet my pants, I was so scared. Did I happen to mention that?"

"*Aw* . . ." Ophelia patted her shoulder.

Scarlet leaned forward. "So what happened next?"

"Finally—after what literally felt like forever—my cousins and my grandma found me. By then, the butterflies had gone back up in the tree—except for the ones I murdered, of course. When they found out what happened, my cousins laughed and called me 'butterfly bait' for the rest of the weekend. In fact, they still call me that today. It's become a little family joke, that nickname."

"That's terrible!" said Scarlet.

Arden nodded. "Yeah, it is."

"I hope you call them something back!" Scarlet said. "I know some good names, by the way, if you need any suggestions."

"Oh, but I'm sure they don't mean to be mean," said Ophelia. "They probably just don't understand."

Arden hung her head, shaking it slowly. "They sure don't. Nobody does."

"We do," Ophelia said softly. "We know exactly how you feel." She glanced over Arden's shoulder at Scarlet. *What should I do next?* she mouthed.

Scarlet tried to think. . . .

Just keep going! she told Ophelia—not with words but by rolling her arm.

"You know what I think?" said Ophelia.

Arden waited to hear.

"I think . . . I think anybody would be scared of butterflies after that happened to them."

"Thanks," said Arden. She smiled a little. "And thanks for this. . . ."

"For what?"

"For letting me talk about it. To be honest, it feels kind of good. Do you know, I don't think I've ever told anyone that story before? Never, in all these years. And in a way, I think the story I actually remember was a little better than the one I was trying to forget."

"What do you mean?"

"Well, I mean, the butterflies were scary—for sure. But for some reason I'd remembered them biting me, like they had little teeth. Now, though, I realize that they didn't do much more than tickle me."

"Hey! It's our turn!"

Scarlet turned, along with the others, to find a long line of young Wishling children standing behind them, looking as if *they* might bite.

"You can't hog the swings!" said the first one.

"Yeah! No hogging!" chirped another. "Besides, you're too old. My mom said."

"Swings are for kids!" they started chanting. "Swings are for kids! Swings are for kids!"

Ophelia shuffled her swing toward Arden's. "Um, can we get out of here? They scare me."

Arden laughed. "Yeah, sure. Let's go."

CHAPTER 13

"I can't believe I'm doing this," said Arden.

Behind her back, Scarlet and Ophelia leaned in to share a smile of so-close-they-could-taste-it success. They were standing on the path that led to the butterfly exhibit, in front of a sign that read BUTTERFLIES! 200 FEET AHEAD.

"My stars," Ophelia whispered to Scarlet. "Did you know butterflies had two hundred legs?"

Scarlet studied the sign. "I didn't," she whispered back. "It's kind of starmazing that they can fly. . . ."

The wooden sign also had a carving of a butterfly, which Arden was regarding with an anxious expression.

"Don't worry," said Ophelia. "Like we said, if you don't want to go in, you don't have to."

"No, of course not. . . . But let's keep going," Scarlet said.

The path turned, and as it did, the exhibit itself came into view.

"Ooh! It's such a pretty structure!" said Ophelia.

Scarlet had to agree. The side they could see had multiple rising and falling arches, almost like the curves of a cloud. The walls appeared to be made of some kind of netting and were decorated with large colorful pictures of butterflies. No two were the same. Through the net, it was easy to see a veritable jungle of trees, vines, and blooming bushes growing inside. What they couldn't yet see—from such a distance, Scarlet figured—was any butterflies.

"Just imagine if that place glittered!" said Ophelia. "How stunning it would be!"

"I think they might light it up at night on the weekends," said Arden.

"*Really?*" Ophelia's face brightened at the thought (as much as a face on Wishworld could).

"Yeah, but I'm not sure. I've never actually seen it. It's just something I've heard."

"Ooh! I'd love to stay and see it. Scarlet, do you think we can?"

"Why couldn't you?" asked Arden.

"Let's just keep going," said Scarlet. "Shall we? I mean, if that's okay?"

Arden nodded. She took a deep breath and moved forward, ever so slowly. Her feet seemed to fight her for every step. Scarlet could hear Arden telling herself, "I can do this. I can . . ." between rapid shallow breaths.

Yes, Scarlet thought. She *was* going to do this. She was going to overcome her fear. Scarlet looked at Ophelia and pointed to her bracelet. *Be ready!* she mouthed. What was crazier, Scarlet wondered: that Ophelia's mission just might be successful or that Scarlet just might be happy for her?

As they got closer to the exhibit, they found themselves walking among dense vibrant flower gardens dotted with butterfly-shaped signs bearing various facts.

One showed the process a caterpillar went through to become a butterfly.

"'Metamorphosis,'" read Arden. "That's what our project is about."

"Wait? Is that really how butterflies are made? They start out as *those*?" Ophelia pointed to a caterpillar, then to a butterfly. "You'd think something that delicate and pretty would be made of flower petals and stardust."

"You're funny," Arden said. She suddenly looked more relaxed.

Scarlet could see how Ophelia had taken Arden's mind off her fear—without even meaning to—so she decided to try it herself. After all, she *was* there to help.

"This is interesting," she said. "Did you know butterflies don't eat? They can only drink. And they taste with their feet. That's uncommon, right?"

Arden laughed again.

It worked! Scarlet could practically feel the wish energy ready to come out of this Wisher, and she could tell that Ophelia was sensing it, too.

"Oh," Ophelia went on, not really getting the humor in anything but still happy to play along. "And look here. This says that they have four wings, two on each side, and only *six* legs. Not two hundred?" She paused to frown, seriously confused.

"Two *hundred*! You're so funny!" Arden giggled. "Both of you." She stopped in front of another sign. "Ooh," she said. "Check this out. According to this, butterflies can see ultraviolet colors. It helps them know which flowers have the nectar they want. *Hmmm.* What's so special about seeing ultraviolet colors?" She grinned. "I mean, can't everyone?"

"I don't get it," Ophelia whispered to Scarlet.

"You don't have to," Scarlet murmured back. "Just so it works. How about this one?" she said more loudly, pointing to another sign. "This is also about what butterflies see. It says butterflies are attracted to bright colors, especially yellow and red. *Hee-hee!*"

She waited for Arden to laugh . . . or chuckle . . . or at least smile. Instead, though, she looked over to see Arden staring down at her bright yellow T-shirt. She touched the hem of her ruby red skirt.

"Er, what's wrong?" Scarlet asked.

"I can't do this."

"But you have to—I mean . . . yes, you *can*."

"Maybe. But not today. Not dressed like this. What if they land on me? Uh, I thought I was ready. I did. But I'm not. I'm really not." She held out her hands. "Look." They were trembling like leaves in a solar storm.

Scarlet looked over at Ophelia. Did she have an idea? Any idea at all? Scarlet had done everything she could think of to help grant this wish in time, but it just wasn't enough in the end.

With the tiniest nod, Ophelia lowered her eyes back to Arden's hands and gently picked one up. "You know, you're not alone. We're here for you. Whatever you need. Would it help at all if Scarlet and I stayed right by your side and maybe held your hands?" She looked back at Scarlet warmly, clearly expecting her to reach out and take Arden's other hand. "Scarlet?"

"Well . . . I don't know. Here's the thing. *Would* it help?" Scarlet was skeptical at best. She'd never bought into that whole Starland hand-holding-all-the-time thing. What was the point? She didn't know. To other Starlings, linking arms and holding hands came as naturally as glowing, but to Scarlet it always felt forced. In fact, getting that close to others just made her feel more alone.

But Ophelia wasn't letting go, and neither was Arden.

Oh, why not? Scarlet finally thought.

She reached out and put her hand lightly on Arden's, surprised at how warm and soft it felt. Arden squeezed, and Scarlet nearly jumped. Instead, though, without even thinking about it, she flashed Arden a smile and squeezed back.

"You know . . . it's so weird how I met you today," Arden said with a small but grateful smile. "It's almost like a fairy godmother sent you or something."

"Well, *that* sure didn't happen," Scarlet said.

"Close, though." Ophelia grinned, then caught Scarlet's "*Really?*" face. "What? Oh. That's a *joke*."

"So, shall we try this again?" Scarlet said. "Together?"

"Okay." Arden took a deep breath. "Just . . . don't let go."

Hand in hand, they walked down the last bit of path toward the butterfly building and up to the wide glass door. Inside, they could see the stars of the exhibit: hydrongs and hydrongs of butterflies. Some were tiny, no bigger than a pinky. Others were almost as big as a hand. Some were yellow and black, some were orange, and some were all white. And some were the exact same blue as Vega's hair!

"Now, just so we're clear, if I start to scream or faint or anything like that, we're coming right back out."

"Of course," said Ophelia.

"We've got you," said Scarlet. She placed her other hand on Arden's, as well.

"Okay." Arden took a long and slow breath in, held it, then let it out quickly. "I think I'm ready."

"Wait . . . what? Oh, no . . ." groaned Scarlet.

"What's wrong?"

"We have a problem, I'm afraid." Scarlet nodded toward the door—to the sign hanging in the middle, right over the handle, where it was impossible to miss. In the most unsparkly black block letters, it read very simply CLOSED.

"What? What does that mean?" said Ophelia as she read it. "Does that mean we can't go in?"

"That's totally what it means," said Arden. "Look." She pointed to another sign to the side of the door that listed the operating hours. "They're closed every

Thursday. Oh, well. I guess this fear just wasn't meant to be conquered all in a day. But at least I got a little closer to facing it, right?"

"Right," Scarlet sighed.

A little closer. Great, she thought. If only energy could be captured from that.

But no. They needed a wish to be fully granted. And they needed it granted soon. Not the next day or that weekend, when Arden suggested they return.

"We're going in today. Right now," said Scarlet as she worked to unlock the entrance with her mind. She clasped Arden's hand more tightly and pulled her toward the door. "We've come this far. We can't stop now. C'mon, Ophelia. You too."

"What? How? But we can't. It's closed!" said Arden, confused but stubbornly holding her ground.

"Um, Scarlet. Scarlet." On the other side of Arden, Ophelia tried to get Scarlet's attention by waving wildly with her hand. "*Scarlet!*"

"What? It's no big deal. We'll go in and come right back out."

"But that's just it. I don't think we have to," said Ophelia, pointing.

Scarlet followed her finger to Arden's shoulder. . . .

"Freakin' fireballs!" she gasped.

Ophelia grinned. "I know! Right?"

"What? What is it?" Arden asked. She started to turn her head.

"No, no. Don't move," Scarlet calmly warned her.

Arden froze. "What is it? Tell me, please."

"Okay . . . there's a . . . there's a *butterfly* on your shoulder," Scarlet said as gently as she knew how.

"What?"

"It's very small."

"How small?" asked Arden.

Scarlet held up her first finger and thumb two inches apart. "It's kind of light gold," she said, "with black outlines. . . . There's even some orange and a little blue."

"It sounds kind of pretty," said Arden.

"Oh, it is!" said Ophelia.

"I think . . . I don't know. . . . Should I look?"

"Yes!" said Scarlet and Ophelia together.

"But slowly," said Scarlet. "Don't scare it away."

Slowly, very slowly, Arden swiveled her head to the right, until she could just barely see the butterfly out of the corner of her eye. Her heart must have been racing, Scarlet thought, if her own fluttering heart was any gauge. And Ophelia . . . Scarlet glanced at her and saw she was smiling at Arden. How excited she must be. . . .

"How do you feel?" asked Ophelia gently.

"I feel okay. . . ." Arden's eyes left her shoulder for just an instant to flit from Ophelia to Scarlet. "And you know what's even better? What I don't feel is afraid!"

Scarlet was ready for the wish energy to flow out of Arden, but she wasn't prepared for such an intense and powerful stream. It burst forth with such force that Scarlet staggered back, and Ophelia did, as well. Arden just stood there, oblivious, as Wishlings always were. She could only assume it was the butterfly they were reacting to, so she smiled and said, "Don't worry. It won't hurt you."

Of course, that was the last thing Scarlet was worried about. The first thing was making sure every drop of energy made it into Ophelia's Wish Pendant, which Ophelia seemed to have forgotten all about. Scarlet held her own hand out and pointed to her wrist to try to remind her, but Ophelia replied by shaking her head. That was when Scarlet realized the wish energy was already flowing into a Wish Pendant.

Not Ophelia's at all—but Scarlet's.

CHAPTER 14

Scarlet was so happy about all the wish energy she had collected that she didn't even mind giving Ophelia a ride back home on her star. Scarlet hadn't planned on holding Ophelia's hand the whole time, but somehow it turned out that way, and they were still holding hands when Lady Stella's door opened to welcome the returning Starlings in.

Maybe that was why every jaw in the room seemed to drop. Or maybe it was Scarlet's smile, which she couldn't hold back and for once didn't even try to.

"Scarlet . . ." Lady Stella walked forward, her stardust-flecked silver robe flowing behind her in a shimmering diaphanous cloud. "I owe you star salutations and, more importantly, star apologies." She stood before Scarlet and humbly bowed. "Clearly, you always were—and always will be—meant to be a Star Darling. If there was any doubt whatsoever left, this resolves it once and for all."

With that, the headmistress extended her arm. In her upturned palm was the Wish Orb, which she handed to Scarlet. It felt heavy and warm and then began to transform into a flower. "It's a punkypow," said Scarlet with a smile. The burgundy star-shaped petals were aglow.

And then her Power Crystal, the ravenstone, emerged. It was so beautiful and made Scarlet feel very special, indeed. "Take it, and hold it dear," said Lady Stella.

"Oh, I will. I will," said Scarlet. Her own heart seemed to stop as she received the gem and felt the pulse of its energy through her hands.

Meanwhile, Lady Stella, still smiling, but more sadly, turned to Ophelia. As she spoke, she shook her head. "To you, Ophelia, I must also offer star apologies. It is clear you are not a Star Darling, as we had believed."

Scarlet looked down. She remembered how those words had crushed her, and she could only imagine they'd wound Ophelia the same way. When Scarlet finally made herself look at the Starling, however, the words seemed instead to have lifted a great weight off Ophelia. Her whole aura had changed. Not only was she brighter and more sparkly, she looked almost happy—content and relieved. Her eyes skipped from Lady Stella to Scarlet, then around to each of the dumbstruck Star Darlings, who hadn't moved since the two Starlings had glided in.

"*What the stars?* Who's next?" Gemma suddenly blurted. "*Starf!* Hey!" she cried as Tessa elbowed her ribs.

Lady Stella clasped her now empty hands tightly in front of her, as if in prayer. "I know this is quite a lot for you to take in, particularly on such an . . . intensely emotional day. We've all been through quite a lot—especially, of course, Scarlet and Ophelia—which is why I think it's best to retire for now. Rest assured that Lady Cordial and I will work diligently to ensure that nothing like this happens again." She turned her head respectfully toward the admissions director, who'd stood off to the side in semi-shadow throughout the whole Wish Blossom presentation.

Lady Cordial took a step forward and bowed to the headmistress. Her deep purple bun looked especially tight. "We most c-c-certainly will," she said, her eyes still on the floor. "No mis-s-stakes like this. Ever again."

As fast as Scarlet had fled from the other Star Darlings when she'd learned she'd been dismissed from the group, she fled even faster now that she was back in. She could see everyone waiting to congratulate her and *embrace* her (*ugh!*) outside Lady Stella's office, and suddenly, it all seemed too much for her to bear. She would deal with them all later—be sociable—Scarlet thought as she rushed past them, but right then, more than anything, she needed to be by herself. She'd already hugged and held hands more in one day than she had in the whole rest of her time at Starling Academy. She was overwhelmed. She needed to breathe.

The holo-text came as she was descending the spiral staircase into the Star Caves.

WHERE DID YOU GO? it flashed as Vega's picture appeared in the upper corner of the screen.

Scarlet almost didn't answer, but then another line came through . . . and another after that:

WE HAVE TO TALK!

YOU WERE RIGHT!

AND SO WAS CASSIE!

THE LAB RESULTS CAME IN WHILE YOU WERE GONE!

And . . . ? Scarlet waited. *Well?* she thought. What had they found out?

Finally, she texted back:

WHAT DID THEY SAY?!

She realized she was holding her breath as she stared at her Star-Zap, waiting for Vega's reply. At last, the screen flashed again, this time with both Cassie's and Vega's faces, one in each corner. Cassie's picture coyly winked.

HERE'S A HINT: ISLE OF MISERA.

FOR MORE, MEET US IN THE HEDGE MAZE.

ASAP!

So as fast as possible, Scarlet spun and ran back up the stairs.

The Isle of Misera? That sad, barren, negative-energy dumping ground? Could it be that the Star Darlings' flowers had come from there?

Glossary

Afterglow: The Starling afterlife. When Starlings die, it is said that they have "begun their afterglow."

Age of Fulfillment: The age when a Starling is considered mature enough to begin to study wish granting.

Bad Wish Orbs: Orbs that are the result of bad or selfish wishes made on Wishworld. These grow dark and warped and are quickly sent to the Negative Energy Facility.

Big Dipper Dormitory: Where third- and fourth-year students live.

Boingtree: A shrublike tree with tickly aromatic needles.

Booshel Bay: A vacation destination.

Bot-Bot: A Starland robot. There are Bot-Bot guards, waiters, deliverers, and guides on Starland.

Bright Day: The date a Starling is born, celebrated each year like a Wishling birthday.

Celestial Café: Starling Academy's outstanding cafeteria.

Cocomoon: A sweet and creamy fruit with an iridescent glow.

Cosmic Transporter: The moving sidewalk system that transports students through dorms and across the Starling Academy campus.

Countdown Clock: A timing device on a Starling's Star-Zap. It lets them know how much time is left on a Wish Mission, which coincides with when the Wish Orb will fade.

Crystal Mountains: The most beautiful mountains on Starland. They are located across the lake from Starling Academy.

Cycle of Life: A Starling's life span. When Starlings die, they are said to have "completed their Cycle of Life."

Druderwomp: An edible barrel-like bush capable of pulling up its own roots and rolling like a tumbleweed, then planting itself again.

Floozel: The Starland equivalent of a Wishworld mile.

Flutterfocus: A Starland creature similar to a Wishworld butterfly but with illuminated wings.

Galliope: A sparkly Starland creature similar to a Wishworld horse.

Garble greens: A Starland vegetable similar to spinach.

Glitterbees: Blue-and-orange-striped bugs that pollinate Starland flowers and produce a sweet substance called gossamer.

Globerbeem: Large, friendly lightning bug–type insects that are sparkly and lay eggs.

Glorange: A glowing orange fruit. Its juice is often enjoyed at breakfast time.

Glowfur: A small, furry Starland creature with gossamer wings that eats flowers and glows.

Glowsow: A large farm animal that is prized for the light it emits at night—perfect for working after dark.

Good Wish Orbs: Orbs that are the result of positive wishes made on Wishworld. They are planted in Wish-Houses.

Green globules: Green pellets that are fed to pet glowfurs. They don't taste very good to Starlings.

Halo Hall: The building where Starling Academy classes are held.

Halo-harp: A melodious stringed instrument played by striking its strings with a small mallet.

Holo-text: A message sent or received on a Star-Zap and projected into the air. There are also holo-albums, holo-billboards, holo-books, holo-cards, holo-communications, holo-diaries, holo-flyers, holo-letters, holo-papers, holo-pictures, and holo–place cards. Anything that would be made of paper or contain writing or images on Wishworld is a hologram on Starland.

Hydrong: The equivalent of a Wishworld hundred.

Illumination Library: The impressive library at Starling Academy.

Impossible Wish Orbs: Orbs that are the result of wishes made on Wishworld that are beyond the power of Starlings to grant.

Isle of Misera: A barren rocky island off the coast of New Prism.

Kaleidoscope tree: A rare and beautiful tree whose blossoms continuously change color.

Keytar: An instrument that is held like a guitar but has keys instead of strings.

Lightning Lounge: A place on the Starling Academy campus where students relax and socialize.

Little Dipper Dormitory: Where first- and second-year students live.

Luminous Lake: A serene and lovely lake next to the Starling Academy campus.

Microjoule: A tiny amount.

Mirror Mantra: A saying specific to each Star Darling that when recited gives her (and her Wisher) reassurance and strength. When a Starling recites her Mirror Mantra while looking in a mirror, she will see her true appearance reflected.

Moonium: An amount similar to a Wishworld million.

Old Prism: A medium-sized historical city about an hour from Starling Academy.

Power Crystal: The powerful stone that each Star Darling receives once she has granted her first wish.

Shooting stars: Speeding stars that Starlings can latch on to and ride to Wishworld.

Shortsnip: A tiny unit of measurement, generally referring to distance.

Silver Blossom: The final manifestation of a Good Wish Orb. This glimmering metallic bloom is placed in the Hall of Granted Wishes.

Solar Springs: A hilly small town in the countryside where Tessa and Gemma are from.

Sparkle shower: An energy shower Starlings take every day to get clean and refresh their sparkling glow.

Star ball: An intramural sport that shares similarities with soccer on Wishworld. But star ball players use energy manipulation to control the ball.

Starcar: The primary mode of transportation for most Starlings. These ultrasafe vehicles drive themselves on cushions of wish energy.

Star Caves: The caverns underneath Starling Academy where the Star Darlings' secret Wish-Cavern is located.

Starf!: A Starling expression of dismay.

Star flash: News bulletin, often used starcastically.

Starland City: The largest city on Starland, also its capital.

Starlicious: Tasty, delicious.

Starlings: The glowing beings with sparkly skin who live on Starland.

Star Quad: The center of the Starling Academy campus. The dancing fountain, band shell, and hedge maze are located here.

Star salutations: The Starling way to say "thank you."

Staryear: A period of 365 days on Starland, the equivalent of a Wishworld year.

Star-Zap: The ultimate smartphone that Starlings use for all communications. It has myriad features.

Stellation: The point of a star. Halo Hall has five stellations, each housing a different department.

Supernova: A stellar explosion. Also used colloquially, meaning "really angry," as in "She went supernova when she found out the bad news."

Time of Applying: The very busy time of year when Starlings work on and send out applications to schools.

Time of Letting Go: One of the four seasons on Starland. It falls between the warmest season and the coldest, similar to fall on Wishworld.

Time of Lumiere: The warmest season on Starland, similar to summer on Wishworld.

Time of Shadows: The coldest season of the year on Starland, similar to winter on Wishworld.

Toothlight: A high-tech gadget that Starlings use to clean their teeth.

Wish Blossom: The bloom that appears from a Wish Orb after its wish is granted.

Wish energy: The positive energy that is released when a wish is granted. Wish energy powers everything on Starland.

Wisher: The Wishling who has made the wish that is being granted.

Wish-Granters: Starlings whose job is to travel down to Wishworld to help make wishes come true and collect wish energy.

Wish-House: The place where Wish Orbs are planted and cared for until they sparkle. Once the orb's wish is granted, it becomes a Wish Blossom.

Wishlings: The inhabitants of Wishworld.

Wish Mission: The task a Starling undertakes when she travels to Wishworld to help grant a wish.

Wish Orb: The form a wish takes on Wishworld before traveling to Starland. There it will grow and sparkle when it's time to grant the wish.

Wish Pendant: A gadget that absorbs and transports wish energy, helps Starlings locate their Wishers, and changes a Starling's appearance. Each Wish Pendant holds a different special power for its Star Darling.

Wishworld: The planet Starland relies on for wish energy. The beings on Wishworld know it by another name—Earth.

Wishworld Outfit Selector: A program on each Star-Zap that accesses Wishworld fashions for Starlings to wear to blend in on their Wish Missions.

Wishworld Surveillance Deck: Located high above the campus, it is where Starling Academy students go to observe Wishlings through high-powered telescopes.

Zing: A traditional Starling breakfast drink. It can be enjoyed hot or iced.

Acknowledgments

It is impossible to list all of our gratitude, but we will try.

Our most precious gift and greatest teacher, Halo; we love you more than there are stars in the sky . . . punashaku. To the rest of our crazy, awesome, unique tribe—thank you for teaching us to go for our dreams. Integrity. Strength. Love. Foundation. Family. Grateful. Mimi Muldoon—from your star doodling to naming our Star Darlings, your artistry, unconditional love, and inspiration is infinite. Didi Muldoon—your belief and support in us is only matched by your fierce protection and massive-hearted guidance. Gail. Queen G. Your business sense and witchy wisdom are legendary. Frank—you are missed and we know you are watching over us all. Along with Tutu, Nana, and Deda, who are always present, gently guiding us in spirit. To our colorful, totally genius, and bananas siblings—Patrick, Moon, Diva, and Dweezil—there is more creativity and humor in those four names than most people experience in a lifetime. Blessed. To our magical nieces—Mathilda, Zola, Ceylon, and Mia—the Star Darlings adore you and so do we. Our witchy cuzzie fairy godmothers—Ane and Gina. Our fairy fashion godfather, Paris. Our sweet Panay. Teeta and Freddy—we love you all so much. And our four-legged fur babies—Sandwich, Luna, Figgy, and Pinky Star.

The incredible Barry Waldo, our SD partner. Sent to us from above in perfect timing. Your expertise and friendship are beyond words. We love you and Gary to the moon and back. Long live the manifestation room!

Catherine Daly—the stars shined brightly upon us the day we aligned with you. Your talent and inspiration are otherworldly; our appreciation cannot be expressed in words. Many heartfelt hugs for you and the adorable Oonagh.

To our beloved Disney family. Thank you for believing in us. Wendy Lefkon, our master guide and friend through this entire journey. Stephanie Lurie, for being the first to believe in Star Darlings. Suzanne Murphy, who helped every step of the way. Jeanne Mosure, we fell in love with you the first time we met, and Star Darlings wouldn't be what it is without you. Andrew Sugerman, thank you so much for all your support.

Our team . . . Devon (pony pants) and our Monsterfoot crew—so grateful. Richard Scheltinga—our angel and protector. Chris Abramson—thank you! Special appreciation to Richard Thompson, John LaViolette, Swanna, Mario, and Sam.

To our friends old and new—we are so grateful to be on this rad journey that is life with you all. Fay. Jorja. Chandra. Sananda. Sandy. Kathryn. Louise. What wisdom and strength you share. Ruth, Mike, and the rest of our magical Wagon Wheel bunch—how lucky we are. How inspiring you are. We love you.

Last—we have immeasurable gratitude for every person we've met along our journey, for all the good and the bad; it is all a gift. From the bottom of our hearts we thank you for touching our lives.

Shana Muldoon Zappa is a jewelry designer and writer who was born and raised in Los Angeles. She has an endless imagination and a passion to inspire positivity through her many artistic endeavors. She and her husband, Ahmet Zappa, collaborated on Star Darlings especially for their magical little girl and biggest inspiration, Halo Violetta Zappa.

Ahmet Zappa is the *New York Times* best-selling author of *Because I'm Your Dad* and *The Monstrous Memoirs of a Mighty McFearless.* He writes and produces films and television shows and loves pancakes, unicorns, and making funny faces for Halo and Shana.

Sneak Peek

Cassie Comes Through

"Well, there you are, Bitty!" Cassie cooed as her pet glowfur landed on her shoulder and gave her pale cheek a nuzzle. Bitty's soft fur tickled her face and made the girl giggle. Cassie finished twisting her long, glimmering pinkish-white hair into a second pigtail bun, fastened it in place with a starpin, and reached over to give the creature a quick pat. She was rewarded with Bitty's Song of Contentment, and Cassie, who had heard it many times before, hummed along.

"That's really pretty," someone said. Cassie turned around to find her roommate smiling at her. Sage was freshly gleaming from her sparkle shower, wrapped in a soft lavender towel that matched her hair and eyes.

Cassie nodded in agreement. "Did you know that glowfurs have twenty-six distinct songs?" she asked. "And that each glowfur has her own version of each tune? This is one of my favorites. After the Song of Joy and Song of Enchantment, of course."

"I can't believe it," said Sage. Then she laughed. "Actually, I'm pretty sure you've told me that before."

Not letting go of her towel, Sage opened her closet door with her wish energy manipulation skills and quickly got dressed behind it. Cassie, who was a private person herself, was grateful to have a similarly modest roommate. When Sage emerged, she was wearing a loosely woven, shimmery sweater over a long sleeveless dress that flickered and changed color as she moved—exhibiting more shades of purple than Cassie knew even existed.

Sage shook her head in mock seriousness. "Actually, what I really can't believe is you still haven't gotten caught with that thing," she said with a laugh.

Bitty gave a squeak of indignation and Cassie said, "She's just kidding, Bitty." To Sage she said, "This *thing* is my pride and joy." Bitty gave another squeak, this time of approval. Cassie knew Sage was just teasing. She was actually quite fond of Bitty, and even smuggled dessert leftovers out of the Celestial Café with the intent to entice the little creature to eat out of her hand. Plus, of course, she willingly kept Cassie's secret to herself.

"That's because Bitty and I are very careful," said Cassie, smoothing her silver tunic with the ruffled hem. Bitty took off from Cassie's shoulder and circled the room, still singing her song. Cassie smiled at Sage. "And because I have a very discreet roommate."

Sage nodded as she crouched to buckle her sandals. "I *am* discreet, aren't I?"

"You are," said Cassie. She had read the Starling Academy Student Manual from cover to cover and knew quite well that pets were expressly forbidden in the student dormitories. She told herself that she had taken Bitty to school with her because the creature would have been lonely back at her uncle's mansion. He was away on book tours more often than he was home. But the truth was that Cassie simply couldn't part with her pet, who had once belonged to her dear departed mother. When Bitty sang her evening song, Cassie knew that her mother had fallen asleep to the very same tune many staryears before. It wasn't much, in the grand scheme of things, but it brought her great comfort. So Cassie had packed up Bitty and a case of green globules and successfully smuggled her past the Bot-Bot guards on the first day of school.

Sage stood and walked over to the door, her lavender braids gleaming.

"Ready to start the starday?" she asked Cassie.

"Ready!" said Cassie. Bitty zoomed in for a kiss on her furry head and began her good-bye song, but it was the shortened version, not the one she'd sing if Cassie ever left her behind to go on a long voyage. She knew Cassie would be back in mere starhours.

Cassie hurried to the door. "Oh, let me," she begged, so Sage stepped aside. Cassie concentrated on opening the door with her wish energy manipulation skills and the door began to tremble, almost imperceptibly, as if it were trying to decide whether it wanted to be opened or stay closed. A starmin or so later, after Cassie's pale face got quite pink from the effort, the door slid open fluidly.

Cassie grinned and turned to Sage. "You're like my good luck charm, Sage," she said. "I wish I was as good in Wishful Thinking class as I am in our room." She shrugged. "I guess I get stage fright or something."

Sage nodded and for a starsec Cassie thought she caught a flicker of a smile on her roommate's face. But it disappeared as they stepped into the hallway and onto the Cosmic Transporter, and soon the observation slipped from Cassie's mind.

Cassie's stomach grumbled. "I wonder what to order for break—"

"Stop right there!" someone barked.

Cassie rolled her eyes and shook her head. They were standing on the Cosmic Transporter and couldn't stop even if they wanted to, for stars' sake.

But Sage laughed merrily. "Hurry up, Mojo!" she cried.

The Bot-Bot guard zoomed after them eagerly. His official name was MO-J4, but Sage thought that was too formal and had settled on the nickname, which he had embraced wholeheartedly. Mojo had taken an instant starshine to Sage during her orientation tour and had been delighted by everything Sage did and said ever since. Cassie later discovered that Bot-Bots generally acted by the holo-book, with a preset vocabulary and a limited range of programmed reactions. But Mojo was special. He had a personality that was silly and fun, and he often greeted Sage with special jokes and occasionally left a gift on her doorstep.

Cassie couldn't help feeling a small stab of jealousy as Mojo excitedly told Sage about the morning's star-rise and showed her the holo-video he had taken just for her. Sometimes Cassie wished that she and Bitty could talk like Sage and Mojo did. Though she wasn't quite sure what Bitty would say. Most likely, "More green globules, please." Or maybe, "Rub my glowbelly for another star-hour if you don't mind." The only present (besides the gift of music) that Bitty had ever given Cassie was a half-eaten green globule, left in the toe of her silver slipper. And by the time Cassie had found it, it was as hard as a meteorite. Cassie had tossed it into the vanishing garbage can. She knew exactly what green globules tasted like, even at the peak of freshness. Horrible.

Still, she wouldn't trade Bitty for all the wish energy on Starland. She half-listened to Sage and Mojo chat away. She smiled, remembering that Sage had initially confided in her that she found MO-J4's slavish devotion a bit annoying. But then the silvery creature had started to grow on her. Sage was used to small annoying creatures, she had told Cassie, who laughed, knowing she was referring to her younger twin brothers, who could be quite a handful. As an only child, and an orphaned one at that, Cassie had nodded along in apparent sympathy. But Cassie would have liked nothing more than an annoying sibling (or two or even three) to liven things up around her uncle's quiet home. That's why she liked it there at Starling Academy so much, she realized. It was lively and there was always something going on to keep her entertained. Like that time when Astra had bet everyone that she could do a triple flip off the starbounce—while eating a half-moon pie. It had looked like she was going to win the wager, too, when Leona had—

Just then she realized Sage was trying to get her attention. "Cassie!" she was saying, snapping her fingers in Cassie's face. Cassie blinked. "We haven't even discussed Scarlet's return yet! I mean, that was so unexpected. So what do you think about—"

Cassie held up her hand. She turned to MO-J4. "I'm going to shut off your hearing," she told the Bot-Bot. Even though he was extremely devoted to Sage, the Star Darlings couldn't take any chances with anyone—or anything—learning about their secret missions.

MO-J4's eyes flashed as if he was annoyed by the request, but he politely acquiesced. "Certainly, Cassie," he said smoothly.

Sage nodded her thanks. "Though I'm sure he wouldn't say a word," she hurriedly said.

"I know," said Cassie. "But as loyal as he is, we really can't take any chances. Lady Stella would want it this way."

Sage nodded solemnly. "So what do you think about Scarlet's return?" she asked. "What does it mean?"

FEVER AT DAWN

PÉTER GÁRDOS

Translated from the Hungarian
by Elizabeth Szász

BLACK SWAN

TRANSWORLD PUBLISHERS
61–63 Uxbridge Road, London W5 5SA
www.penguin.co.uk

Transworld is part of the Penguin Random House group of companies
whose addresses can be found at global.penguinrandomhouse.com

Originally published in Hungary by Libri Kiado in 2015
First English-language edition published in Australia by Text Publishing in 2016

First published in Great Britain in 2016 by Doubleday
an imprint of Transworld Publishers
Black Swan edition published 2017

Fever at Dawn is a work of fiction. In some cases true life figures appear but their actions and conversations are largely fictitious. All other characters, and all names of places and descriptions of events, are the products of the author's imagination and any resemblance to actual persons or places is entirely coincidental.

Every effort has been made to obtain the necessary permissions with reference to copyright material, both illustrative and quoted. We apologize for any omissions in this respect and will be pleased to make the appropriate acknowledgements in any future edition.

A CIP catalogue record for this book
is available from the British Library.

ISBN
9781784161408

Typeset in Electra
Printed and bound by Clays Ltd, Bungay, Suffolk.

Penguin Random House is committed to a sustainable future for our business, our readers and our planet. This book is made from Forest Stewardship Council® certified paper.

1 3 5 7 9 10 8 6 4 2

FEVER AT DAWN

One

MY FATHER, Miklós, sailed to Sweden on a rainy summer's day three weeks after the Second World War ended. He was twenty-five years old. An angry north wind lashed the Baltic Sea into a three-metre swell, and he lay on the lower deck while the ship plunged and bucked. Around him, passengers clung desperately to their straw mattresses.

They had been at sea for less than an hour when Miklós was taken ill. He began to cough up bloody foam, and then he started to wheeze so loudly that he almost drowned out the waves pounding the hull. He was one of the more serious cases, parked in the first row right next to the swing door. Two sailors picked up his skeletal body and carried him into a nearby cabin.

The doctor didn't hesitate. There was no time for painkillers. Relying on luck to hit the right spot between two ribs, he stuck a large needle into my father's chest. Half a litre of fluid drained from his lungs. When the aspirator arrived, the doctor swapped the needle for a plastic tube and siphoned off another litre and a half of mucus.

Miklós felt better.

When the captain learned that the doctor had saved a passenger's life, he granted the sick man a special favour: he had him wrapped in a thick blanket and taken out to sit on the deck. Heavy clouds were gathering over the granite water. The captain, impeccable in his uniform, stood beside Miklós's deckchair.

'Do you speak German?' he asked.

'Yes.'

'Congratulations on your survival.'

In different circumstances, this conversation might have led somewhere. But Miklós was in no state to chat. It was all he could do to acknowledge the situation.

'I'm alive.'

The captain looked him up and down. My father's ashen skin was stretched over his skull, and there were ugly warts on his face. His pupils were magnified by his glasses, and his mouth was a dark yawning void. He virtually hadn't a tooth to call his own. I'm not quite sure why. Maybe three burly louts had beaten his scrawny frame to a pulp in an air-raid shelter lit by a naked bulb swinging from the ceiling. Maybe one of these thugs had grabbed a flat iron and used it over and over to bash Miklós in the face. According to the official version, which was rather short on detail, most of his teeth had been knocked out in the prison on Margit Street in Budapest in 1944, when he was arrested as a deserter from a Jewish forced-labour unit.

But now he was alive. And despite the slight whistle when he took a breath his lungs were dutifully processing the crisp salty air.

The captain peered through his telescope. 'We're docking in Malmö for five minutes.'

This didn't really mean anything to Miklós. He was one of 224 concentration-camp survivors who were being shipped from Lübeck in Germany to Stockholm. Some of them were in such bad shape that they wanted nothing more than to survive the journey. A few minutes in Malmö was neither here nor there.

The captain, however, continued to explain the decision, as if to a superior. 'The order came over the radio. This stop wasn't part of my itinerary.'

The ship's horn sounded as the docks of Malmö harbour became visible in the mist. A flock of seagulls circled.

The ship moored at the end of the pier. Two sailors disembarked and started jogging along the pier. Between them they carried a big empty basket—the kind washerwomen use to haul wet laundry up to the attic to hang out.

A crowd of women on bicycles was waiting at the approach to the pier. There must have been fifty of them, motionless and silent, gripping their handlebars. Many wore black headscarves.

They looked like ravens perched on a branch. It was only when the sailors reached the barrier that Miklós noticed the parcels and baskets hanging from the handlebars.

He felt the captain's hand on his shoulder. 'Some mad rabbi by the name of Kronheim dreamed this up,' the captain explained. 'He placed an ad in the papers saying that you people were arriving on this ship. He even managed to arrange for us to dock here.'

Each of the women dropped her parcel into the big laundry basket. One standing slightly back let go of her handlebars and her bicycle fell over. From where he sat on deck, Miklós heard the clang of the metal on the cobblestones. Given the length of the pier, this is quite inconceivable, yet whenever my father told this story he always included the clang.

Once they had collected all the packages, the sailors jogged back to the ship. This scene remained fixed in Miklós's mind: an improbably empty pier, the sailors running with the basket, and in the background the strange motionless army of women and their bicycles.

The parcels contained biscuits that these nameless women had baked to celebrate the arrival of the survivors in Sweden. As my father tasted the soft, buttery pastry in his toothless mouth, he could detect vanilla and raspberry, flavours so unfamiliar after years of camp food that he almost had to relearn them.

'Sweden welcomes you,' grunted the captain, as he turned away to give orders. The ship was already heading out to sea.

Miklós sat savouring his biscuits. High among the clouds, a

biplane drew away, dipping its wings in salute. When he saw it, my father began to feel he was truly alive.

~

By the end of the first week in July 1945, Miklós was in a crowded sixteen-bed hospital ward, a barracks-like wooden hut in a remote village called Lärbro on the island of Gotland. Propped up against a pillow, he was writing a letter. Sunlight poured through the window and nurses in crisply starched blouses, white bonnets and long linen skirts darted between the beds.

He had beautiful handwriting: shapely letters, elegant loops and just a hair's breadth between each word. When he finished his letter he put it in an envelope, sealed it and leaned it against the jug of water on his bedside table. Two hours later a nurse called Katrin picked it up and dropped it in the postbox with the other patients' mail.

Miklós rarely got out of his hospital bed, but two weeks after writing his letter he was allowed to sit out in the corridor. Each morning the post was handed out, and one day a letter came for him—straight from the Swedish Office for Refugees. It contained the names and addresses of 117 women, all of them young Hungarians whom nurses and doctors were trying to bring back to life in various temporary hospitals across Sweden. Miklós transcribed their details into a thin exercise book with square-ruled paper he had found somewhere.

By this time he had recovered from the dramatic pronouncement he had received a few days earlier.

~

Pressed against the X-ray machine, Miklós had done his best not to move. Dr Lindholm shouted at him from the other room. The doctor was a gangling figure, at least six foot six tall, and he spoke a funny sort of Hungarian. All his long vowels sounded the same, as if he were blowing up a balloon. He had run the Lärbro hospital—now temporarily enlarged to accommodate the intake of camp survivors—for the last dozen years. His wife, Márta, a tiny woman whom Miklós reckoned couldn't be more than four foot six, was a nurse and worked in the hospital too; she was Hungarian, which explained why the doctor tackled the language with such bravado.

'You hold breath! No frisking!' he bellowed.

A click and a hum—the X-ray was ready. Miklós relaxed his shoulders.

Dr Lindholm walked over and stood beside him, gazing with compassion at a point slightly above his head. Miklós was slumped, his sunken chest naked against the machine, as if he never wanted to get dressed again. His glasses had steamed up.

'What you say you occupied with, Miklós?' the doctor asked.

'I was a journalist. And poet.'

'Ah! Engineer of the soul. Very good.'

Miklós shifted from one foot to the other. He was cold.

'Dress. Why you stand around?'

Miklós shuffled over to the corner of the room and pulled on his pyjama jacket. 'Is there a problem?' he asked the doctor.

Lindholm still didn't look at him. He started walking towards his office, waving at Miklós to follow him. He was muttering, almost to himself, 'Is a problem.'

Erik Lindholm's office looked onto the garden. On these warm midsummer evenings the island glittered in a bronze light that bathed the countryside. The dark furniture radiated comfort and safety.

Miklós sat in a leather armchair. Opposite him, on the other side of the desk, sat Dr Lindholm. He had changed into a smart waistcoat. He was flicking anxiously through Miklós's medical reports. He switched on the sea-green glass desk lamp, though there was no real need for it.

'How much you weigh now, Miklós?'

'Forty-seven kilos.'

'You see. It works like a clock.'

As a result of Dr Lindholm's strict diet, Miklós had gained eighteen kilos in only a few weeks. My father kept buttoning and unbuttoning his pyjama jacket, which was far too big for him.

'What temperature you have this morning?'

'Thirty-eight point two.'

Dr Lindholm put the reports down on his desk. 'I won't beat away the bush any longer. Is that what they say? You are quite strong now to face facts.'

Miklós smiled. Almost all his teeth were made of a

palladium-based metal alloy that was acid-resistant, cheap and ugly. The day after he'd arrived in Lärbro, a dentist had come to see him. He took moulds of his mouth and warned him that the temporary plate he was getting would be more practical than aesthetic. In a trice the dentist had fitted the metal into his mouth.

Although Miklós's smile was anything but heart-warming, Dr Lindholm forced himself to look directly at him.

'I come straight at the point,' he said. 'It is easier. Six months. You have six months to live, Miklós.' He picked up an X-ray and held it to the light. 'Look. Come closer.'

Miklós obligingly stood up and hunched over the desk. Dr Lindholm's slender fingers roamed over the contoured landscape of the X-ray.

'Here, here, here and here. You see, Miklós? See these patches? This is your tuberculosis. Permanent damage. Nothing to be done about them, I'm afraid. Terrible thing, I have to say. In everyday words, the illness…gobbles the lungs. Can one say "gobble" in Hungarian?'

They stared at the X-ray. Miklós held himself up against the desk. He wasn't feeling very strong, but he managed a nod, thus confirming that the doctor had found a way through the tangle of his language. 'Gobble' was accurate enough to show what the future had in store for him; he didn't need technical terminology. After all, his father had owned a bookshop in Debrecen before the war. It was housed in Gambrinus Court in the Bishop's Palace, under the arcades, a few minutes' walk from the main square. The shop was named Gambrinus Booksellers and consisted of three narrow, high-ceilinged rooms. In one room you could also buy stationery, and there was a lending library too. As a teenager Miklós would perch on top of the high wooden ladder and read books from all over the world—so he could certainly appreciate Lindholm's poetic turn of phrase.

Dr Lindholm continued to stare into my father's eyes. 'As matters stand,' he explained, 'medical science says that you are too gone to come back. There will be good days. And bad ones. I will always be next to you. But I don't want to lead you up the path. You have six months. Seven at most. My heart is heavy, but that is the truth.'

Miklós straightened up, smiling, and then flopped back into the roomy armchair. He seemed almost cheerful. The doctor wasn't quite sure that he had understood or even heard the diagnosis. But Miklós was thinking of things far more important than his health.

Two

TWO DAYS after this conversation Miklós was allowed out for short walks in the beautiful hospital garden. He sat on one of the benches in the shade of a big tree with spreading branches. He rarely looked up. He wrote letter after letter, in pencil, in that attractive looping hand of his, using the hardcover Swedish edition of a novel by Martin Andersen Nexø as a desk. Miklós admired Nexø's political views and the silent courage of the workers in his books. Perhaps he remembered that the famous Danish author had also suffered from tuberculosis. Miklós wrote swiftly, placing a stone on the finished letters to stop the wind blowing them away.

The next day he knocked on Dr Lindholm's door. He was determined to charm the good doctor with his frankness. He needed his help.

At this time of day it was Dr Lindholm's custom to talk to his patients while seated on his sofa. He sat at one end in his white coat, while Miklós sat at the other end in his pyjamas.

The doctor fingered the stack of envelopes with surprise. 'Is not in tradition to ask patients who they write to and why. And not curiosity now that…' he mumbled.

'I know,' said Miklós. 'But I definitely want to let you in on this.'

'And there are 117 envelopes here? I congratulate you for diligence.' Dr Lindholm raised his arm as if he were gauging the weight of the letters. 'I ask the nurse to buy stamps for them,' he said obligingly. 'Always feel free to apply me for help in any financial matter.'

Miklós nonchalantly crossed his pyjama-clad legs, and grinned. 'All women.'

Dr Lindholm raised an eyebrow. 'Is that so?'

'Or rather, young women,' my father corrected. 'Hungarian girls. From the Debrecen region. That's where I was born.'

'I see,' said the doctor.

But he didn't. He hadn't a clue what Miklós intended with that pile of letters. He gave my father a sympathetic look—after all, this was a man who had been sentenced to death.

'A few weeks ago,' Miklós went on eagerly, 'I made an enquiry about women survivors convalescing in Sweden who were born in or near Debrecen. Only those under thirty!'

'In hospitals? My God!'

They both knew that in addition to Lärbro there were a number of rehabilitation centres operating in Sweden. Miklós sat up straight. He was proud of his strategy. 'And there are loads of girls in them,' he went on excitedly. 'Here's the list of names.'

He took the sheet of paper out of his pocket and, blushing, handed it to Dr Lindholm. The names had been carefully assessed. He'd put a cross, a tick or a small triangle beside each one.

'Aha! You look for acquaintances,' exclaimed Dr Lindholm. 'I'm in favour of that.'

'You're mistaken,' said Miklós with a wink and a smile. 'I'm looking for a wife. I'd like to get married!'

At last it was out.

Dr Lindholm frowned. 'It seems, my dear Miklós, that I did not speak myself clearly the other day.'

'You did, you did,' Miklós reassured him.

'The language is against me! Six months. Is all you have left. You know, when a doctor must say something like this, is dreadful.'

'I understood you perfectly, Dr Lindholm,' said Miklós.

They sat in uncomfortable silence, each on his end of the sofa. Dr Lindholm was trying to work out whether he should lecture someone who had been sentenced to death. Was it his job to beg his patient to think sensibly? Miklós was wondering whether it was worth trying to persuade Dr Lindholm, with all his experience, to look on the bright side of things. The upshot was they left each other in peace.

That afternoon Miklós got into bed as prescribed and lay back on his pillows. It was four o'clock—nap time. Some of the patients in his hut were asleep, and others were playing cards. His friend Harry was practising the trickiest part of the last movement of a romantic sonata on his violin, over and over, with aggravating zeal.

Miklós was sticking stamps on his 117 envelopes. He licked and stuck, licked and stuck. When his mouth became dry he took a sip from the glass of water on his bedside table. He must have felt that Harry's violin was an appropriate accompaniment to this activity. The 117 letters could have been written with carbon paper. They were identical except for one thing—the name of the addressee.

~

Did Miklós ever wonder what these girls might feel when they opened the envelopes addressed to them? What did they think when they took out the letters and began to read his neat, swirling handwriting?

Oh, those girls! Sitting on the edges of their beds, on garden benches, in the corners of disinfected corridors, in front of thickened glass windows, stopping for a moment on worn staircases, under spreading lime trees, on the banks of miniature lakes, leaning against cold yellow tiles. Did my father see them in his mind's eye as they unfolded the letters in their nightdresses or in the pale grey uniforms they wore in the rehabilitation centres? Confused at first, later smiling perhaps, heartbeat accelerating, skimming the lines over and over in astonishment.

> Dear Nora, Dear Erzsébet, Dear Lili, Dear Zsuzsa, Dear Sára, Dear Seréna, Dear Ágnes, Dear Giza, Dear Baba, Dear Katalin, Dear Judit, Dear Gabriella…
>
> You are probably used to strangers chatting you up when you speak Hungarian, for no better reason than they are Hungarian too. We men can be so bad-mannered. For example, I addressed you by your first name on the pretext that we grew up in the same town. I don't know whether you already know me from Debrecen. Until my homeland ordered me to 'volunteer' for forced labour, I worked for the *Independent* newspaper, and my father owned a bookshop in Gambrinus Court.
>
> Judging by your name and age, I have a feeling that I might know you. Did you by any chance ever live in Gambrinus Court?
>
> Excuse me for writing in pencil, but I'm confined to bed for a few days on doctor's orders, and we're not allowed to use ink in bed.

~

Lili Reich was one of the 117 women who received a letter. She was an eighteen-year-old patient at the Smålandsstenar rehabilitation hospital. It was early September. She opened the envelope and scanned its contents. The young man from distant Lärbro did have lovely handwriting. But he must have mixed her up with someone else. She promptly forgot the whole thing.

Besides, she was terribly excited about her own plans. A few days earlier she and her two new girlfriends, Sára Stern and Judit Gold, had decided to put an end to the grey days of slow recuperation and set their hearts on staging an evening of Hungarian music in the hospital hall.

Lili had studied piano for eight years, Sára had sung in a choir and Judit had taken dance lessons. Judit had a large, pale face with fine dark hairs above her thin, rather severe lips. Quite the opposite of Sára, who was blonde and light boned with narrow shoulders and shapely legs. Two other girls, Erika Friedmann and Gitta Pláner, joined in just for fun. They banged out three copies of the thirty-minute program on the typewriter in the doctors' room and pinned them up around the hospital. On the night of the performance, the creaky wooden chairs in the hall filled with patients and curious visitors from the nearby village of Smålandsstenar.

The concert was a resounding success. After the last piece, a lively Hungarian dance, the *csárdás*, the audience gave the five blushing girls a standing ovation.

As she ran offstage, Lili felt a sudden unbearable pain in her stomach. She hunched over, pressing her hand to her belly, moaning. And then she lay down; her forehead was bathed in sweat.

'What's the matter, Lili?' asked Sára, who had become her closest friend, crouching down beside her.

'It hurts dreadfully,' she said, and passed out.

Lili couldn't remember being put in the ambulance. She could only recall Sára's blurry face saying something she couldn't hear.

Later, she would often think that without this pain, which had something to do with her kidneys, she might never have met Miklós. If that hulking white ambulance hadn't taken her to the military hospital more than a hundred kilometres away in Eksjö; if, when she came to visit, Judit hadn't brought Miklós's letter, along with her toothbrush and diary; if, on that visit, Judit hadn't persuaded her, against all common sense, to write a few words to the nice young man (for the sake of humanity if nothing else); that's where the story would have ended.

But as it happened, on one of those interminable hospital evenings, once the noise filtering in from the corridor and the clanging of the old-fashioned lift with its grating doors had ebbed away and the bulb above her bed was casting a pale light onto her blanket, Lili took a sheet of paper and, after a bit of thought, started to write.

> Dear Miklós,
>
> I'm unlikely to be the person you were thinking of, because, though I was born in Debrecen, I lived in Budapest from the age of one. Nonetheless, I've

> thought a lot about you. Your friendly letter was so comforting that I would be happy for you to write again.

That was a half-truth, of course. Confined to bed with a strange new illness, out of fear, by way of escape or just to stave off boredom, Lili allowed herself to daydream.

> As for myself, neatly ironed trousers or a smart haircut don't do anything. What touches me is the value inside someone.

~

Miklós had grown a little stronger. He could now walk into town with Harry. Each of the patients received five kronor a week pocket money. There were two cake shops in Lärbro. One of them had small round marble tables just like a café in Hungary. On the way there, Miklós and Harry ran into Kristin, a plump Swedish hairdresser, and Harry urged her to join them. So now the three of them were sitting at a marble table in a corner of the cake shop. Kristin was politely eating apple pie with a fork. The men each had a glass of soda water. They were speaking German, because the Hungarians were only just getting used to the melodic Swedish language.

'You are two very nice guys,' declared Kristin, the sugar from the icing trembling on her pale moustache. 'Where were you born exactly?'

Miklós sat up. 'In Hajdúnánás,' he boasted, as if he had uttered a magic word.

'And I was born in Sajószentpéter,' said Harry.

Kristin naturally attempted the impossible—to repeat what she'd heard. It sounded as if she were gargling. 'Haydu…nana… Sayu…sent…peter…'

They laughed. Kristin nibbled her apple pie. This gave Harry time to think up a joke. He was good at jokes.

'What did Adam say to Eve when they first met?' he asked.

So keen was Kristin to work out the answer that she forgot to chew. Harry waited a bit, then stood up, miming that he was now stark naked.

'Please, my lady, stand aside, because I'm not sure how much this thingamajig will grow!' he declared, pointing down towards his fly.

Kristin didn't understand at first, but then she blushed.

Miklós felt ashamed and took a sip of his soda. Harry, though, was just getting started.

'Here's another one,' he blurted. 'The lady of the house asked the new chambermaid if her references were good. The chambermaid nodded. "Yes, madam, they were satisfied with me everywhere." "Can you cook?" The chambermaid nodded. "Do you like children?" The chambermaid nodded. "Yes, I do, but it's better when the master of the house is careful."'

Kristin giggled. Harry grabbed her hand and kissed it fervently. Kristin was about to remove her hand, but Harry had a tight grip and she decided not to resist for a moment or two.

Miklós took another sip of soda and looked away.

Then Kristin freed herself and got up, smoothing her skirt. 'I'm off to the ladies' room,' she announced, walking demurely across the café.

Harry switched to Hungarian right away. 'She only lives two blocks away.'

'How d'you know?'

'She said so. Don't you listen?'

'She likes you.'

'You, too.'

'For all I care,' replied Miklós, giving Harry a stern look.

'You haven't been in a café for years. You haven't seen a naked woman for years.'

'What's that got to do with it?' asked Miklós.

'At last we can get out of the hospital. We should start living!'

Kristin was now sashaying back to the table.

'What do you say to a sandwich?' whispered Harry, still in Hungarian.

'What sort of sandwich?'

'The two of us and her. Kristin in the middle.'

'Leave me out of it.'

Harry switched to German, almost in the same breath, and began to stroke Kristin's ankle under the table. 'I've been telling Miklós that I've fallen head over heels for you, dear Kristin. Do I have any chance?'

Kristin put a warning finger coquettishly on Harry's mouth.

~

Kristin rented a tiny flat on the third floor of a building in Nysvägen Street. The low rumble of traffic filtered in through the open window. She sat on the bed so that Harry could get to her more easily. The first test she set him was to mend a tear in the strap of her bra. 'Are you finished yet?' she asked, monitoring the process in the mirror.

'Not quite. It'd be easier if you took it off.'

'I wouldn't dream of it.'

'You're torturing me.'

'That's the point. You should suffer. Restrain yourself. Do a bit of housework,' replied Kristin, giggling.

Harry finished at last, breaking the thread off with his teeth. Kristin went over to the mirror, turning around and fingering the mended strap.

Harry grew redder and redder. Then he hugged her and clumsily tried to undo the bra. 'I can cook, do the washing, scrub. I am a workhorse,' he whispered.

By way of an answer Kristin kissed him.

~

When Harry came back an hour later, he found Miklós at the same marble table in the corner of the café. He was writing a letter and didn't even look up when Harry flopped down beside him. The tip of his pencil seemed to glide over the white paper. Harry gave a deep dejected sigh.

When at last Miklós raised his head, he showed no surprise

at Harry's dismal expression.

'Aren't you in love any more?'

Harry swigged the remains of the soda in Miklós's glass. 'In love? I'm a wreck.'

'What happened?'

'She made me mend her bra. Then I undressed her. Her skin was so silky and firm!'

'Good. Now don't interrupt me, I've got to finish this,' said Miklós, returning to his letter.

Harry envied the way that Miklós could cut himself off from everything with the merest flick of his finger. 'But *I* wasn't firm. It doesn't work,' he muttered. 'It simply doesn't work.'

Miklós kept writing. 'What doesn't work?'

'I don't. And I used to do it five times a day. I could walk up and down with a bucket of water hanging from it.'

'Hanging from what?' Miklós enquired, biting the end of his pencil.

'Right now…a slug hangs between my legs. Soft, white and useless.'

Miklós found the right word. He smiled to himself and wrote it down, satisfied. Now he could comfort Harry.

'That's quite normal. Without feelings it doesn't work.'

Harry was chewing the side of his mouth in irritation. He slid the letter across the table and started to read. '"Dear Lili, I am twenty-five—"'

Miklós snatched at the letter. There was a brief tug of war, which Miklós won. He thrust the letter into his pocket.

> Dear Lili,
>
> I am twenty-five. I used to be a journalist until the First Jewish Law got me thrown out of my job.

Miklós had a special gift for poetic licence. The truth was that he had been a journalist for exactly eight and a half days. He was taken on at the Debrecen *Independent* on a Monday, more as messenger boy on the police rounds than an actual journalist. It was the worst possible moment. The following week a law banning Jews from certain professions came into force. His newspaper career was over. But he kept that brief apprenticeship on his CV for the rest of his life. It can't have been easy for a nineteen-year-old to get over such a setback. One day he had a pencil behind his ear; the next he was shouting, 'Soda! Come and get your soda water!' as he leaned out from a horse-drawn cart and a bitter wind whistled around his ears.

> After that I worked in a textile factory, then as a bloodhound in a credit agency; I had a job as a clerk, an advertising salesman and other similar excellent posts until 1941, when I was called up for forced labour. At the first opportunity, I escaped to the Russians. I spent a month washing dishes in a big restaurant in Csernovic before I joined a partisan group in Bukovina.

There were eight Hungarian deserters. The Red Army gave them a crash course in spying and dropped them behind

German lines. Looking back, it's obvious that the Russians didn't trust them. The lessons of history teach us that the Soviets didn't trust anybody. But when those Hungarian deserters turned up, they decided to enlist them.

I can imagine my father wearing a quilted jacket and a knapsack, clinging to the open door of an aeroplane. He looks down. Below him there's vertical space, clouds, and spreading countryside. He suffers from vertigo, feels dizzy, turns away and starts to vomit. Rough hands grab him from behind and shove him into the void.

On that dawn morning, somewhere in the vicinity of Nagyvárad, Hungarian soldiers with submachine guns were waiting in open woodland. When the parachute team floated just a few metres above the ground, the soldiers casually fired off a few rounds for target practice. Miklós was lucky. He was the only one they didn't hit. But as soon as he landed, they pounced on him and put him in handcuffs. That night he was transported to a prison in Budapest where, in the space of barely half an hour, he was relieved of most of his teeth.

~

In the café in Lärbro, Harry looked at Miklós with admiration. 'How many have replied?'

'Eighteen.'

'Are you going to write back to all of them?'

'Some of them, but she's the one,' Miklós answered, patting the pocket where he had hidden the letter.

> I've introduced myself, now it's your turn, Lili. First of all, please send a photo! Then tell me everything about yourself.

'How do you know?'

'I just do.'

Three

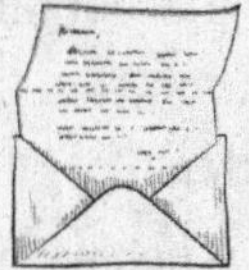

LILI BLEW her nose and wiped away her tears. It was the end of September. She was in a four-bed ward on the third floor of the Eksjö hospital. Outside the window stood a lonely birch tree that had already shed its leaves for winter.

Dr Svensson had started going bald early. He wasn't yet forty, but pink skin, reminiscent of a baby's bottom, was already shining through his colourless hair. He was short and stocky, and his hands were like a child's. His thumbnails were the size of cherry-blossom petals.

He removed his protective apron of leather and wire mesh, and wandered into the bleak X-ray room. Beside the ugly apparatus there was a single chair on which Lili was sitting. She looked pale and scared in her washed-out striped hospital overall.

Dr Svensson squatted down beside her and touched her hand. It was encouraging that the Hungarian girl spoke excellent German. Nuances counted a lot in this context.

'I've assessed your last X-ray. This new one will be ready tomorrow. We suspected scarlet fever at first, but we've excluded that now.'

'Something worse?' whispered Lili, as if they were in the audience at the theatre.

'Worse in some ways. It's not an infection. But there's no need to worry.'

'What's the matter with me?'

'That kidney of yours is behaving badly. But I'll cure you, I promise.'

Lili started to cry.

Dr Svensson took her hand. 'Please don't cry! You'll have to stay in bed again. This time we'll have to be stricter.'

'How long?'

'Two weeks to start with. Or three. Then we'll see,' he said, taking out his handkerchief.

> I haven't got a photo of myself. I've been back in hospital again for the past few days.

~

I hate dancing, but I love having fun—and eating stuffed peppers (in thick tomato sauce, of course).

The story goes that Miklós wasn't even nine years old when, with his hair dampened down and wearing a suit that felt like armour, he was dragged along to a dance at the Golden Bull Hotel. He was already having trouble with his eyes, and due to some sort of refraction error he had to wear glasses with thick, ugly lenses that did nothing for his looks.

At an energetic moment in the dance, the young Miklós and a little girl named Melinda were shoved into the middle of a circle of girls. The crowd of dancers clapped wildly and urged the pair to start spinning. Melinda came to life. Swept up by the wave of good cheer, she grabbed Miklós's hands and swirled round with him, until he slipped on the waxed parquet floor. And from this ignominious position he watched Melinda become the belle of the ball.

Now Miklós and Harry hurried back to the hospital. A strong wind was blowing. Miklós turned up the collar of his thin spring coat.

Harry stopped and took Miklós's arm. 'Ask her if she's got a girlfriend.'

'Not so fast. We're only at the beginning.'

That day the men had a party. They turned the barracks upside down, pushing the beds into the corners. They borrowed a guitar from somewhere, and it turned out that Jenö Grieger could at least strum the latest hits.

The dancing began. At first they just threw themselves around with abandon, then the urge to play different characters took over. They didn't discuss parts or assign roles, but began to act out dashing hussars and flirtatious girls. They clicked their heels. They curtsied; they whispered sweet nothings. They fawned over each other, swirling and spinning. Instincts that had been buried for months erupted.

Miklós didn't take part in this childish game. In silent lonely protest, he settled himself on his barricaded bed. He leaned his back against the wall, put his favourite book by Nexø across his knees, and began to write.

> You didn't say anything about your appearance!
> Now you're probably thinking that I'm some shallow
> Budapest type who only cares about that sort of thing.
> I'll let you in on a secret: I'm not.

~

Someone was knocking. Lili didn't even look up. She was reading a dog-eared German edition of *Dick Sand: A Captain at Fifteen* by Jules Verne, which Dr Svensson had given her the day before.

Sára Stern was standing in the doorway. Lili stared in shock. Sára rushed over to the bed, kneeled down and gave her a hug. The novel slipped to the floor.

'Dr Svensson gave me a referral. Right here, to this ward. Though there's nothing wrong with me.' Sára swirled round like a ballroom dancer. She undressed quickly, pulled on her nightdress and got into the bed next to Lili's.

Lili laughed and laughed as if she'd gone mad.

> Now I'll try to describe myself, since I don't have a photo. As far as my figure goes, I'd say I was plumpish (thanks to the Swedes), medium tall, with dark brown hair. My eyes are greyish-blue, my lips are thin, and my complexion is dark. You can imagine me as pretty or ugly, as you like. For my part, I make no comment. I have a picture of you in my mind. I wonder how close to reality it is.

~

On Sunday Dr Lindholm organised three buses to take his patients to the Gotland coast twenty kilometres away. Miklós and Harry wandered off from the others and found a deserted, sandy bay where they could be on their own. The radiant afternoon was a gift from heaven. The sky was like a stretched cobalt canvas. They took their shoes off and paddled in the shallows.

Later, Harry, who had taken to putting his virility to the test at every opportunity, disappeared behind a rock. Miklós pretended not to notice. The late afternoon cast long shadows. The silhouette of the invisible man, doggedly trying to satisfy himself, was projected onto the sand like a drawing by Egon Schiele. Miklós, meanwhile, tried to concentrate on the waves and the endless blue horizon.

> I'd be interested to know what your views are about socialism. I gather from what you write about your family that you are middle class, just as I was until I became acquainted with Marxism—which the middle class tend to have very strange notions about.

~

Autumn came early in Eksjö. It came at night with unexpected swiftness, bringing with it sleet and a howling wind. The two girls watched in alarm as the lone birch tree swayed in the storm. The two beds were close enough for them to hold hands.

'If only I had twelve kronor!' whispered Lili.

'What would you do with it?'

Lili closed her eyes. 'There used to be a greengrocer on the corner of Nefelejts Street. My mother always sent me there to buy fruit.'

'I know the one. He was called Mr Teddy!'

'I don't remember that.'

'I do. His name was Mr Teddy. Though I called him Bear. What made you think of him?'

'Nothing really. Last month, before I got sick, I saw a dish of green peppers in a shop window in Smålandsstenar.'

'Really? I didn't think they had green peppers here.'

'Nor did I. They were twelve kronor—for a kilo, I suppose. Or was it half a kilo?'

'You had a craving for one?'

'I know it's silly, but I dreamed about those peppers yesterday. I bit into one. It was crisp. Fancy dreaming such a crazy thing.'

The sleet kept beating against the window. The two girls looked on wistfully.

> My friend Sára has been telling me a lot about socialism. I must admit I haven't taken much notice of politics so far. I'm reading a book about the show trials in Moscow in the 1930s. You probably know all about them.

~

A week or two later, in the middle of October, Miklós again felt he was going to suffocate. He didn't have time to shout out. He stood in the middle of the barracks, his body rigid, his mouth open, trying to suck in some oxygen. Then he collapsed.

This time they drained two litres of fluid from his lungs. He spent the rest of the night in a tiny room beside the surgery. Harry lay on the cold pinewood floor beside the bed so that he could let Dr Lindholm know right away if Miklós suffered another attack—though the doctor had tried to reassure him that another emergency was unlikely for a while now.

'What happened?' My father's voice fluttered in the air like a bird with a hurt wing.

'You fainted,' replied Harry. 'They siphoned off the fluid. You're in the room next to the operating theatre.'

The wooden floor was hurting Harry's side, so he sat up

cross-legged. Miklós lay in silence for a long time. Then he mumbled, 'You know what, Harry? I'll develop gills. They won't get the better of me.'

'Who won't?'

'No one will. No one knows just how stubborn I can be.'

'I envy you. You're so strong.'

'You'll be all right too. I know it. Your slug will turn into a pine tree rising to the sky. And then there'll be no stopping you.'

Harry was rocking back and forth, thinking about what Miklós had said. 'Are you sure?'

'Test my sword, ladies!' said my father, trying to smile, and remembering what he had written to Lili.

> Now for a strange question. How are you placed in the love department? Is that irritatingly indiscreet of me?

~

One afternoon, having asked a nurse where to find the best greengrocer in Eksjö, Sára took the lift to the ground floor and escaped from the hospital. In the persistent drizzle she made a dash for the old town, which still had its charms. Fate rewarded her: the only thing in the grocer's window was a wicker basket, and in the basket were several fleshy green peppers. Sára stared at them in amazement while she got her breath back. Then, fishing her small change from her pocket, she sauntered in.

> The answer to your 'strange' question is simple: I've had a few boyfriends. Does that mean I've had a lot or just one special one? You'll have to guess!

~

Harry was the dandy of the barracks. He loved swaggering around like some grand seducer, and his enigmatic smile suggested that he'd already broken the hearts of umpteen women. Naturally, Miklós was the only one who knew about his little 'problem'.

Then someone discovered that Harry kept a precious, shapely bottle of cologne hidden under his mattress. No one knew where he'd got it from but sometimes, before he walked into town, the whole barracks was filled with the pungent scent of lavender. One evening, when Harry was about to set out on one of his jaunts, he discovered the bottle was missing.

Soon it was flying through the air and, desperate to get it back, Harry was rushing in every direction. The men would wait for him to come close, and then throw the bottle to each other over his head. Tiring of that game, they unscrewed the top and splashed each other with the scent. Harry, tears in his eyes, pleaded with them. 'I bought it on borrowed money,' he shouted.

> My fellow patients are horrible. That's why this letter is such a mess. Hungarians, the lot of them! And there's such chaos in here that I can't even write. They've drenched the place in the cologne belonging

> to our resident Don Juan. Some of it even landed on my writing paper. We're in such high spirits it's almost dangerous. Harry and I may have to break out and trek across the country to see you and your friends.

~

When Sára got back from her expedition to the old town Lili was asleep. This was a stroke of luck. She delicately laid the two peppers on the pillow next to Lili's cheek.

> How thrilling, dear Miklós, that you and your friend may come and visit us.

~

Miklós and Harry often exercised by striding around the hospital grounds. Now that a trip to Eksjö might be on the cards—Miklós was cooking up some story about a family reunion—Harry was full of curiosity. He was determined to get his own penfriend, or at least to make certain of going on the visit with Miklós. 'How many kilometres is it exactly?' he enquired.

'Almost three hundred.'

'Two days there, two days back. We won't get permission.'

Miklós led the way, keeping his eyes on the path.

'Yes, we will.'

Harry felt this was the time to banish all doubt about his virility. 'I'm in much better shape. Every morning I wake up with a stiff, like this!' he said, showing the length with his hands.

But Miklós didn't react.

> Whatever happens, don't forget that I'm your cousin and Harry is Sára's uncle. I have to warn you, though, that at the station, yes, right there at the station, you'll be getting a kiss from your cousin. We must keep up appearances!
>
> I send you a friendly handshake plus a kiss from your cousin, Miklós.

~

One rare sunny morning in Eksjö, the door swung open and there stood a grinning, chubby Judit Gold! She dropped her belongings and threw her arms out wide. 'Dr Svensson gave me a referral too. Severe anaemia. We can all be together!'

Sára flew over to Judit and they hugged each other. Lili clambered out of bed, though it was strictly forbidden, and, linking arms, the three of them danced in front of the window. Then they sat on Lili's bed.

'Does he still write to you?' asked Judit, taking Lili's hand in hers.

Lili waited a moment. She had recently learned the subtle advantage of pausing for effect. She stood up and in a dramatic gesture pulled open the drawer of her bedside table. She took out a sheaf of letters and held it high.

'Eight!'

Judit applauded. 'How industrious of him.'

Sára patted Judit on the knee. 'You should see how clever he is! And a socialist, too.'

That was a little too much for Judit, who pulled a face. 'Ugh, I hate socialists.'

'Lili doesn't.'

Judit took the letters out of Lili's hands and smelled them. 'Are you sure he's not married?'

Lili was taken aback. Why did she have to smell them? 'Dead sure.'

'We ought to check him out somehow. You know, I've been burnt so many times.'

Judit was at least ten years older than the other two, and she knew more about men. Lili took the letters from her, slipped off the rubber band and picked up the top one.

'Listen to what he says: "I've got good news for you. We can send cables to Hungary now. But you have to use special forms. You can get them either from the consulate or from the Red Cross in Stockholm. Each form can fit twenty-five words." How about that?'

This was wonderful to hear. They thought about it for a while. Lili lay back in her bed, put the letters on her stomach and stared at the ceiling. 'I haven't heard anything from Mama. Or Papa. I can't bear it. Aren't you worried too?'

The girls avoided each other's eyes.

~

Autumn had by now slunk across the island of Gotland too. It was a bleak overcast day when Dr Lindholm summoned the inhabitants of the barracks together at noon. He briskly gave them the good news that none of them remained infectious. And that early the following morning the Hungarian patients were being transferred to a temporary hospital in Avesta, north of Stockholm. Dr Lindholm would be travelling with them.

~

Avesta was a few hundred kilometres away. After a day and a half of chugging along on steam trains they arrived. At first sight, their new rehabilitation camp was a shock. Situated in the middle of thick forest, seven kilometres from the town, it was surrounded by a wire fence and, worst of all, a tall chimney rose from its centre.

They were housed in brick barracks. They might have settled in better if the weather had not been so terrible. The wind always blew in Avesta. Everything was covered in frost, and the sun, the colour of an overripe orange, never peeped out for more than a few minutes.

Outside their window was a small concrete courtyard full of weeds. Its long wooden table and benches gave it a certain spartan charm. The convalescents sat here in the evenings wrapped up in blankets.

Dr Lindholm had arranged for a Hungarian newspaper to be delivered every few days, even if it was three weeks old. The men instantly tore the shoddily printed paper into four parts. Huddled in groups, they devoured every word. A single light bulb swung overhead. Then they swapped pages in the pale light, their mouths moving soundlessly. In spirit they were far away.

THE REBUILT 250-HORSEPOWER SCREW STEAMER SETS OUT ON ITS MAIDEN VOYAGE

SOVIET PAINTER ALEXANDR GERASIMOV IS CELEBRATED IN THE HOTEL GELLÉRT

THE TOWN OF KECSKEMÉT RECEIVES A GIFT OF 300 PAIRS OF OXEN FROM THE OCCUPYING RUSSIAN FORCES

BICYCLE RACE IN SZEGED

SHOOTING STARTS ON THE FILM *THE TEACHER*

> Just imagine! We got hold of an August edition of *Kossuth's People*. We even read all the ads. The theatres back home are full. A four-page newspaper costs two pengö, a kilo of flour fourteen. The people's court is sentencing members of the Arrow Cross Party one after the other. There are lots of new street names. Mussolini Square is now Marx Square. The whole country is full of hope. People want to work. Teachers have to attend re-education courses. The first lecture was given by party boss Mátyás Rákosi. But I'm sure you're sick of politics.

~

The tiny X-ray room in Avesta was no different from the one in Lärbro. Except perhaps for the hairline crack that ran the length of the ceiling. It was a symbol of something and it gave Miklós a feeling of hope. In this room he once again pressed his sunken chest and narrow shoulders up against the machine. And once again it gave out a high thin beep when the X-ray was done. Miklós always covered his eyes when the door opened and light streamed into the darkness. And it was always Dr Lindholm who stood in the doorway in his radiation-proof leather apron.

The X-rays were read the following day. Miklós entered Dr Lindholm's office and sat down in front of the desk. He leaned back until the front legs of his chair rose into the air. It was to become an annoying habit in Avesta. He had made a bet with himself. If something of vital importance was being discussed, he would pivot on his chair like a naughty child—all the while concentrating like mad.

'The X-rays came out well. Sharp, easy to read,' Dr Lindholm said, looking into my father's eyes.

'Any change?'

'I can give no encouraging.'

Miklós let the chair drop back on all four legs.

'And forget about going to Eksjö. Is too far away from Avesta. God knows how long to get there.'

'I only want three days.'

'You have always fever at dawn. There are no miracles.'

Miklós had his own thermometer. Each morning, at half past four on the dot, an inner alarm clock woke him up. The mercury always reached the same point. Thirty-eight point two. No more, no less.

'This is not about me. My cousin is lonely and depressed. It would mean the world to her.'

Dr Lindholm gave him a thoughtful glance. He and Márta, who was now head nurse in their section in Avesta, had settled into their new home. He decided to invite Miklós, who got on well with his wife, for supper. Perhaps over a family meal he could dissuade this charming and stubborn young man from his crazy scheme.

~

The Lindholms' house was next to the railway line. Trains regularly shrieked past the window. Miklós dressed for the occasion, having borrowed a jacket and tie, but he felt ill at ease. At the beginning, conversation was awkward. Márta dished out the stuffed cabbage. Dr Lindholm tucked his napkin into his shirt.

'Márta cook this dish especially for you. Hungarian, she tell me.'

There was the banshee noise of a passing train.

'It's one of my favourites,' replied Miklós when it was quiet again. He broke a crust of bread and carefully gathered up the crumbs.

Márta smacked his hand. 'If you don't stop cleaning up, I'll send you out to wash the dishes.'

He blushed. For a while they blew on the hot cabbage in silence.

Miklós started to cough. After he caught his breath, he said, 'Dr Lindholm speaks beautiful Hungarian.'

'I won on that score. In everything else Erik is the boss,' said Márta, smiling at her husband.

They continued to eat in silence. Fatty cabbage juice started to trickle down Miklós's chin. Márta handed him a napkin. He wiped his mouth in embarrassment.

'Can I ask you how you two met?'

Márta, who could barely reach the table from her chair, stretched her hand out between the glasses and laid it on Lindholm's arm. 'Can I tell him?'

Dr Lindholm nodded.

'It was ten years ago. A delegation of Swedish doctors came to visit the Rókus Hospital in Budapest. None of them was tall. I was the head nurse there,' Márta said, then stopped.

Dr Lindholm sipped his wine. He was not going to help her out.

'Since I was a teenager people have always teased me. Look at me, Miklós, you can see why, can't you? If I was asked to open a window, I had to get someone in the class to do it for me. When I was sixteen I told my mother that, as soon as I could, I would move to Sweden and find a husband. So I started learning Swedish.'

A passenger train clattered past. It felt as if it had passed between them and the plates.

'Why Sweden?'

'Is common knowledge that very short men live here,' Dr Lindholm retorted.

It was five seconds before Miklós dared to laugh. It was as if a plug had been pulled out: now the conversation flowed.

'By 1935 I could speak Swedish fluently. By coincidence Dr Lindholm had had enough of his previous wife. She was a giant—six foot. That's right, isn't it, Erik?'

Dr Lindholm nodded gravely.

'What was I to do? One evening I seduced him. In the hospital. Next to the operating theatre. I haven't left anything out, have I, Erik? Now it's your turn, Miklós. Did you tell the girl in Eksjö about your condition?'

My father, who until now had been preoccupied with his napkin, picked up his knife and fork and started to wolf down the cabbage. 'More or less.'

'Erik and I differ on this. I think you should go. To cheer up your…cousin. And yourself.'

Dr Lindholm sighed and poured more wine into everybody's glasses. 'Last week I receive letter from my colleague who work in Ädelfors,' he said. He jumped up and hurried into the other room. A moment later he returned clutching a sheet of paper.

'I read you parts, Miklós. There is women's hospital in Ädelfors, a rehabilitation centre for four hundred inmates. Well, about fifty girls were transferred to different hospital with stricter regime. What you think reason?' he asked, brandishing the letter.

Miklós shrugged. Lindholm didn't wait for the answer.

'Their loose life. I read it to you. Listen. "The girls received men in their bedrooms and in clearings in the nearby forest."'

No one had anything to say.

After a while the tiny Márta asked, 'Were they Hungarian girls?'

'I don't know.'

But Miklós knew the answer. 'They were spoilt upper-class girls!' he announced triumphantly.

Márta put down her fork in alarm. 'What's that supposed to mean, Miklós?'

My father was at last on familiar ground. He intended to enjoy himself. The dusty world of the past had been blown away by the fresh wind of socialism.

'Women like that adhere to a certain type of morality. They smoke, wear nylon stockings and chatter away about superficial things. *While from the depths not a word.*' Miklós couldn't resist quoting the poetry of Attila József.

'I'm not sure about that,' said Dr Lindholm. 'All I know, opportunity makes a thief.'

But Miklós was not so easily deterred. 'There's only one way to cure those bourgeois morals.'

'And that is?'

'By building a new world! From the foundations.'

From that point on, the supper was overwhelmed by my father's rousing manifesto in praise of the redeeming trinity of *liberté, égalité, fraternité*. He didn't even notice that they had polished off the dessert.

After midnight Dr Lindholm's car swung into the entrance of the hospital. Miklós clambered out and waved goodbye. He was buoyant, full of hope that he would soon be off to Eksjö. As soon as he got back to his barracks, he lit a candle, crouched down at his bed and excitedly condensed his world-saving ideology into a four-page letter.

> It will make me happy if you write and tell me what you think about all this. I'm especially interested because you are middle class, and probably look at this question from the point of view of the bourgeoisie.

Four

IN THE third week of October, Dr Svensson allowed Lili to get up. She forlornly roamed the tiled corridors of the hospital. The acrid smell of disinfectant mingled with the stench of gutted fish. The women's section was on the third floor, but otherwise the place seemed to be full of surly Swedish soldiers.

Lili was about to spend her first Sunday with the Björkmans. Two months earlier, at Smålandsstenar, each of the Hungarian girls had been introduced to a Swedish family who would help them find their feet. Sven Björkman ran a small stationery shop. He and his family were practising Catholics.

Lili wasn't assigned to the Björkmans by chance. It was five months since her 'betrayal'. In May, just after the war ended, when she regained consciousness in a hospital in the town of Belsen after being rescued from the concentration camp, she immediately renounced her Jewish faith. The truth is that she chose Catholicism quite randomly. But it meant that later, thanks to the thoroughness and the sensitivity of the Swedish authorities, the Björkman family was chosen to support her.

Björkman, his wife and their two sons made the long drive to Eksjö at dawn the next Sunday. They waited for Lili at the hospital entrance, hugged her joyfully on seeing her again, and then took her straight to mass in Smålandsstenar.

The Björkman family sat in the third pew of the simple but spacious church. And the convalescent Hungarian girl, Lili Reich, sat with them. Their radiant faces turned towards the pulpit. Lili understood only a few words of Swedish so the sermon washed over her with the same solemnity as the organ fugue that followed it. Then she, too, kneeled in the line before the young priest with the piercing blue eyes, so he could place a wafer on her tongue.

> Dear Miklós,
>
> I'd like to ask you not to hurry so much next time you write, but rather to think over what you're writing and to whom. Our relationship isn't that close. Mind what you say to me! Yes, I'm a typical bourgeois girl. And if, among four hundred girls, 'about fifty' fit your description of them, why should you be surprised?

~

That same Sunday morning Miklós and Harry were sitting in front of a few scones and glasses of soda water in the Avesta canteen. They should have been celebrating the fact that they had the place to themselves, but Miklós was in such a bad mood that he didn't even notice.

'I've ruined it,' he muttered.

Harry waved him down. 'Of course you haven't. She'll calm down.'

'Never. I've got a feeling.'

'Then you can write to someone else.'

Miklós looked up, shocked. 'There isn't anyone else. It's either her or I die.' How could Harry be so insensitive?

Harry burst out laughing. 'Words, just words?'

Miklós dipped his finger in the glass of water and wrote 'LILI' on the wooden table. 'This'll dry up too,' he said sadly.

'Send her one of your poems!'

'Too late.'

'I don't like sorrowful Jews,' said Harry, getting up. 'I'll find you something sweet. I'll bribe someone or steal something for you. But wipe that glum look off your face.'

Harry crossed the dreary hall to the swing door and entered the kitchen. There was no one there either. He opened cupboards until he found a jar of honey buried deep in one of them.

He hurried back in triumph. 'No spoon. You'll have to dip your finger in, like this.'

My father was staring at the table. The stem of the second 'L' was still visible.

'Right.' Harry sucked his finger. 'Have you got paper and a pencil? I'll dictate.'

'What?' asked Miklós, looking up at last.

'A letter. To her. Are you ready?' He dipped his finger in the honey.

Puzzled, Miklós took some paper and a pencil out of his pocket. Harry's cheerfulness had managed to strike a tiny crack in the armour of his despair.

'Dear Lili,' Harry dictated, licking his finger, 'I have to tell you that I despise and deride those stupid women who are ashamed to talk about such things—'

Miklós slammed down his pencil. 'This is lunacy! You want me to send this to Lili?'

'You've been writing to each other for a month now. It's high time you became more intimate with her. I'm an outsider, I can gauge things better.'

~

The following Sunday, after Sven Björkman had said grace, and the two Björkman boys had more or less settled down, Mrs Björkman began ladling out the soup with her usual precision.

'Where have you hidden your crucifix, Lili?' Björkman asked, without so much as a glance at Lili.

Either he spoke little German or he wanted to test Lili's

knowledge of Swedish. When she looked at him blankly, he repeated the question, in Swedish, and pointed to the crucifix round his own neck.

Lili blushed. She fished the little silver cross out of her pocket and put it round her neck.

'Why did you take it off?' he asked, looking at her pleasantly. 'We gave it to you for you to wear. Always.'

The reproach was clear. The meal passed without further conversation.

> The tone and content of your last letter were rather strange but you seem like a kind man, so I'll answer this one too. On the other hand, I'm not sure that a 'bourgeois' girl like me is the right friend for you. This time I think you went too far.

~

It was dawn. Miklós felt for the thermometer in the drawer of his bedside table, and with his eyes still shut he stuck it in his mouth. Then he counted to 130. He opened his eyes for a split second: there was no need for him to study the delicate markings in detail. The fever, as stealthy as a thief, crept up, stole his confidence, and then vanished in the half-light of dawn. He put the thermometer in the drawer again, turned over and went back to sleep.

When he got up at eight o'clock his temperature was normal.

Dear Lili,

What a fool I am! I'm sorry. Why do I bother you with all my stupid thoughts? I send you a warm handshake.

Miklós

P.S.: Is that still allowed?

~

It took two days for a letter to arrive by Swedish mail train. When Miklós's apology arrived, Lili and Sára were huddled on Lili's bed.

'"P.S. Is that still allowed?"'

'Now you should forgive him,' said Sára after some thought.

'I already have.'

Lili scrambled across the bed and took an envelope from her bedside table.

'I purposely left it open,' she said as she searched for the bit she wanted to show Sára. 'Here it is: "Yes, Miklós, you really are a fool! But if you behave yourself we can be friends again."' She gave Sára a jubilant look.

'Men!' said Sára, smiling.

~

Four bicycles were kept in the entrance to Avesta, so patients could ride from the forest to the town. Now that the weather had turned cold and even the midday sunshine didn't melt the snow on the fir trees, Miklós and Harry had to rug up to prevent their ears and hands from freezing on the hour-long ride.

Even so, it took a long time, as they sat waiting at the post office, for the feeling to return to their fingers, though they tried to keep them warm under their thighs.

Miklós was anxious. From where they sat he could see the glass doors of the three telephone booths, which at that moment were all occupied. He was beside himself. It was his turn next.

After what seemed forever one of the booths became vacant. At the counter, an operator lifted the receiver to her ear. She looked at Miklós, said something into the phone and waved at him. He stood up and staggered into the vacant booth.

~

Judit Gold dashed up the stairs at full speed, practically knocking over the nurses and doctors hurrying in the opposite direction. Lili and Sára were reading in the open window of the ward. Judit stormed through the door. 'Lili! Lili!' she shouted. 'You've got a phone call!'

Lili gaped at her, not understanding.

'Hurry! Miklós is on the phone!'

Lili turned red and leapt off the windowsill. She flew downstairs to the basement, where a telephone room had been set up for patients. A nurse was on her way out of the room, and she looked at Lili in surprise. Lili saw the receiver lying on the table. She made herself slow down. She touched the receiver gingerly, and cautiously lifted it to her ear. 'It's me.'

In the post office Miklós gave a small cough, but his voice still came out an octave higher than its usual baritone. 'You sound exactly the way I imagined you would,' he managed to say. 'How mystical!'

'I'm out of breath. I ran. There's just one telephone, in the main building, and we…'

Miklós started to babble. 'Catch your breath. I'll do the talking, all right? Remember I told you how you can already send cables home? I'm calling because—just imagine—now we can send airmail letters too, via London or Prague. At last you can find your mother! Isn't it great! I thought I'd call and tell you right away.'

'Oh dear.'

'Did I say something wrong?'

Lili was clutching the receiver so tightly that her fingers had turned white. 'Mama…I don't know…I don't know her address…She had to leave our old flat and move to the ghetto… and now I don't know where she is living.'

Miklós's voice recovered its silky tone. 'Oh, I'm a fool. Of course you don't! But we can place a notice in a newspaper. We'll send her a message through *Világosság*. Everyone reads that. I've got a bit of money saved up. I'll arrange it.'

Lili was surprised. There was no way he could afford to do that on five kronor a week.

'How have you been able to save any money?'

'Didn't I tell you, my darling? Oh, sorry, have I gone too far? I'm sorry, Lili.'

Lili blushed furiously. Now her temperature had shot up. 'I wish I could see you.'

The post office felt like a palace to Miklós. Thrilled, he punched the air with his fist, signalling to Harry through the glass. 'Well, it's like this, what if I had a Cuban uncle…but that's a long story, I'll put it in a letter.'

No one spoke for a while. They pressed the receivers tightly to their ears.

'How are you?' Lili started up again. 'Your health, I mean.'

'Me? I'm fine. All my tests are negative. There was a tiny spot on my left lung. Some fluid. A touch of pleurisy. But not serious. I'm more or less in the middle of my treatment. And you?'

'I'm fine, too. Nothing hurts. I have to take iron tablets.'

'Have you got a temperature?' Miklós asked.

'Very slight. A kidney infection. Nothing to worry about. I've got a good appetite. I'm so looking forward to seeing you… seeing you both,' said Lili.

'Yes. I'm working on it. But in the meantime I've written you a poem.'

'Me?' Lili blushed again.

Miklós closed his eyes. 'Shall I recite it?'

'You know it by heart?'

'Of course.'

He had to think quickly. The truth was that he had already

written six poems for Lili, to Lili. Now he had to choose one. 'The title is "Lili". You still there?'

'Yes.'

Miklós leaned against the booth wall. He kept his eyes closed.

I stepped on an icy puddle
the rime crunched under me.
If you touch my heart, beware,
a single move will be
enough to crack apart
my secret frozen sea.

'Are you still there?'

Lili held her breath.

He couldn't hear her, but he could sense her presence.

'Yes.'

Miklós was frightened by something, too, or perhaps he was just hoarse. The distance made the receiver hiss, and the words of the poem sounded like breaking waves. 'I'll go on then,' he said.

So come to me gently,
with the smiles that we lost.
Seek out the places
where pain has chilled to frost
so the warmth of your caress
melts to dew within my chest.

Five

THE GROUND-FLOOR meeting room, which the hospital in Eksjö had made available to the Red Cross, was tiny and embarrassingly bare. It had no window. There was just room for a desk and a bentwood chair for visitors.

Madame Ann-Marie Arvidsson was the local Red Cross representative. She sharpened her pencil after almost every sentence she wrote. She spoke German slowly, enunciating every syllable to make it easier for Lili to understand the finer points. And she was set on explaining everything to this charming Hungarian girl. Even things that were out of her hands. Such as the risk Sweden had taken by allowing in so many sick people. Such as the fact that the International Red Cross never had enough money, because all sorts of unforeseeable expenses were always cropping up. She didn't even get to the question of accommodation. The main thing was, like it or not, she couldn't support this kind of private initiative.

'You ought to know, Lili, I don't agree with this type of visit even in principle.'

Lili tried again. 'Just a few days. What harm will that do anyone?'

'It won't do any harm. But what would be the point? To come from the other side of the country. That's a lot of money. And once the men are here? Among three hundred patients. This is a hospital, not a hotel! Have you considered that, Lili?'

'I haven't seen them for a year and a half.' She gave the woman an imploring look.

Madame Arvidsson thought she saw a speck of dust on the immaculate surface of the desk. She wiped it off. 'Let's say I give permission. What will your relatives eat? The Red Cross has no funds for extra food.'

'Something. Anything.'

'You are not facing facts, Lili. These men are patients too. I can't even imagine how they'll buy the tickets for the train.'

'We've got a Cuban relative.'

Ann-Marie Arvidsson raised an eyebrow. She jotted down a few words, then sharpened her pencil. 'And this relative is financing the visit, all the way from Cuba?'

Lili looked deep into Madame Arvidsson's eyes. 'We're a loving family…'

This, at last, made Madame Arvidsson laugh. 'I admire your determination. I'll try to do something. But I can't make any promises.'

Lili got up, leaned awkwardly over the desk and gave Madame Ann-Marie Arvidsson a kiss. Then she ran out of the room, knocking over her chair on the way.

Ann-Marie Arvidsson got up, set the chair on its legs, took out her handkerchief and wiped all trace of the kiss off her cheek.

~

A few days later Rabbi Emil Kronheim climbed briskly onto a train in Stockholm. The rabbi was an ascetic figure, small and thin, in an old grey suit. His hair was like a haystack. Ever since the Swedish government had called on him to give moral support to his fellow Jews in these hard times, his name and address had been pinned on the noticeboard of every rehabilitation centre in Sweden.

He travelled up and down the country for three weeks of each month. Sometimes he talked to people in groups. Other times he would listen to a single person for hours on end, hardly moving, giving strength with just the bat of an eyelid, until they were engulfed by the early evening twilight. He never grew tired.

His one excess was herring. It was almost comical. He couldn't resist pickled herring. Even on the train, reading the newspaper, while the snow-covered countryside raced past, he ate pieces of herring out of greasy paper.

At the station in Eksjö he clambered out of his carriage. It was pouring. He hurried across the wet platform.

According to his information there were three young Hungarian women in the hospital. A few days ago he had received a letter from one of them. A single soul is a soul. Without a moment's hesitation he had set out on the mind-numbing journey from Stockholm.

Now he was sitting in the same windowless room that had confined Madame Ann-Marie Arvidsson. He was concentrating on a fly that was crawling around the desk between the pencils, the sharpener.

There was a knock. Judit Gold stuck her head round the door. 'Can I come in?'

The rabbi smiled. 'Just as I imagined you. You see, dear—'

'I'm Judit Gold.'

'You see, dear Judit Gold, on the basis of your handwriting I formed a mental picture of you. Now comes my pat on the back: I've scored a bullseye. Incidentally the world is built on this kind of presentiment. Before the Battle of Waterloo, Napoleon…Oh, you look so pale. Can I get you some water?'

There was a jug on the desk. Rabbi Kronheim filled a glass.

Judit Gold drank greedily, then sat down. She spoke in a whisper. 'I'm ashamed of myself.'

'So am I. We all are. And we've reason to be. What's the reason for your shame, Judit?'

'I'm ashamed of writing you that letter. And of being forced to tell tales.'

'Don't tell tales then! Forget the whole thing.'

'I can't.'

'Of course you can. Shrug it off and throw what you wanted to tell me into the bin. Don't give it another thought. Forget it. Let's talk about something else. Let's talk about flies, for example. What's your attitude to flies?'

Emil Kronheim pointed to the fly buzzing over the desk.

'They disgust me.'

'You want to be careful with disgust. It can easily turn into hatred. And right after that comes conflict. Later, it becomes ideology. And in the end you'll be pursuing flies all your life.'

Judit couldn't take her eyes off the fly that had now landed on the rim of her glass. 'I've got a friend,' she said.

Judit paused. She was in need of a question or a gesture, but Kronheim seemed interested only in the fly, the crazy, fidgety fly.

She had to start somewhere. 'It's about my friend Lili. She's eighteen. Inexperienced and naïve.'

The rabbi shut his eyes. Was he listening at all?

'She has been completely ensnared by a man from Gotland. Well, he has now been transferred to Avesta. I can't stand by and do nothing. I can't bear seeing Lili getting all worked up about him. There's no way I can keep calm or stay out of this.'

The rabbi, who had been so chatty to start with, was now sitting still, his eyes closed. Had he fallen asleep?

Judit started crying. 'She is my best friend. I've grown to

love her. She was skin and bone when she arrived. She was so down. So alone. Then she started writing letters to this good-for-nothing. He's a gangster. He promises her everything under the sun. Right now he wants to come and visit her in the hospital. Sorry, I'm not making any sense. All I know is that Lili's too young.'

Judit felt that she had lost the thread. She should tell the story from the beginning. Tell him why she was anxious and why her fears were real. But, instead of helping her out, the rabbi was confusing her. He sat there with his eyes closed, his back straight. He wasn't paying attention.

A minute passed. Then Rabbi Kronheim ran his fingers through his untidy hair. So he hadn't been asleep.

Judit snivelled and sniffed. 'I've lived through so much horror. I've given up so many times. But I'm alive. I'm still here. And Lili is so young.'

Emil Kronheim put his hand in his pocket. 'I always have a clean handkerchief on me for such occasions. Here you are.'

~

Around this time Miklós began to figure out how he could trick fate. He had no illusions about his looks. Even though he now weighed fifty kilos, and the nasty warts were starting to disappear, he remained self-conscious.

Dr Lindholm was surprised by his request, but for once it wasn't about going to Eksjö, and it was something that would make Miklós happy, so he agreed right away. He went over to the cupboard and took out a small camera. Then he got a roll of film out of his desk drawer. He handed them both to Miklós, who was standing in the middle of the room, beaming.

Miklós, Harry and Tibor Hirsch headed across to a spacious, breezy tract of land between the barracks where hundred-year-old pine trees rose up high. Miklós solemnly handed the camera to Tibor, who at over fifty was the oldest of the patients. His hair didn't seem to want to grow; irregular-shaped purple patches could be seen on his scalp.

'You were a photographer,' Miklós said, looking at him. 'I trust you. My life's in your hands.'

Hirsch spent a long time examining the camera. 'I know this type. It'll be perfect, I promise.'

Miklós interrupted. 'No, it shouldn't be perfect.'

'What?'

'It should be fuzzy. That's what I want.'

Hirsch looked puzzled.

'That's why I asked you. Because you know what you're doing.'

'Only to a point. I'm an electronic radio technician and photographer's assistant. Or used to be. What *do* you want?'

Miklós now pointed at Harry. 'We both should be in the picture. Harry and me. Harry should be in focus. I should be blurred, somewhere in the background. Could you do that?'

'That's nuts!' Hirsch protested. 'Why on earth do you want to be out of focus?'

'Never you mind. Can you do it?'

Tibor Hirsch, electronic radio technician and photographer's assistant, hesitated. But Miklós was his friend, and was giving him begging looks, so he put aside his professional pride.

Within five minutes he had worked out how to take a photograph in which my father would be more or less unrecognisable. He posed Harry in the foreground. In half-profile, at the most flattering angle. A watery sun came out for the briefest moment. Hirsch positioned them with backlight for an artistic feel. He instructed Miklós to run up and down a few metres behind Harry. Hirsch took several shots while Miklós ran.

> Dear Lili,
>
> What a sorceress you are! You enchanted me on the telephone. Now I'm even more keen to see whether you are as I imagine you from your letters. There'll be trouble if you aren't, but even more trouble if you are. I've found a photo of myself and Harry, who's standing in the front. Granted I look like I've been crushed by some sort of Cyclops and I'm in a hurry to get to the smallest room in the house—but I'm sending it anyway.

~

An artificial palm with lush tropical foliage stood in front of an alcove window on the third-floor corridor of the Eksjö hospital. The three girls sat there, hidden from sight.

Lili was examining the photograph with a magnifying glass. She handed it to Sára and Judit. There was nothing wrong with their eyesight. But was that indistinct shape running away behind Harry's back, that almost unidentifiable figure, Miklós?

A shadow loomed over them. 'Ah ha, so that's why you needed my magnifier.'

The three girls jumped as one. Dr Svensson pointed to the photo. 'Men? Hungarians?'

Lili held out the photo in embarrassment. 'It's my cousin.'

Svensson took a good look. 'Handsome. An open face.'

Lili hesitated, but then she pointed at the hazy figure in the background. 'That's him, the one who seems to be running away.'

Dr Svensson lifted the photograph close to his eyes, trying to identify the young man loping out of the frame, but it was hopeless. 'I thought he was in the picture by mistake. How mysterious.'

Miklós's idea was a success. The mysterious figure had kept the promise of the future alive. The girls were laughing as Svensson handed back the photo in disappointment, and they returned his magnifying glass to him.

~

> Now I'm going to be very cheeky, partly to you and partly to your friend Sára, to whom I send friendly greetings. You see, the thing is my friend Harry and I have acquired some rather ghastly muddy grey wool

> that nimble-fingered girls could conjure into passable sweaters. I'd like to ask you to do this for me—as soon as possible, of course.

At dawn the next day Lili sat up in bed and took a handkerchief from under her pillow. She folded it carefully and slipped it into the envelope on the bedside table.

> Accept this trifle from me with love. I'm afraid it isn't quite as fine as I'd have liked, and since I haven't got an iron I had to press it under my pillow. How did you find the wool? By the way, it's getting colder and colder here, and since they haven't given us winter coats I always put on two cardigans if I go out for a walk.

At that moment Judit Gold stuck her head out from beneath her eiderdown and couldn't help but see Lili's look of peaceful happiness. She wasn't a bit pleased.

~

The mail was distributed every afternoon after the men had rested. It was usually Harry who went to get the letters from the caretaker's office and he would read out the names. 'Misi, Adolf, Litzman, Jenö Grieger, Jakobovits, Józsi, Spitz, Miklós...'

My father got lots of letters, perhaps too many, but only one person's letters excited him. If he saw that Lili had written, he didn't have the patience to wait until he was back in bed, but greedily tore open the envelope on the way. Now a handkerchief slipped out onto the floor. He picked it up and smelled it over and over again.

> The fact that you pressed your handkerchief under your head just enhances its value for me...Tell me, why is it that your letters bring me more and more joy?
>
> Sorry about the pencil, but I wanted to write back straight away and someone has taken the ink.
>
> I send you a long warm handshake.
>
> Miklós

~

In Eksjö there was a hall on the ground floor of the hospital, with a yellow-sided platform where a red velvet curtain could be let down to make a stage. When Sára had the idea that they should give an evening concert, she and the girls hoped that the women living on the third floor would come and listen to them. In actual fact almost all of the two hundred chairs were taken up by the soldiers. The occasional Swedish nurse, with her braided hair, crisply starched cloak and bonnet, was squeezed in between them like a raisin in a bun.

The girls performed four numbers. Sára sang, while Lili accompanied her on the harmonium. After three Hungarian songs, Sára began to sing the Swedish national anthem. She was halfway through it when the soldiers, unshaven and in pyjamas, kicked back their two hundred chairs, jumped to their feet and joined in, none of them in tune.

> These Swedes are starting to get on my nerves. They expect us to sing their praises all the time. I am indescribably homesick!

Six

KLÁRA KÖVES arrived unexpectedly on the midday train. She had just enough money to buy a rail ticket from her camp near Uppsala to Avesta. That didn't worry her in the slightest—she was convinced that Miklós would take care of everything.

At the station she arranged a lift in the mail van, which meant that she travelled the last few kilometres in style. It was early afternoon when she arrived at the hospital.

Klára was a large girl—her friends called her 'bear woman'. Her walk was more like a trudge. Her handshake was like a man's. A good part of her body was covered with a silky down that, in a certain light, looked a lot like fur. She had full, sensuous lips, a hooknose and a mop of unruly, dark brown hair.

She blew into the barracks like a whirlwind. 'I'm here, dear Miklós!' she shouted. 'I've come to you!'

The men froze. Miklós couldn't connect this hefty woman with the amusing, quick-witted girl he'd been exchanging letters with for the past two months. There must be some misunderstanding.

Klára Köves, it turned out, was one of nine women apart from Lili with whom my father had been corresponding after he sent out his initial batch of 117 letters. He couldn't help himself. He took great joy in the process of writing; it helped him understand things, and he was genuinely curious about the lives of these girls. Of course the letters he wrote to the nine women were nothing like his outpourings to Lili. He and Klára, for instance, merely shared their views on world issues. Klára had distributed socialist pamphlets during the war—that's how she got caught.

She made a beeline for my father, threw her arms around him and kissed him on the lips. 'I've been wanting to do that for weeks.'

The other men hadn't moved an inch. What an entrance! A real flesh-and-blood woman, all ninety kilos of her, had materialised before them, despite all the regulations, restrictions and prohibitions. Their dreams had become three-dimensional.

Miklós shuddered, trapped in Klára's embrace. 'Wanting to do what?'

'To tie our lives together! What else?'

At last Klára let go of him. She took some letters out of her handbag and threw them in the air. She turned to the other men, who by this time were scrambling off their beds and gathering around her. 'Do you know who you've got in your midst? A new Karl Marx! A new Friedrich Engels!'

The letters fell like confetti. The men were enchanted.

Miklós wanted to die on the spot.

Klára took his arm and led him out of the barracks. My father signalled urgently for Harry to follow. The three of them set off down the path that led to the forest. It was as if Klára had taken possession of Miklós, as if she were hugging a doll. Harry walked behind them, hoping for his turn. It began to drizzle.

'Look here, Klára,' said Miklós in what he hoped was a quiet but authoritative voice. 'You should know that I write to other girls. Lots of them, in fact.'

Klára laughed. 'Are you trying to make me jealous, sweetie?'

'Heavens, no. I just want to be clear with you. Letter-writing is our only entertainment. Not only for me, but for the whole barracks. But it may have caused you to misunderstand certain things.'

'Misunderstanding, my foot! I've fallen for you, honey! You're as clever as they get. I look up to you. You'll be my teacher and my lover! You're full of hang-ups, but I'll be your saviour.'

'I write tons of letters. I want you to know that.'

'All geniuses are complex. I had two before the war, so I know. You don't mind my coming clean, do you? I'm not a virgin. Hell, no! I'm many things, but no virgin. But I will be faithful to you, I can feel it. The thoughts and ideas you come up with! I know them by heart. Would you like to test me?'

She grabbed Miklós by the waist and covered his face with kisses. His glasses misted up. But even through the fog he could see the desperation in her eyes, her fear of rejection.

This unexpected discovery had a soothing effect on Miklós. 'Could I get a word in, please, Klára,' he said calmly.

'I just wanted to say,' Klára raced on, 'that I'll nurse you if you need it. I've completely recovered. I'm going to work! I'll move to be near you. Now, what did you want to tell me?'

Miklós extricated himself from Klára's grasp and turned to her. 'All right. Now for the facts. I write many letters, but only because I've got beautiful handwriting. People have noticed it. The men in the barracks take advantage of it, so to speak. Your letters, I'm afraid, were composed by Harry, not me. He dictated them to me because my writing is so much better than his. That's the sad truth. You fell for Harry's brain through me.'

Klára's eyes widened. She spun around to Harry. The drizzle was getting heavier. 'So it turns out you're my genius. Is that right, sweetheart?'

Harry cottoned on. He hoped his lonely preparation for the manly tasks that lay ahead would prove sufficient. 'He…just did the writing,' he improvised, pointing to Miklós. 'The thoughts…' Harry gave his forehead a modest tap.

Klára looked from one man to the other. Miklós was short, wore glasses and had metal teeth. Harry was tall, with a neat moustache, and she must have detected the look of genuine desire in his eyes. She decided she was better off believing my father. She took Harry's arm.

'I'm going to get to know you, sweetheart. I don't give a damn about appearances. I don't care about the shape of a mouth, the colour of a man's eyes, whether he is handsome or not. It's the mind I go for, if you see what I mean. I get high on progressive, soaring ideas—I can't get enough of them.'

Harry turned the girl towards him, putting one hand on her ample bottom, and holding her chin in the other. 'I won't disappoint you,' he said boldly, and kissed her on the lips.

Miklós felt it was time to make his exit. At the end of the path he looked back and saw them locked in an embrace as they wandered towards the thick of the forest behind an increasingly heavy curtain of rain.

~

To atone for this episode with Klára, Miklós inflicted three days' penitence on himself. During this time he didn't write a word to Lili. On the fourth day, after getting the key from the caretaker, he ran a full bath of hot water in the only private bathroom on the grounds. It was in a separate building far from the barracks, so Miklós didn't bother to lock the door. He got into the bath, lit a cigarette and started bellowing out a workers' marching song. He wasn't exactly famous for his musical ear.

The door swung open. There was the tiny Márta, the head nurse, trying to wave the thick smoke away. In shock, Miklós tried to cover his penis with his left hand.

Márta was in a rage. 'What do you think you're doing here, Miklós? Hiding away to smoke in secret? You ought to be ashamed! How old are you? You're behaving like a naughty schoolboy!'

My father dropped his cigarette in the water. He tried to wave the smoke away with his right arm but only managed to stir it up. He was shy about being naked and in his embarrassment covered himself with both hands.

Márta, in her huge nurse's cap, came right over to the bath. 'For you, Miklós, every cigarette means death,' she shouted. 'Each one costs you a day of life. Is it worth it? Answer me, you foolish man! Is it worth it?'

> Lili, my dear little friend,
>
> It's time for a confession. Not the one that I'm afraid to write down—but another one. I have to tell you that my ear for music is atrocious and my singing voice is deplorable. But, like all pacifists, I belt out marching songs at the top of my voice in the bath.
>
> It's terrible the way they watch over us here. We have to keep to a strict daily routine: with silent rest times and other fun and games. The chief tyrant is Márta, the Mickey Mouse–like head nurse, Dr Lindholm's Hungarian wife. She's always fussing around us.

The Mickey Mouse–like head nurse stomped across the

garden. It was five minutes' walk to the caretaker's office, and Márta's anger grew with every step.

She practically tore the office door off its hinges.

Four days earlier, not least as a result of Klára Köves's patience, Harry had regained his lost masculinity. Although Klára went away slightly disappointed, they agreed to go on writing to each other. Harry, on the other hand, had worked up an appetite. This time it was big-boned Frida, the daytime caretaker—nicknamed 'baby elephant' by the men—who took his fancy. Harry meditated on the devious whims of his desire. It seemed that the days when only pale, wasp-waisted girls made an impression on him were inexplicably over.

When Márta appeared like an avenging angel in the caretaker's office, Frida and Harry (in his pyjamas) hadn't got past cuddling. But there was no time to break away from each other. Harry was grateful that the conversation took place in Swedish, of which he understood next to nothing.

'Did you sell Miklós cigarettes, Frida?'

Frida's plump arms held Harry in a tight clasp, which she didn't relax for a moment. 'Just two or three.'

'This is your last chance! If I catch you again I'll report you!' shouted Márta, and she turned on her heel, slamming the door behind her.

Of course, Frida was not just being generous by handing out cigarettes. The tiny mark-up she added went to supplement her meagre wages.

> Honestly, I like a man who smokes, but you're an exception now. Please don't overdo it. I don't smoke, by the way.

~

Lili came into the ward like a sleepwalker. She sat down on her bed without a word, radiating despair. Judit, who was in bed reading *Tess of the d'Urbervilles* for the third time, closed the book and sat up.

Sára was pouring herself a cup of tea. She hurried over to Lili. 'Has anything happened? '

Lili, sitting there with drooping shoulders, didn't answer.

Sára put her hand on Lili's forehead. 'Your temperature's up again. Where's the thermometer?'

Judit got out of bed to get the thermometer, which they kept in a dish on the windowsill. Lili let the girls lift her arm then press it tightly to her side. They sat opposite her on the bed and waited.

The wind beat against the windowpane. Lili's soft voice sounded like a lone violin over the beat of its thrumming and creaking. 'Someone reported me.'

Judit straightened her back slightly. 'What?'

'I've just come from the Red Cross woman. She told me I'd been lying…' Lili stared at her slippers.

Silence. Sára remembered her name. 'Ann-Marie Arvidsson?' she queried.

'...That she knows Miklós isn't my cousin, he's an unknown letter-writer...'

Judit started to pace the room. 'Where did she get that from?'

'...and she's refusing to give permission. He can't come. Can't come!'

Sára kneeled down in front of Lili and kissed both her hands. 'We'll work something out. Get a hold on yourself, your temperature's up.'

Lili couldn't look up. 'She showed me a letter. It was written here, by one of us.'

'Who on earth?' Judit Gold was shouting now.

'She didn't say. She only told me it said that I had lied. Miklós isn't my cousin, as I had claimed, and that's why she is refusing permission for his visit.'

'We'll apply again,' Sára said. 'We'll go on putting in requests to receive visitors until they're sick of the sight of them.'

'Dearest Lili!' Judit collapsed at Lili's feet.

At last, Lili raised her head and looked at her friends. 'Who could hate me so much?'

Sára got up and took the thermometer from under Lili's arm. 'Thirty-nine point two. Get into bed this minute. We'll have to tell Svensson.'

The two girls laid Lili on her back and covered her with the eiderdown. She seemed incapable of moving on her own. They had to treat her like a baby.

'He's attracted to you,' remarked Judit by way of distraction.

Sára didn't understand at first. 'Who's attracted to Lili?'

'Svensson. You should see the looks he gives her.'

'Come off it!' Sára scoffed.

But Judit couldn't leave it alone. 'I'm never wrong in these matters.'

~

Miklós was standing on the iron girders of the bridge over the railway, staring at the tangle of tracks that snaked their way towards the horizon. The sky was steel grey.

A figure came into sight on the road. It was running. At the bridge it climbed the iron steps two at a time. Even so, Miklós only noticed it was Harry when he was standing beside him, puffing and panting.

'You going to jump?'

Miklós smiled. 'What makes you think that?'

'Your eyes. And the way you rushed off after we got the mail.'

A goods train pulled away below them. Its thick black smoke enveloped them like sorrow. Miklós grasped the bridge railings.

'No. I'm not going to jump.'

Harry leaned his elbows on the railings next to Miklós. They watched the departing train. When it had shrunk to a narrow streak in the distance, Miklós took a crumpled letter out of his pocket and handed it to Harry.

'I received this.'

> Dear Sir,
>
> In answer to your notice in today's *Szabad Nép*, I regret to inform you that your mother and father were the victims of a bombing raid on the Laxenburg camp in Austria on 12 February 1945...I knew them very well. It was me who guided them to the best place in the camp, the Coffee Factory, where they would be treated as humans and could get decent food and accommodation. I'm extremely sorry that I am the bearer of such sad news.
>
> Andor Rózsa

Miklós had a confused and contradictory relationship with his father. The owner of Gambrinus, the famous bookshop in Debrecen, was a domineering character, prone to shouting and often to violence too. He didn't spare his wife—and he didn't even need to be drunk to attack her. Unfortunately he drank a lot. In spite of this, my grandmother often came into the bookshop with a sandwich or an apple or a pear for him.

My father always remembered a wonderful afternoon in spring when, as a small boy, perched on the top rung of the bookstore ladder, he became so engrossed in Alexei Tolstoy's *Peter the Great* that, spellbound by the intrigues of the tsar's court, his ears flaming red, he forgot all about the time.

In the evening his mother showed up, wearing a wide-brimmed maroon hat. 'Miki, it's seven o'clock. You forgot to come home for dinner. What are you reading?'

He looked up. The woman in the wide-brimmed maroon

hat was familiar, but he couldn't quite place her.

Harry folded the letter and gave it back to Miklós without a word. They leaned against the railings and kept their eyes on the tracks. Some birds were circling overhead.

> Dear Miklós,
>
> I am terribly sorry that the letter from Szolnok contained such dreadful news. I can't find the words to comfort you.

That afternoon Miklós rode a bike to the cemetery in Avesta. It started to rain. He wandered aimlessly along the headstones, sometimes leaning over an inscription to try to sound out the Swedish name.

> I'm sorry I'm so cold and that I'm taking this calamity so damn hard. Yesterday I went to the local cemetery. I hoped perhaps my loved ones, at the bottom of a mass grave, might be stirred by a cosmic memory… That's all.

~

Lili sat up in bed. It was late at night; the bulb above the door gave off a faint light. Her forehead was drenched in sweat. In the next bed Sára was lying uncovered in the foetal position. Lili slipped out of bed and kneeled beside her.

'Are you asleep?'

Sára turned over, as if she had been expecting her. 'I can't sleep either!' she whispered back.

In a moment Lili was lying beside her; she held Sára's hand. Together they watched the strange patterns on the ceiling made by the birch tree swaying in the wind.

'He got some news,' Lili said. 'About his parents. They were bombed.'

Sára's eyes flickered; she could see the letter lying on Lili's bedside table. 'Good God!'

'I've worked it out. It's 373 days since I had any news of my mother or my father.'

With wide eyes they stared at the windblown expressionist images above them.

Seven

THE MAIL van arrived in Avesta soon after lunch. A man in a fur-collared coat jumped out, went round to the back, propped the door open and sorted the letters. It usually took him a few minutes. Then he went over to the yellow letterbox—which looked more like a large suitcase—opened the door at the bottom with a key and scooped all the outgoing mail into an empty canvas sack. After that he tipped all the incoming mail into the letterbox.

It was part of my father's daily routine to monitor this tedious ritual from beginning to end. He had to be absolutely convinced that his letter—as a result of some insidious plot—didn't fall out of the canvas sack.

> Lili, dear,
>
> I'm sure that, if not today, then tomorrow, you will get good news. The letter is sitting in your father's pocket, and he's waiting for the chance to try out this more or less impossible feat of sending a letter to Sweden.

~

In the Eksjö hospital there was one place you could smoke without getting caught. It was a bathroom on the second floor, which was used every morning for taking showers, but was then empty until the evening.

Judit Gold smoked at least half a pack a day; that's where all her pocket money went. But Sára, too, smoked three cigarettes a day. Lili went along to keep them company.

Sára inhaled pensively. 'We could go into town this afternoon. I begged for permission,' she announced after a while.

Judit was sitting on the edge of the shower cubicle, her legs drawn up under her. 'What for?'

'We could get a photo of Lili taken for Miklós.'

Lili was shocked. 'God forbid! He'll take one look and flee.'

Judit could blow excellent smoke rings. 'That's a good idea. A photo of the three of us, so we can remember all this, later on.'

'Later on when?' asked Sára.

'One day, when we're somewhere else. When we're happy.'

They meditated on this.

Then Lili said, 'I'm ugly. I don't want a photo.'

Sára smacked her hand. 'You're stupid, my friend, not ugly.'

Judit smiled enigmatically, her eyes following the smoke rings until they reached the ventilator.

~

In the post office Miklós leaned against the glass cubicle. He spoke in German to prevent any misunderstanding.

'I'd like to send a telegram.'

The clerk, who also wore glasses, gave him an encouraging look. 'Address?' she asked.

'Eksjö, Utlänningsläger, Korungsgården 7.'

She started to fill in the form. 'Message?'

'Two words. Two Hungarian words. I'll spell them.'

She took offence at that. 'Just say them, and I'll write them down.'

Miklós breathed in. He pronounced the words clearly, syllable by syllable, in his melodious Hungarian. '*Sze-ret-lek, Li-li.*'

The girl shook her head. Quite a language. 'Spell them, please.'

Miklós went letter by letter. They progressed patiently. Then they got stuck. Whereupon Miklós reached under the glass, grabbed the girl's right hand and tried to guide her pencil.

It wasn't easy. At the capital L, the girl threw down her

pencil and shoved the form across to my father. 'You write it.'

Miklós crossed out the mishmash and in his gorgeous, swirling script wrote in Hungarian: *I love you, Lili!*

He pushed the form back.

The clerk look nonplussed at the unfamiliar word. 'What does it mean?'

Miklós hesitated. 'Are you married, miss?'

'I'm engaged.'

'Oh! Congratulations. Well, it means…it means…'

He knew exactly how to translate into German the simplest and most beautiful declaration in the world. Even so he was reluctant to give himself away.

The girl was adding up. 'That'll be two kronor. So, are you going to tell me?'

Miklós suddenly lost his nerve. He turned pale. 'Give it back, please!' he shouted at her. 'Give it back!'

She shrugged and pushed the form across the counter. Miklós grabbed it and tore it to pieces. He felt utterly stupid and cowardly. How could he explain? Instead he grinned in embarrassment, nodded at the girl and fled the post office.

~

Late that evening the men, wrapped in their blankets, sat around the wooden table in the courtyard. Many of them had their eyes closed in the drowsy silence, or stared vacantly at the bare red-brick wall opposite.

Miklós was standing with his back against the wall, his eyes closed, as if he were asleep.

> I won't send any new poems now, just a sonnet. I've got bigger plans: I'm working out the plot for a novel. It's about twelve people—men, women, children, German, French and Hungarian Jews, cultured people and peasants—travelling in various railway freight wagons to a German concentration camp. From the security of life to certain death. That would be the first twelve chapters. The next twelve would describe the moment of liberation. It's still rather vague, but I'm very keen on the idea.

Pál Jakobovits—who couldn't have been much more than thirty, though his hands were constantly shaking and the doctors no longer comforted him by saying that one day he would get better—rocked back and forth mumbling: 'Dear God, hear my prayers. Dear God, send me a girl, a beautiful dark girl, let her be dark, a beautiful blonde girl, let her be blonde.'

Tibor Hirsch, radio technician and photographer's assistant, could only take so much. From the other end of the table he lashed out at Jakobovits. 'You make yourself ridiculous with that prayer.'

'I can pray for whatever I like.'

'You're not a kid any more, Jakobovits. You're over thirty.'

Jakobovits looked down. He grasped his left hand in his right as if somehow to stop the shaking. 'What's it got to do with you?'

'A man of thirty doesn't drool over women.'

'What does he do then?' Jakobovits yelled. 'Jerk off?'

'Don't be vulgar.'

Jakobovits sank his nails into his arm to overcome the cursed shaking. 'What does a man of thirty do?' he wailed. 'I'm waiting for the answer!'

'He stifles his desires. He asks for bromide. He waits his turn.'

Jakobovits thumped the table. 'I'm not waiting any more! I've waited enough.' He rushed into the barracks.

Standing at the wall, Miklós winced. He kept his eyes shut.

> Lili, dearest,
> I would swear like hell if I weren't so ashamed. That helps me cope with things in the way crying helps girls. We're getting dreadfully out of hand here. I'd like to get hold of a book by August Bebel for you, *Woman and Socialism*. I hope I'll manage it.

~

Lili was curled up under her eiderdown, sobbing. It was past midnight. Sára woke up to the sound of her weeping and climbed out of bed. She lifted the eiderdown and started to stroke Lili's hair.

'Why are you crying?'

'No reason.'

'Did you have a bad dream?'

Sára got into bed beside Lili. They stared at the ceiling—this was becoming a habit. And then Judit Gold appeared hovering over them.

'Is there room for me too?'

The two girls made room, and Judit slipped in with them.

'Who is this Bebel fellow?' asked Lili.

Judit made a face. 'Some sort of writer.'

Sára sat up. This was her field. At times like this she acted like a schoolmistress and even wagged her index finger. 'Not "some sort of writer"! He was a wonderful person.'

'Apparently he wrote a book, *Woman and Socialism*.' Lili dried her eyes.

Judit, who was irritated by Sára's schoolmarmy manner, and in any case loathed left-wing thinking, couldn't help being sarcastic. 'Judging by the title I'll be rushing off to read it. Try stopping me!'

'It's Bebel's finest book. I learned a lot from it,' Sára insisted.

Judit gave Lili's arm a squeeze under the eiderdown. But since she never allowed herself to be beaten in literary debates she opened a new front. 'I'll bet your poet keeps stuffing your head with leftist ideas.'

'He wants to send me this book as soon as he can.'

'Learn chunks of it by heart. That'll impress him.'

Sára was still sitting up with her index finger raised. 'In *Woman and Socialism* Bebel claims that in a just society women have equal rights with men. In love, in war, in everything.'

'Bebel is a prat. He never had a wife.' Judit gave a scathing smile. 'No doubt he had syphilis.'

This made Sára see red. All sorts of retorts churned around in her head, but she couldn't choose the right one. So she lay down again.

> I can't wait to receive the book. Sára has read it already, but she'll happily read it again.

~

In Avesta the patients had been given two board games and a chess set. The instructions for the board games were in Swedish and the games themselves seemed rather primitive, so after trying to play them once the men gave up.

The chess set, on the other hand, they fought over. Litzman and Jakobovits were the best players. Apparently Litzman had been chess champion in his home town. He and Jakobovits played for money, and this gave them certain prerogatives over the board. Litzman gave a running commentary on the game for the benefit of the onlookers. He picked up the bishop, drew circles with it in the air and chanted, 'I'll ta-ha-ha-hake it! Che-he-heck!'

Jakobovits thought about this for long minutes.

In the tense silence, Hirsch's exclamation hit them like the celebratory chime of a bell. 'She's alive!' Hirsch was sitting up in bed waving a letter. 'She's alive! My wife is alive!'

Everyone stared.

He stood up and looked around with a radiant face. 'Do you hear? She's alive!' He set out, marching between the beds, waving the letter like a flag above his head and shouting, 'She's alive! Alive! Alive!'

Harry was the first to join him. He fell in behind Hirsch with his hands on his shoulders, taking up the rhythm. They marched round and round between the beds, belting it out like the beat of a drum. 'She's alive! Alive! Alive!'

Then Fried, Grieger, Oblatt and Spitz joined in. There was no resisting the *joie de vivre* that swept them along, Miklós too, until all sixteen survivors were in a line. Hirsch led the way, holding the letter-flag up high, and behind him came the rest, Jakobovits and Litzman bringing up the rear.

They swirled around the room, finding different routes each time, like an endless snake. They clung to each other's shoulders and soon discovered they could tramp over everything, beds, tables, chairs—the main thing was not to break the rhythm.

'Alive! Alive! Alive! Alive! Alive! ALIVE! ALIVE! ALIVE!'

> Today one of my friends, Tibor Hirsch, got a letter from Romania. It said that his wife was alive and at home. Yet three people have already told me they are absolutely certain they saw her being shot in Belsen.

This triumphant episode inspired Miklós to make one last attempt to win permission for his journey.

He knew that Dr Lindholm spent Wednesday evenings working in his office in the main building. So he borrowed a coat to put on over his pyjamas, walked across the yard and knocked on his door.

Dr Lindholm motioned for him to sit down while he finished his sentence, and then looked up. The room was lit by a desk lamp, and its circle of light ended just under the doctor's eyes. This put Miklós off slightly.

'I'd like to speak to you about the soul, doctor.'

Lindholm's chin and nose were in the light. 'Yes, is a strange thing.'

My father took off his coat and threw it on the floor. He was sitting there in his frayed stripy pyjamas like a mediaeval saint. 'Sometimes it's more important than the body,' he said.

Dr Lindholm clasped his hands. 'A psychologist is coming next week.'

'No, I want to discuss this with you. Have you read *The Magic Mountain*?'

Dr Lindholm leaned back, his face disappearing in the darkness. He became headless. 'Yes, I have.'

'I'm a bit like Hans Castorp. The wry envy that I feel for the healthy almost hurts…'

'Is understandable.'

'Give me permission. Please.'

'How does that fit in?'

'If I could go and see my cousin, just for a few days. If I could pretend to myself that I was cured.'

Dr Lindholm interrupted. 'Is becoming obsessive, Miklós. Drop it, for goodness sake!'

'Drop what?'

'This travel madness! This stubborn behaviour. Come to senses!' Dr Lindholm was almost shouting. He got up and stepped out of the light.

Miklós jumped up too. He also raised his voice. 'I have come to my senses. I want to travel!'

'But you will die. You will die soon!'

Dr Lindholm's terrifying diagnosis circled them like a bird of prey. Miklós could see only the doctor's two well-lit legs in their suit trousers, and decided that his verdict could therefore be ignored.

In the ensuing silence only their rapid breathing could be heard.

Dr Lindholm turned round, ashamed, and went to the cupboard. He opened the door. Shut it. Opened it again. Shut it.

Miklós stood still, growing pale.

'I'm sorry. I'm sorry. I'm sorry,' Lindholm said softly in Swedish.

He opened the cupboard again, took out a file, went over to the backlit wall and flicked the switch there. The room was flooded with cold, sterile light. The doctor removed some X-rays from the file and held them in front of the pane of glass on the wall. There were six of them. He didn't turn round. He didn't catch my father's eye.

'By the way, where is your "cousin" being treated?'

'In Eksjö.'

'Take off pyjama jacket. I listen to your chest.'

Miklós slipped out of his jacket.

Lindholm took out his stethoscope. 'Deep breathings. In, out, in, out.'

They avoided each other's eyes. Miklós breathing. Dr Lindholm listening. He listened for a long time, as if he were enjoying some distant, celestial music.

'Three days,' Dr Lindholm said. 'To say goodbye.'

Miklós pulled on his pyjama jacket. 'Thank you, doctor.'

> Lili,
>
> Now you have to be quick and nimble because we're going to trick the Red Cross. I need a letter in Swedish from your doctor in which he recommends my visit on medical grounds. I've already managed to persuade my doctor!

Dr Lindholm fiddled awkwardly with his stethoscope. In the strange, intimate glow he was brave enough to take his wallet out of his back pocket. 'Finish with her. Is my opinion as a doctor, but what matters my opinion? The soul…sometimes you have to bury it.'

He took the X-rays down from the wall and put them back in the file. He switched off the backlit wall. Now, he took a small, creased photo out of his wallet and handed it to Miklós. It showed a fair-haired little girl with a ball in her hands, gazing warily into the lens.

'Who's that?' Miklós asked.

'My daughter. Not now. She die in an accident.'

My father hardly moved. Lindholm shifted from leg to leg. The floor creaked. His voice became husky. 'Life sometimes punish us.'

Miklós stroked the face of the little girl with a finger.

'Her name is Jutta. From my first marriage. Márta related second part of story to you. Jutta is first part.'

~

This time Lili and the others had planned a longer program. Sára sang eight songs with Lili accompanying her on the piano. They included two Hungarian songs, one Schumann, two Schubert and some of the popular songs from operettas.

The soldiers, in their pyjamas, and the nurses applauded loudly. On stage, Lili and Sára gave a modest and graceful bow after each song. It was to Lili's credit that Dr Svensson came too. He sat in the middle of the front row with a little girl on his lap, and after every song he stamped his feet.

At the end of the evening he went on stage to congratulate Lili, who was standing tensely by the piano. Lili looked longingly at the little girl, who hadn't been the slightest bit fidgety, but nor had she fallen asleep. In fact, she had clearly enjoyed the concert.

'Can I hold her?'

Svensson handed the girl over to Lili, and she chuckled as Lili hugged her.

Meanwhile Sára was surrounded by soldiers. It didn't take much asking for her to sing them an encore, just like that, unaccompanied. She chose 'Crane Bird High in the Sky'. A few soldiers wept, though they didn't understand a word.

Lili caught the mood too—a kind of sorrow overwhelmed her.

~

> One evening a few days ago I went into town and wandered around on my own in the snowy streets.

It was dusk. Miklós was tired by the time he reached the top of the hill and he couldn't pedal any more. He got off his bike, pushed it about twenty metres, then stopped.

There were no curtains in the windows of the house; from where he stood beside the fence he could easily look in. The scene was like a nineteenth-century realist painting. The man reading, the woman sitting at her sewing machine, and lying between them in a wooden cradle a young child. He could even see that the child was playing with a doll and smiling.

> I could see into a worker's home. I feel very tired. Twenty-five years and so many awful things. I can't look back on a good and harmonious family life: I never had one. Perhaps that's why I long for one so much. I couldn't bear to see them any more, and hurried away.

Eight

LILI KEPT hugging Dr Svensson's little girl. The soldiers, moved by Sára's song, still surrounded her.

> *Crane bird high in the sky*
> *Is flying homewards*
> *The gypsy boy is walking on his way*
> *His staff in his hand.*

Dr Svensson touched Lili's arm. 'I've received a letter from the Avesta rehab centre. A colleague of mine wrote it, the head doctor. He's got a Hungarian wife.'

Lili blushed and stammered something. 'Yes.'

'It was about your cousin.'

'Oh, yes.'

'I'm not quite sure how to tell you. It's a disturbing letter.'

The little girl suddenly felt heavy in Lili's arms. She put her down. 'We've been planning for him to come and visit me.'

The doctor took his daughter by the hand. 'That's what it's about. I agree with the visit. I shall certainly give my permission.'

Lili shrieked, and grabbed at Dr Svensson's hand to kiss it. The doctor did all he could to pull his hand away.

Down among the audience Sára was singing, 'If I could only be with you once more, I'd lie beside you on your violet couch.'

Svensson held his arm behind his back. 'But there's something you should know.'

'I know everything.'

'You don't know about this.' Svensson waited. 'Your cousin is seriously ill.'

'Is he?' Lili felt a tiny pang in her heart.

'It's his lungs. Very serious. Irreversible. Do you understand? Irreversible.'

'I do.'

'I was in two minds whether to tell you. But since he's family I think you should know. It's not contagious.'

'I see. It's not contagious,' repeated Lili, as she stroked the little girl's hair.

Sára had finished her song and there was a hush except for the sound of Svensson's daughter humming, the effect of which was like a fading echo. Svensson put his finger to her lips, and the echo died away too.

'Take care of yourself, dear Lili. You're not well either. Far from it.'

Lili's mouth was dry; she couldn't say anything.

~

Miklós tried to conceal it, but Lindholm's diagnosis nagged at him. He didn't really believe the doctor, but for his peace of mind he felt it would be good to get a second opinion. So he asked Jakobovits, who in peacetime had worked in a hospital as a theatre assistant, to assess the X-rays. That meant breaking into Lindholm's office. Harry happily joined the mission; he was up for anything that had the tang of adventure.

The narrow corridor of the main building was lit by the yellow glow of a night light. Miklós, Jakobovits and Harry crept towards Lindholm's office like three hobgoblins.

Harry was carrying a piece of wire. He often boasted of having belonged to a gang of thieves before the war. Apparently he was an expert at picking locks.

He fiddled about in the keyhole for ages, giving Miklós time to regret the whole idea. Their escapade seemed almost laughable. But eventually Harry succeeded in opening the door and they were inside.

They went into action like a crack military unit. Miklós gestured to Harry which cabinet to open, and Harry fiddled around with his wire once again. They didn't dare turn on the light, but there was a full moon and Lindholm's room was bathed in an unearthly phosphorescent glow. The three men might have felt like heroes in a fairytale.

The cabinet lock clicked. Miklós reached in and ran his fingers over the files; he remembered that his was somewhere around the middle. He breathed out when he found it, took the X-rays and handed them to Jakobovits.

Jakobovits settled himself comfortably in Lindholm's armchair and, holding the images up to the light of the moon, began to study them.

Someone flung the door open, flicked the switch and flooded the room with the unforgiving light of three hundred-watt bulbs.

Márta stood in the doorway, her tiny bosom heaving. 'What are you gentlemen doing here?'

The gentlemen, all wearing uniform striped pyjamas beneath their makeshift coats, leapt to their feet. The X-rays slipped out of Jakobovits's hands. No one answered. The situation spoke for itself. Márta added to the pantomime by strolling over to the X-rays and picking them up one by one.

Then she turned to the honourable company. 'You may go.'

The men began to tramp out in single file.

'You stay here, Miklós,' Márta said.

The relief felt by the other two was palpable. The door shut behind them. Miklós turned round with the most penitent expression he could summon. Márta had already taken up residence in Lindholm's armchair.

'What do you want to find out?'

'My friend Jakobovits is some kind of doctor,' Miklós stammered. 'Or used to be. I wanted him to take a look at the X-rays.'

'Didn't Erik assess them for you?'

Miklós looked down at his shoes with their sloppy laces. 'Yes.'

Márta stared at him for such a long time that he was forced to return her gaze. Then the head nurse nodded, as if she had taken note and understood. She stood up, put the X-rays back in the file and the file back in the cabinet. 'Erik does all he can for you. You are his favourite patient.'

'I always have a fever at dawn: thirty-eight point two.'

'New medicines are becoming available all over the world every week. Who knows what might happen?'

Something burst in my father. It happened so swiftly that he didn't even have time to turn away. It was as sudden as an earthquake. He collapsed to the floor and buried his face in his hands, sobbing.

Márta turned away discreetly. 'You've been through terrible things. You survived them. You survived, Miklós. Don't give up now, at the finishing post.'

Miklós couldn't speak. He wasn't crying any more—the sound he made now was more like the whimpering of a wounded animal. He tried to form intelligible words, but it was as if his voice had abandoned him.

At last, he said, 'I'm not giving up.'

Márta looked at him in despair. He was huddled on the floor, his arms covering his head. She stepped closer to him. 'Good. So now pull yourself together.'

They gave each other some time. Miklós was quiet now, but he was hiding behind his arms and had curled himself up even smaller.

'Right,' he said when he could speak normally again.

'Look at me, Miklós.' Márta crouched down beside him.

My father peered out between his two bony elbows.

Márta adopted her cold, bossy head-nurse voice. 'Take deep breaths.'

He attempted to breathe evenly.

Márta conducted. 'One, two. One, two. Deep breaths. Slowly.'

Miklós's chest was rising and falling regularly. One, two. One, two.

'Slowly. Deep breaths.'

> My dearest little Lili,
>
> I'm not stupid, I know that the illness that keeps me here will gradually disappear. But I also know my fellow patients. I hear the terrible pity in their voices when they say, 'It's his lungs.'

~

It was November and an icy wind blew leaves around the Eksjö hospital. There was an open, circular pavilion in its grounds, an attractive building with a dark green wooden roof supported by graceful white pillars. For Lili, forbidden to leave the grounds during the week, this pavilion was a refuge. When she couldn't stand the smell of the hospital any longer she escaped there. On fine days she leaned against a column and bathed her face in the fitful sunshine.

But now, hostile winds were blowing. In their dejection, Lili and Sára were walking obsessively round and round the columns in their thick woollen uniforms.

> My dear Miklós,
>
> I am very cross with you! How can a serious, intelligent man of twenty-five be so foolish? Isn't it enough for you that I am fully aware of your illness and can hardly wait to meet you?

~

Late one afternoon, two men in suits and ties arrived in Avesta and were taken straight to the Hungarian section. It turned out they were from the Hungarian embassy. One of them held up a radio bound with a ribbon, and the other made an announcement.

'This radio has been sent to you, on loan, by the Orion factory in Hungary. Happy listening!'

Tibor Hirsch accepted the radio on behalf of the men. 'Thank you! News from home is more effective than any medicine.'

They put the radio on a table and my father looked for a

socket. Harry switched it on. The tuning eye glistened green, and the radio crackled and hissed.

'Search for Budapest,' ordered one of the suited men.

Within half a minute they could all hear Hungarian. 'Dear listeners, it is five minutes past five. We are transmitting a message to Hungarians abroad from Sándor Millok, Minister for Repatriation. "Every Hungarian scattered around the world who is listening to this program should know that we are thinking of them and have not forgotten them. In the next few minutes I will outline to them and to our listeners at home the regulations devised to simplify the administrative requirements for our compatriots' return home."'

That evening the men sat out in the courtyard with the radio on the long wooden table. The light bulb swung eerily in the wind. The men usually spent half an hour before bed in the open air. By now they had been playing the radio for six hours without a break. They had put on sweaters and coats over their pyjamas and wrapped blankets around themselves. They sat right up close to the radio. The green tuning light winked like the eye of an elf.

They were listening to Senator Claude Pepper talking from Washington. The Hungarian presenter whispered his translation every few sentences. Then they listened to the news from Budapest. The fragments of sound whirled around in their heads like the wind sweeping down from the North Pole.

The second transport of major war criminals had arrived at Keleti railway station.

The pontoon bridge at Boráros Square had been officially opened.

The training of the first unit of policewomen had been successfully completed.

A competition testing the skill of waiters had taken place on Nagy Körút.

In the second round of the boxing team championship Mihály Kovács, boxing for Vasas, had knocked out Rozsnyó from Csepel.

~

It was Sunday. The Björkmans' dark grey car swung round in front of the hospital, and Lili, who had been waiting in the caretaker's office, climbed into the back seat.

After mass the Björkmans took Lili home to Smålandsstenar. They sat at the table for lunch, and Sven Björkman said grace. Mrs Björkman ladled out the soup, and her husband was pleased to see Lili's silver cross sparkling around her neck. Language difficulties kept the conversation brief.

'No news from home, Lili?' Björkman asked her in Swedish.

Lili didn't look up. She understood every word. She shook her head.

Björkman took pity on her. 'You know what? Tell us something about your father!'

Lili winced. How could she possibly?

Björkman misunderstood: he thought Lili was struggling with his Swedish. Using his spoon for emphasis he hammered out the words. 'Your papa! YOUR PA-PA! Papa! Daddy! Father! Get it?'

Lili nodded. 'I could try to tell you in German, but I don't speak it well enough.'

'It doesn't matter,' Björkman said. He wasn't to be put off. 'Tell us in Hungarian. We'll listen. Believe me, we'll understand. Just tell us about him. In Hungarian. Come on! Fire away!'

The spoon was shaking in Lili's hand. The whole Björkman family was looking at her, even the two boys. Lili wiped her mouth on her napkin, put her spoon on the table and her hand in her lap. She glanced down at the cross hanging from her neck. 'My father, my dear father, has blue eyes…blue eyes that shine,' she said in her soft Hungarian. 'He's the kindest person in the world.'

The family listened, transfixed. Sven Björkman sat motionless, his head slightly to one side, enchanted by the music of the unfamiliar language. What did he understand in the melody, in the rhythm?

'My father isn't tall, but he isn't short either. He loves us dearly. He's a salesman by occupation. A suitcase salesman.'

Every Monday at dawn Lili's father, Sándor Reich, trudged down Hernád Street in Budapest carrying two huge Vulkan cabin-trunks. In each one, like the layers of an onion, dozens of smaller and smaller cases and bags lay one inside the other.

This picture was so vivid that, even without shutting her

eyes, Lili could see the shadow of her father creeping along the walls of the buildings in the spring sunshine.

'My father travels in the country all week. But at the weekend, on Fridays, he always comes home to us. We rented a flat to be near Keleti train station. On Monday mornings, Father sets out on foot with his wares and he walks down Hernád Street to the station. On Fridays, when he comes home, we are waiting for him.'

These words swept Lili into the past. They were sitting at the specially laid table in Hernád Street: Mother, Father and eight-year-old Lili. At the head of the table sat somebody else: an unshaven man, his scruffy coat buttoned up to hide his grimy, ragged shirt and torn trousers. Father had tried to take his coat from him, but he gave up. The stranger fingered the saltcellar with his dirty nails in embarrassment.

'On Friday evenings we always had a special supper to which Father invited a poor Jew. This was how he greeted the Sabbath. More often than not he invited a man from around the station.'

It was as if Sven Björkman understood Lili's words. A tear danced in the corner of his eye, but he remained hunched on his chair. His wife had an ecstatic smile on her face, and even the two boys were listening with wide eyes, between spoonfuls of soup.

'So every Friday evening we are a family of four.'

Lili didn't dare look down at the silver cross hanging round her neck.

In the evening, during the long drive back to Eksjö, Mrs Björkman described to Lili the complicated process of Swedish adoption. It didn't seem to bother her that Lili could not understand the subject of her excited monologue. She was simply relieved that at last she could speak out about what she and Sven had been planning for weeks.

The Björkman family was still waving goodbye to Lili long after she had disappeared behind the double wooden doors of the hospital.

Dear Miklós,

Don't forget your promise to find a partner for my best friend Sára. She is older than I am. She has just turned twenty-two.

~

Crazed by nicotine deprivation, my father ran the short distance to the caretaker's office. He barged in without knocking. Frida and Harry shot apart.

'I just came for cigarettes,' Miklós said.

Frida leapt off Harry's lap and, not even doing up her blouse, went to the cupboard and took out a box. Its compartments were filled with various brands of cigarettes. She grinned, her breasts swinging all over the place. 'How many do you want?'

Miklós was ashamed, for her sake as well. He wanted four. Frida licked her fingers and picked out the cigarettes. Miklós fished out his coins. They swapped.

Harry embraced Frida from behind, kissing her neck. 'Give them to him free, darling. He's my best friend. It's thanks to him that I'm up to it again.'

Frida gave Miklós a coquettish look, shrugged and gave him back the coins.

> I'm really struggling with your request. There are sixteen of us Hungarians here, but there's not one that I'd choose for Sára. I wanted to take Harry with me to see you, for instance, but I've given up on that idea.

~

In Eksjö, the musical evenings were becoming more frequent. Dr Svensson even allowed Lili and Sára to skip half their afternoon rest. At two o'clock the girls shut themselves in the main hall and practised. The doctor had found some sheet music for them, too.

One of these albums included a selection of works by Leoncavallo. That week they performed his best known aria, 'Mattinata'. On the wings of this lofty song, Sára's soprano floated to the heights. She waved her arms about, enraptured. Lili took on this exaggerated romantic manner too, swooping down on the keys like a falcon.

It was a huge pity for them that they didn't have any suitable clothes to perform in. In fact they didn't have suitable clothes for any occasion. They took the stage in their hospital gowns, which were just long enough to cover their nightdresses.

Judit Gold sat among a row of soldiers, the only woman. She pulled herself up proudly; it felt good to be Hungarian.

L'aurora, di bianco vestita,
Già l'uscio dischiude al gran sol.
Dawn, dressed in white,
Already opens the door to broad daylight.

There must have been something in the atmosphere, because on the same evening in Avesta, hundreds of kilometres to the north, everyone was in high spirits.

Unaware of this synchronicity, the men began to sing the identical Leoncavallo aria. It was as if a celestial conductor had given a sign to his herald angels and called on his choir to sing the same song. Their rendition of 'Mattinata' in the barracks, at the suggestion of Jenö Grieger who spiced their performance with his accomplished guitar accompaniment, might have been slightly out of tune, but they gave the Italian everything they had.

For the soldiers in the Eksjö hospital the song's rousing power was irresistible. The hall was all smiles. Sára raised her arms high; Lili practically floated above the piano stool.

The men in the barracks were by now standing on beds and tables. Harry wormed himself in beside Grieger and conducted.

Ove non sei la luce manca,
Ove tu sei nasce l'amor!
There is no light where you are not,
Love is born where you are!

Miklós stood in the front row. He was flushed; the future seemed radiant. After all, 'Mattinata' was a hymn to love; he was certain that the others were celebrating *him* with this song.

~

> I'm sending the wool, with our measurements. You don't mind, do you?

Miklós had hinted to Lili on the telephone that he wasn't short of funds, courtesy of a Cuban uncle. The truth was that Uncle Henrik was my grandmother's elder brother, and his claim to fame was that in 1932 he absconded with the family jewels and emigrated to Cuba. He mustn't have felt too many pangs of conscience, because as soon as he got to Havana he sent a postcard to the family in Hungary raving about the wonders of his new homeland.

As a little boy my father often studied that black-and-white picture of the crowded Havana harbour on a rainy afternoon. He could only vaguely remember Uncle Henrik's face. He seemed to think he had a jaunty moustache and sparkling eyes, and that now and then he wore a monocle, but he couldn't swear to that.

On the Havana postcard, which for years members of the family pointed at as proof of Uncle Henrik's unforgivable disloyalty, a three-funnelled ocean steamer was visible, as well as a number of Ford cars clustered on the dock. A few skinny stevedores loafing about gazed into the camera, so it was easy to identify them with Uncle Henrik's future. But my great-uncle had no intention of loading ships. Quite the contrary, as revealed by a more recent photograph, which he sent years later, with the obvious intention of tantalising his envious relations—a crystal-clear picture of Henrik embracing a mulatto woman with wide cheekbones and a dozen children underfoot.

In the photograph, Henrik and the woman are standing on a wooden veranda and Henrik has a cigar between his lips. On the back two lines were scribbled in his sloping hand: 'I'm fine. I've invested in a sugarcane plantation.'

When Miklós was struck by his passion for letter-writing, he immediately thought of his uncle as a potential source of cash. There was nothing to lose. He wrote to Henrik that he had managed to survive the war and was now being nursed in Sweden. He had an imaginary picture in his mind's eye. As a teenager he had often dreamed about Cuba after leafing through an album from the 1920s that he had found in his father's bookshop. In the picture he now imagined, his uncle was rocking in a hammock on the famous veranda. He had put on weight—he must have been at least 120 kilos. In my father's vision the veranda is set on a hillside overlooking the sea.

Whether or not Uncle Henrik lived like that or in even greater style history doesn't say. He didn't write a single word in reply to Miklós's letter, but three weeks later a cheque arrived to the tune of eighty-five dollars.

This became my father's capital. On the day it arrived, he gave some of it to an old man smelling of vinegar, who palmed off four skeins of mud-coloured wool in return.

Now the owner of the world's ugliest wool, Miklós wrote a touching ad and placed it in *Világosság* to help Lili find her mother in Hungary. Another portion of Uncle Henrik's now less-than-princely sum he spent on three little chocolate cupcakes from an Avesta café and had them wrapped in a smart parcel bound with gold twine. His most serious investment was three and a half metres of material for a winter coat, which, trembling with indecision, he took a great deal of time to choose. Now he was ready for his journey.

Nine

MY FATHER travelled for a whole day. He had to change trains several times. He sat in different compartments: sometimes by the window; sometimes, for lack of space, jammed up against the door. At times he removed his bulky overcoat, folding it up and laying it across his knees. At other times his glasses misted up from the heat so he fished Lili's handkerchief out of his trouser pocket to wipe them. He took the greatest care of his parcel of cakes. He found a safe place for it in every compartment—in no way was it to be damaged.

Occasionally he fell asleep; when he was awake he looked out of the window. The stations flashed by: Hovsta, Örebro,

Hallsberg, Motala, Mjölby.

Sometime after Mjölby he slipped as he entered his compartment and fell on his face. The left lens of his glasses was smashed to smithereens.

> I travelled to Stockholm so that I could buy my train ticket in person at the office for foreigners. You know what? I send you my kisses.
>
> Miklós

> There are two alcoves in the corridor. One of them is particularly secluded. We can sit all day under a huge artificial palm tree without anyone disturbing us. All right, then—I send you a kiss.
>
> Lili

> I want to tell you something the evening I arrive, just before we say goodnight for the first time. As for me, I send special kisses, heaps of them—not in that 'all right, then' mode.
>
> Miklós

> In Sára's repertoire there is another song that I'm sure you know—'The March of the Volunteers'. I'm so looking forward to seeing you! Till we meet, I send you many kisses.
>
> Lili

> I'm glad about the alcove in the corridor because I

don't like talking in full view. I'm stroking your hair in my thoughts (will you let me?) and sending lots of kisses.

Miklós

This morning when I woke up my left eye was itching. I told Sára it was a good sign. See you soon. Kisses.

Lili

I'm arriving on the first of December at 6.17 p.m. I send my love many times over.

Miklós

~

On 1 December 1945 it was snowing hard in Eksjö. The platform and tracks at the tiny station were not covered, but the entrance was protected by a veranda.

Miklós was the only person to alight from the three-carriage train. He didn't quite resemble Don Juan as he hobbled across the platform. He leaned a little to the right because his shoulder was dragged down by the weight of his suitcase, a dilapidated number lent to him by Márta. It was tied up with string. In his left hand he carried the cupcakes.

Lili and Sára were waiting outside the station. Lili clung nervously to her friend's hand. Behind the girls stood a nurse in a full-length black cloak and trademark peaked cap. She had been instructed by Svensson to keep an eye on his patients.

Miklós spotted the reception committee in the distance and smiled. His metal teeth glimmered in the weak light of the platform lamps.

The girls glanced at each other in alarm, then looked guiltily back towards the platform where Miklós was advancing through the thick veil of snow. He had to rest for a moment while he coughed. The left lens frame of his glasses was stuffed with scrunched-up newspaper—that day's *Aftonbladet*—an operation he had performed in desperation half an hour earlier, leaving a crack free so that he could at least see a little. He drew nearer on the snow-covered platform; his borrowed winter coat, two sizes too big for him, floated around his ankles. He seemed to have tears in his visible eye, either from the cold or from excitement. Even from this distance and despite the thick lens, the girls could make that out. And he was smiling broadly, his iron teeth in full view.

Lili was scared stiff. In a matter of seconds he would be in earshot. 'He's yours! Let's swap!' she whispered to Sára out of the side of her mouth, with her teeth clenched, like someone who's had a stroke.

By now Miklós was a few steps away.

'You be Lili! I beg you!' she pleaded.

The nurse at the back of the little group was touched to see the skinny man in his funny coat reach her patients and set his battered case down in the snow.

My father had rehearsed thoroughly for this, the most important meeting of his life. He had put together a short but striking speech—three sentences in all—that he felt would have a magical effect. In the course of his seemingly endless journey, in the stuffy compartments, he had whispered it to himself a thousand times. But now he was struck dumb with happiness. He even seemed to have forgotten his name, but that was only because he was unable to suck air into his lungs. So all he did was extend his hand.

Sára took a quick look. At least his hand was all right. Long fingers, smooth palm. She grasped it. 'I'm Lili Reich,' she said.

Miklós gave her a firm handshake. He turned to Lili. She shook his hand vigorously.

'I'm Sára Stern, Lili's friend,' she said in a bright voice.

Miklós grinned with his metal teeth. He couldn't say a word.

They stood there. Eventually, Miklós handed the parcel of cakes bound with gold twine to Lili.

The nurse stepped forward and snatched the packet out of her hands. 'We must go!' she ordered, giving Miklós a compassionate look.

So they set out. Huge flakes of snow were falling. After a slight hesitation Sára took Miklós's arm. Lili walked beside them, her eyes on the ground. For a moment it occurred to her to take my father's other arm, but she felt it was too intimate. The nurse followed, carrying the elegant parcel of cupcakes.

To get to the hospital they had to cross an enormous park. As they trudged through the virgin snow, Miklós had one arm in Sára's. In his other hand he carried the suitcase tied up with string. Lili and the nurse were a few paces behind.

In the middle of the park, precisely eight minutes after his terrifying dumbness, as if a gift from God, Miklós got his voice back. He cleared his throat, then stopped. He put down the suitcase, withdrew his arm from Sára's and turned to Lili.

It had stopped snowing. The four of them resembled figures out of a Hans Christian Andersen fairytale: dark crumbs on an oval white china plate.

Miklós abandoned the speech he had practised. 'I always imagined you like this,' he said in his pleasant baritone, 'in my dreams. Hello, Lili.'

Lili stood there awkwardly. She nodded. The weight lifted from her; everything seemed natural. She took a step forward and so did Miklós. They hugged each other.

Sára and the nurse instinctively drew back.

Half an hour later Miklós and Lili were in the alcove behind the palm. Two worn upholstered armchairs stood opposite each other. My father draped his overcoat over the back of one of them and put his suitcase down.

They sat and looked at each other, not wanting to speak. At times they smiled. They were waiting.

Miklós took the suitcase onto his lap, undid the string and opened the lid. He had packed the coat fabric on top and now he smoothed it out. He lifted it up like a baby and handed it to Lili. 'I brought this for you.'

'What is it?'

'Material for a winter coat. You just have to get it made.'

'A coat?'

'You wrote that they hadn't given you a coat. Do you like it?'

Apart from the set of clothes she was given on her arrival in Sweden, Lili had one folksy skirt, a spinach-green waistcoat and a rust-red turban-like hat—all presents from the Björkmans. As she ran her hand down the thick, dark-brown, woollen fabric it reminded her of peacetime. She held back her tears.

'I took an hour choosing it,' Miklós added. 'I'm no expert when it comes to winter coats. Or summer coats for that matter.'

Lili again fingered the material, almost as if she were trying to decipher a secret code woven into it. Then she held it to her nose. 'It's got a nice smell.'

'I brought it in that old suitcase. I was afraid it'd get creased. But it hasn't, thank God. I borrowed the suitcase from the head nurse.'

Lili remembered everything. She had read each letter from Miklós at least five times. The first time hastily devouring it, then, escaping to the bathroom, twice more, thoroughly relishing every paragraph. Later, perhaps a day later, she would reread it twice, and behind each word she imagined other words. She knew a great deal about Márta.

'Mickey Mouse?'

'Yes.'

There was so much my father wanted to tell her. The sentences piled up in his head. Where to start?

He found a cigarette in his pocket. He took it out along with a box of matches. 'Do you mind?'

'Of course not. What about your lungs?'

'They're fine. All's well here inside,' he said pointing to his chest. 'It's just my heart! It wants to burst—it's beating so hard!'

Lili stroked the coat fabric with her fingertips.

Miklós lit up. Soon a cloud of grey smoke swirled above their heads.

At last they began to speak, eagerly, hardly finishing their sentences, cutting in on each other. They were excited and impatient, wanting to make up for everything all at once. But they never spoke about certain important things. Neither then, nor later.

~

My father never told Lili that for three months he burned bodies in Belsen concentration camp.

How could he have spoken of the suffocating stench that lingered over the mounds of the dead and clawed at his throat? Is there a word that could describe this work? A phrase that could describe the feeling as bare, scaly arms slipped from their grip, over and over, to land with a senseless thud on top of other frozen bodies?

Lili did not tell Miklós about the day of her liberation from Belsen.

It took her nine hours to drag herself from the barracks to the clothes depot, a distance of about a hundred metres. She was naked and the sun was scorching. The Germans had fled by then. All she could remember was that it was late afternoon when she made it. Then she was sitting in a German officer's tunic, leaning back against a wall and bathing her face in the light.

How did she come to be dressed in a German officer's uniform?

Miklós could never bring himself to tell her of his time, before he burned corpses, as an orderly in the typhoid barracks. In block seventeen, the most ghastly block in the camp, he doled out bread and soup to the half-dead. He had to wear the black band of the *Oberpfleger* on his arm. How could he possibly have told her about the time when Imre Bak knocked on the window? How Imre got down on all fours and barked like a rabid dog? Imre Bak was his best friend in Debrecen. He was hoping to get medicine from Miklós. Perhaps. Or at least a kind word. But he couldn't even walk into the typhoid death block. Through the filthy window, my father watched him topple over. His handsome, clever head landed in a puddle. He was dead.

And Lili never said a word—neither then nor later—about her twelve-day journey to Germany in a freight wagon. On the seventh day she discovered she could lick the condensation that had frozen overnight on the wall of the wagon. She was so thirsty, so dreadfully thirsty! Her friend Terka Koszárik had been screaming beside her nonstop for twenty hours. Perhaps Terka was the luckier of the two: she had gone completely mad.

And my father never described the murderous fight in the Belsen general hospital after the camp was liberated. He weighed twenty-nine kilos at the time. Someone had put him on the back of a truck, which took him to hospital. Afterwards, for weeks, he just lay on a bed. Three times a day a strapping German nurse picked up his featherweight body and poured cod-liver oil down his throat. Lying beside him was a dentist, a Polish Jew. He was thirty-five and spoke several languages. He could talk about Bergson, Einstein and Freud. Six weeks after liberation, this dentist beat an even more unfortunate Frenchman almost to death for half a kilo of butter. My father never spoke about that.

True, Lili never talked about the Belsen general hospital either. It was May, springtime, the war had just come to an end. She was lying there, not far from my father, as it happened, in the women's section. Lili was given paper and pencil. The task was to write down her name and date of birth. Lili thought hard. What was her name? She couldn't remember. Not for the life of her. She was devastated by the thought that she might never again remember her own name.

They didn't speak about any of these things.

Two hours later my father stroked Lili's hair, then got up awkwardly from his armchair and kissed the tip of her nose.

It was past midnight when a nurse took up position at a discreet distance, and Lili realised that it was time to say goodnight. The nurse accompanied Miklós down to the first floor and took him to a four-bed ward where he was to sleep for the next two nights.

Miklós undressed and got into his pyjamas. He was flooded with such happiness that for hours he paced the short distance from the window to the door and back again. Still exhilarated at 3.30 a.m., he had to force himself to get into bed. But he couldn't sleep.

After breakfast, at nine the next morning, they were sitting once more under the palm. When Judit Gold hurried down to the caretaker's office at 11 a.m. to bring up the mail for the women's section, she caught sight of Lili and Miklós in the alcove, their heads together, whispering. She turned away, ashamed of the spurt of breathless jealousy that took hold of her.

Lili was preparing to reveal her deepest secret. She took a breath. 'I've a terrible sin to confess. No one knows about it. Not even Sára, but I'm going to tell you.'

Miklós leaned forward and touched her hand. 'You can tell me anything. Everything.'

'I'm so ashamed…I…I…' Lili faltered.

'You've nothing to be ashamed of,' my father said confidently.

'I can't explain it…it's awful. When we had to give our personal details, before we got on the Swedish ship…I can't bear to tell you…'

'Of course you can!'

'I…I…Instead of my mother's name—her name is Zsuzsanna Herz—instead of her name, for some reason I can't understand, I was incapable of saying her name. I lied! I just couldn't give them my mother's name.'

Lili grabbed Miklós's hand and held it tight. Her face was so pale it seemed almost luminous. My father freed himself and lit a cigarette as he always did when he wanted to think hard.

'It's quite clear: you wanted to change your fate.'

Lili thought about this. 'That's right. What a lovely way of putting it! Changing one's fate. A solution presented itself on the spur of the moment, without my really preparing for it. To be different. Not Jewish. With just one word I was transformed.'

'From a frog to a princess.'

My father always loved images from fairytales. But, perhaps because he felt this was a bit trivial, he added, 'I felt the same way. But I was too much of a coward.'

'Lying on the stretcher there on the quay, I said my mother's name was Rozália Rákosi. Where on earth did I get that name from? Rákosi? I haven't a clue. Rozália Rákosi. That's what I said instead of my mother's real name.'

Miklós stubbed out his cigarette in the tin ashtray. 'Don't worry. It's over and done with.'

Lili shook her head. 'No, it isn't. You see, I also said that my father was a Jew but my mother was Roman Catholic. Not only that, I told them I was Catholic, too. Do you see? I wanted to be done with the whole thing. The Jewish business. Once and for all.'

'Quite understandable.'

Lili started to cry.

Miklós took out his precious handkerchief.

Lili hid her face in her hands. 'No, no, it's a terrible sin! Unforgivable! You are the first person I've ever told. And, if you want to know, every Sunday I go to a Swedish family for lunch. The Björkmans. Everyone thinks I go there because I want to. But that's not true, I go there because they are Catholics, too.

And I go to church with them. I've even got a cross!'

Lili pulled a creased envelope from the pocket of her gown. She unfolded it and took out the silver cross.

Miklós turned it over in his hand. 'That makes things clear.'

'Makes what clear?'

'Why your mother hasn't been in touch yet. Why she hasn't written to you.'

Lili took the cross, slipped it in the envelope and put it back in her pocket. 'Why hasn't she?'

'The list! The one that appeared in so many Hungarian newspapers. The official list. You would be on it as Lili Reich, mother's name Rozália Rákosi. That would be a different girl, not you. I imagine your mother read the list in Budapest and saw your name but didn't realise it was actually you. She was looking for a Lili Reich whose mother's name was Zsuzsanna Herz.

Lili stood up and raised her arms high, like a classical statue. A moment later she fell down on her knees in front of Miklós and started to kiss his hands. He stood up and hid his arms behind his back in embarrassment. Lili stayed kneeling, but she calmed down a little.

'This warrants a celebration!' she said in a whisper, looking up at my father. 'What a clever man you are!'

She was already flying down the corridor. 'Sára! Sára!' she shouted.

Ten

AT MIDDAY, in the cavernous and ugly yellow-tiled canteen where the girls ate their lunch half an hour after the men, Miklós felt that at last the hour had come for him to give an unforgettable account of his view of the world.

That winter twenty-three women were being treated on the third floor of the Eksjö hospital. They were all gathered around Miklós, including the three Hungarian girls, Lili, Sára and Judit. Using a small, sharp, wooden-handled knife Miklós sliced the three little chocolate cakes—gems of a confectioner in Avesta—into pieces. He first cut the cakes in half, then into quarters, then eighths. Soon twenty-four tiny pieces of cake were laid out in front of him, each one hardly bigger than a woman's fingernail.

Miklós stood on a chair—he was in his element. He removed his broken glasses. 'I will now explain communism to you,' he declared in an elevated form of German. 'At the core there is equality, fraternity and justice. What did you see a moment ago? Three small chocolate cakes. Three of you girls could have wolfed them down in no time. Instead, I cut up the three cakes—which, let's say, could stand for bread, milk, tractors or oil fields. I cut them into equal pieces. And, lo! Now I'll divide them among the people. Among you. Help yourselves.'

He pointed to the cakes on the table. It didn't really matter whether or not Miklós's wit had penetrated. Roused by the performance they reached for the plate, and everyone picked up a piece of cupcake. Lili looked at my father with pride.

The morsels of cake disappeared down their throats like breaths of air.

'No one has ever explained the essence of communism so beautifully,' remarked Sára, growing emotional.

Judit was the only one not to eat her now symbolic portion of cake. She turned it over in her hand until it had melted and the sticky, dark-brown goo dripped from her fingers.

~

In the early evening of 3 December, under the supervision of the cloaked nurse, Lili escorted my father to the railway station.

When the train set off, Miklós was hanging off the last step of the last carriage, and he didn't stop waving until the station had vanished.

Her eyes glistening, Lili remained on the snowy, frozen platform for a long time.

~

Miklós shut the door of the carriage behind him. He was on his way.

On the second night of his visit to Eksjö, in the four-bed ward, he had composed a love poem. On the following day, if he was on his own for a moment in the bathroom or the lift, he polished and corrected it. He hadn't dared recite it to Lili. But now, as the wheels of the train knocked against the joints in the tracks, the quickening clatter drew forth the music of his poem.

It yearned to come out of him. It wanted to burst out with such force that Miklós, even if he had wanted to, couldn't fight against it. He walked the length of the train, carrying his suitcase tied up with string. The newspaper jammed in his glasses was by this time in tatters; this didn't worry him in the slightest. He was reciting his poem. Out loud. In Hungarian.

The poem soared above the noise of the wheels. Miklós, like a cross between a troubadour and train conductor, marched the length of the carriages. He left half-empty compartments behind him without regret. He had no intention of sitting down. Instead he wanted to form some sort of bond with his fellow travellers, strangers who were staring in astonishment or sympathy at this passenger holding forth in an unfamiliar language. Maybe some of them could sense in him the lovesick minstrel. Maybe some thought he was a harmless madman. Miklós didn't give a damn; he walked on, reciting his poem.

For thirty hours of endless trails
My life has run on glowing rails
I looked in the mirror seeing how
Wonderfully happy I am now
Thirty hours—the minutes don't linger
Yet with each minute, my love grows stronger
Promise to hold on and never let go
Of my hand that you found thirty hours ago
Arm in arm each storm we'll weather
Smiling as in the alcove together.
You'll be my conscience; you'll urge me to fight
To stand up bravely for all that's right
Justice bids me to battle for all
I'm one of millions to answer the call
With ease and conviction to each task I'll rise
Helped by two stars, your beautiful eyes!

This was the poem that Miklós had been preparing for all his life. Yes, this was poetry itself. It had looped its way out from the pit of his stomach, spiced by the music of his heart and the precise mathematics of his brain. Once he had got to the end of the poem, he went back to the start. He recited it three times and the end flowed into the beginning. The Hungarian lines burning inside him flowed over the icy Swedish tracks.

Later, when he had calmed down, he settled into an empty compartment. He was convinced that the fire inside him was burning him up. Did he have a fever? Even his bones were hurting, and it was as if his skin had thinned, just as it had at dawn every day. He always kept his thermometer with him, in his pocket, in its handsome metal case. He took it out, put it in his mouth, shut his eyes and started counting. He was surprised to find that his symptoms had deceived him. The mercury stood at 36.3—there was nothing to be alarmed about.

Miklós looked through the window. Dark snowy fields and slim pine trees flashed by.

> My dearest, dearest Lili,
>
> How can I thank you for those three wonderful days? They have meant more to me, much more, than anything else ever did.

All he had to do was shut his eyes to see himself and Lili shielded by the palm in the alcove of the corridor. The two armchairs with their worn upholstery. The overcoat lying over the back of one of the chairs, the fibre suitcase on the stone floor. The awkward silence of the first half-hour as they looked at each other, not wanting to speak.

> My darling little Lili,
>
> Now I'm going to tell you about the impressions you left in me.

> First picture: the evening of the first of December.
> The palm, that indiscreet tree, waving its greenery
> as you smile and close your eyes. You're such a good
> person and so awfully charming!

Lili had suddenly thought of a question. If my father had had any talent for music he might even have been able to determine the tone.

'Is that today's paper?' she asked, as if she were a schoolteacher. Miklós wasn't sure what she meant. What paper?

Lili reached across and took off his glasses. She held them up and tried to make out the words on the scrap of scrunched-up newspaper. The awkwardness between them evaporated.

> The next day: your eyes beneath your red turban as
> we walk arm in arm along the street. Oh, for that little
> backstreet where the cinema is!

They had walked down the Kaserngatan in a howling wind, Miklós in the middle. Lili and Sára linked arms with him while he tried to explain things above the noise of the gale. He talked about his mother's special poppyseed pudding and the anthropomorphism of the German philosopher Feuerbach, and he finished up with the Swede Linnaeus's classification of plants. At last he could put to good use all those hours spent perched on the top rung of the ladder in the Gambrinus bookshop.

They were freezing by the time they plunged into the cinema. The remnants of Uncle Henrik's eighty-five dollars were nestled in Miklós's pocket. A soppy American film was playing, and my father felt the title was symbolic—*The Love Letters*. There was hardly anyone in the cinema. The three of them sat in the back row, Miklós between the two girls. He looked at the screen only for a moment or two. The *Aftonbladet* lens now proved a huge advantage: he could stare at Lili's profile, almost unnoticed, without employing any particular artifice. In a brave moment, when the dumb hero slipped on a patch of oil and slid on his bottom to the feet of his giggling love, Miklós tentatively touched Lili's hand. She squeezed his fingers in return.

> I won't write any more—it's suddenly hit me that it's all over. But afterwards, on the walk home, at the crossroads in the park, for a moment…

By the time they were in the park—at the centre of which, carved in stone, sat Carl Linnaeus himself—it was getting dark. Miklós made up his mind.

Sára tactfully walked two or three metres ahead, holding her palms out as if she were undertaking snowflake research for a meteorological institute. Miklós appreciated her tact. They walked past the gaze of Linnaeus's stone eyes. The snow was crisp beneath their boots, and the stars actually sparkled.

My father stopped Lili, stroked her face with his burning fingers—an inexplicable phenomenon in minus ten degrees without gloves—and kissed her on the lips. Lili snuggled into him and returned his kiss. Linnaeus was meditating above them.

Reassured that she could no longer hear the disappointing crunch of two pairs of feet behind her, Sára walked to the edge of the park. She began to count to herself. She was still alone when she got to 132, which gave her a good feeling. She smiled. Her heart, too, was beating hard.

> Monday. A quiet day. Only the photographer. I bet you, too, were wondering what your mother would say about our combined portrait.

The photography studio was at 38 Trädgårdsgatan. Miklós picked up the black-and-white leaflet advertising the place to save it for posterity. The photographer looked like Humphrey Bogart: a tall, handsome young man in a jacket and tie. He fiddled around with the positioning for a while, looking for the right angle. Miklós winced in jealousy every time Bogart gently touched Lili's knee to get her to move to the left or right. Then, from under the black cover behind his camera, he fussed for ages about how they should hold their heads. Eventually he emerged, rushed up to my father and started to read the news-paper stuffed into the frame of his glasses. He asked my father to take off his glasses, and then vanished under the cover again. For five or six minutes he positioned the camera at different angles. Then he came out once again, walked over to my father and whispered in his ear.

Miklós blushed. Bogart, using a very proper form of German, warned him that even if he, as the photographer, could discern that my father was aware of the problem, it didn't alter the fact that those somewhat uninviting metallic teeth were, in this powerful light, shining like mad. As a quality photographer, he felt that it was his responsibility to advise that an ideal family portrait might best be achieved if Lili were to laugh outright while my father was just beginning to form a smile. This is what he for his part would advise.

Half an hour later, the photographer of Trädgårdsgatan had finally taken my mother and father's first photo together.

> That evening you came downstairs with me, then you got into the lift, pulled the grating shut and, before it moved upwards, I leaned in once more.

The second night, Lili had made a foray down to the first floor for a goodnight kiss from Miklós. She was already in her nightdress and dressing-gown. She said goodnight to my father outside the lift, while the nurses were coming and going in the corridor. Lili got in. She pulled the iron grating across. Miklós managed to squeeze his head in between the bars, and in this hopeless position he tried to kiss her. In fact, he pressed his head towards her with such force that the white bars left their outline on his cheeks. The lift went up. Miklós couldn't bring himself to leave. He was still waiting for Lili's slippers to disappear when he felt a hand on his shoulder.

Dr Svensson was standing beside him in his white coat. 'You speak German, don't you?'

'I speak it and understand it.'

'Good. I'd like to call your attention to something.'

Miklós had no doubt what the doctor was referring to. But right now, at this rather special moment, he had no wish to launch into a discussion about the state of his health. 'I'm aware of everything, doctor. Currently my lungs are—'

'I wasn't thinking of you,' Svensson interrupted. 'You misunderstand me.'

Miklós breathed out.

'All I wanted was to ask you to take good care of Lili,' Svensson continued. 'She is no ordinary girl.' Dr Svensson took Miklós by the arm and guided him down the corridor. There was no one else around.

'You see, by a cruel stroke of fate, I happened to be on the international team of doctors present when the women's camp in Belsen was liberated. I'd like to forget that day. But it's impossible. We thought we'd found everyone who showed the tiniest sign of life. Only the dead remained, lying on the bare concrete…nearly three hundred childlike bodies, naked, or in rags. Skeletons weighing twenty kilos.'

Svensson stopped for a moment in the deserted hallway and stared into the distance. He seemed agitated. Miklós looked at him in surprise; the doctor's face was distorted into a strange grimace, as if he were in pain.

'We were on our way out. I looked back once more, just in case…I couldn't decide whether I was seeing things or…if a finger really did move. Do you understand, Miklós? Look…like the last flutter of a dove's wing…or the ripple of a leaf once the wind has died down.' Svensson raised his hand and crooked his index finger. His voice cracked. 'And so we brought Lili back among us.'

~

Years later, it always sent a chill down my father's spine when he recalled Svensson's expression and his hand held up with its quivering finger. And all this merged inseparably with another memory from his visit to Eksjö.

When the train puffed away and he was standing on the last step of the last carriage and waving until the station had disappeared, he was overjoyed that he could summon up Lili's true image. All he had to do was shut his eyes—his last glimpse of her was etched forever into his memory. Lili was waving on the snowy platform. She was crying. And her fingers—my father claimed that he had watched her delicate hand and those slender fingers almost as though they were in close-up on a cinema screen. This, of course, was impossible at such a distance, especially with his smashed glasses, but even so. He was clinging to the open carriage, the train was gaining speed and he, behind his closed eyelids, really did see Lili's fingers as they trembled in the wind like leaves.

~

'Take care of her. Love her,' Svensson instructed Miklós on that last evening in the hospital. 'It would be so good if...'

He fell silent for so long that Miklós wondered if he was searching for the appropriate word in German. 'What would be so good?' he asked.

Svensson still didn't speak. All at once it clicked—Svensson wasn't having trouble with his German. He had arrived at a boundary that he didn't want to cross. He never finished his sentence, but he gave Miklós a hug, which said more than any words could.

~

In Ervalla, Miklós changed trains. He found a window seat. In the foreground of the night landscape, his own tired, stubbly face was reflected in the glass.

> On Tuesday I got up in a bad mood: it was the last day. We walked again to Stadshotell Square like we had on Sunday evening. And I could only steal one or two furtive kisses from you on the way.

That last evening, they sat again in the two armchairs behind the palm. Lili was crying. Miklós held her hand; he couldn't think of anything encouraging to say.

'I dreamed about our flat last night,' Lili said. 'I saw Papa getting his suitcases ready. It was a Monday and just beginning to get light. I knew he would be setting off soon. In my dream I knew we wouldn't see him for a week. Isn't that odd?'

She forgot about crying and that she was in hospital in a foreign country. She talked as if she were recalling the previous day's picnic. When she was a child, her father's routine had seemed like a jigsaw puzzle. Sándor Reich, suitcase salesman, prepared his wares at dawn on Monday. He packed two medium-sized suitcases into two trunks, and the smaller cases into the medium-sized ones. And he crammed the briefcases and handbags into a red children's suitcase. It was quite incredible that all those leather goods could fit into two trunks.

The truth was that Lili's strong attachment to her parents disturbed Miklós. He had only one clear memory of his father. He couldn't quite decide whether the scene remained so vivid because he saw it once or because he saw it many times. Maybe every Sunday lunch had ended in this way.

My grandfather always tucked his damask napkin into the collar of his shirt. His thick hair shone with brilliantine. My grandmother, who always looked rather dishevelled, was taking a spoonful of soup. Pea soup, yes. A white china tureen of yellowy-green pea soup with globules of fat floating on the surface sat in the middle of the table. Beside it was a small dish piled with croutons. Miklós remembered every detail. He was just a boy, sitting opposite his mother in a black waistcoat. His father started shouting; he tore the napkin from his neck, jumped up and with a single movement yanked off the tablecloth.

My father never forgot it. The pea soup shot out of the tureen. The yellowy-green liquid flowed onto his knees, burning him, and the croutons dropped to the floor like tiny winged angels.

He told Lili this story, holding her hand, that evening under the palm.

Lili changed the subject. 'I don't want to be…'

'What don't you want to be?'

'It's so dreadful to say it. But I want to be different.'

'Different?'

'Different from Mama and Papa.'

Judit Gold appeared, carrying cups of tea. She couldn't help overhearing. 'What don't you want to be, Lili?'

Lili looked from her to Miklós. 'I don't want to be Jewish!' she replied in a quiet, resolute tone.

There might have been a hostile edge to her words.

'It's not a question of wanting or not wanting,' retorted Judit, wiping a drop of tea off the table with her finger. She marched off as if Lili had personally offended her.

Miklós was pensive. 'I know a bishop. We'll write to him. We'll apply for a conversion. All right?'

As usual, my father had exaggerated things a bit. He wasn't acquainted with any kind of bishop. But he was convinced that sooner or later, if he looked, he'd find one.

'You don't mind?' asked Lili, stroking my father's hand.

'It had occurred to me, too,' said my father equitably.

~

On the night train back to Avesta, as the stations flashed past, Miklós thought through the problem. For him the question of conversion was irrelevant. It didn't mean a thing to him that he was Jewish. As a teenager, he was so hooked on the new socialist ideology that there was no room left for anything antiquated. If conversion was important for Lili, if that was what she wanted, then he would get hold of a priest. Or a bishop. Or the pope himself, if it came to that.

He had gone through Örebro, Hallsberg, Lerbäck and Motala. Miklós was writing a letter.

> You can see, can't you, dearest Lili, what a devoted soldier I am in the cause of freedom and the oppressed, the cause that has awakened the sons and daughters of every nation. You'll be my companion in everyday life (you will, won't you?), so be my faithful companion in this, too! You were once a bourgeois girl—now you should become a tough and militant socialist! You do feel so inclined, don't you?
>
> I'll contact the bishop as soon as I get back to Avesta. I'm counting the days until Christmas when I hope I'll see you again!
>
> Many, many hugs and kisses,
>
> Miklós

Eleven

THE DAY after Miklós left Eksjö, at the end of the communal breakfast, Dr Svensson came in and tapped a spoon against a glass. The hum of chatter died away.

Svensson seemed nervous. 'I would like you all to remain patient and trusting. I have just received news that will bring certain changes to your lives. The Swedish Ministry of Health has decided to disband the Smålandsstenar rehabilitation hospital with immediate effect. This means that patients who have been cured in our hospital here in Eksjö will be permitted to leave. Others will be moving to another facility at Berga.'

Svensson wanted to say more, but no one could hear him

in the eruption of joy. The girls stood up on their chairs, some of them hugging each other, even screaming. Others tried to get close to Svensson, speaking to him in various languages. He tapped his glass to take control of the situation, but it was hopeless.

> This morning, in the midst of bedlam, they
> announced that the hospital here will be shut down,
> and we are moving to a vast rehab centre several
> hundred kilometres away—very soon. And it is my
> turn to visit you. But at least I'll be a bit nearer to you
> and won't have so far to travel when I come.

The three Hungarian girls went straight to their ward. They were about to start packing when Lili noticed the theft.

Half an hour later, a committee was trying to get the facts of the case, but Lili was in no condition to answer questions. She had one fit of crying after another, and finally she was given a sedative. She lay curled up on her side on her bed and didn't say a word.

So for the hundredth time Sára had to tell those concerned what had happened. 'I said that before. It was open,' she reported, pointing to the only cupboard, in the corner of the room.

The cupboard, which the girls had used to store their things, was still wide open and more or less empty.

A bespectacled man was whispering a translation of Sára's words into Swedish for the benefit of the local head of the Red Cross, a tall blond scowling fellow with amazingly pale skin.

Madame Ann-Marie Arvidsson was also there, writing the report. 'What did the material look like?' she asked.

Sára stroked Lili's curled back. 'What was it like, Lili? I only saw it once.'

But Lili just stared at the birch tree swaying in the breeze.

Sára did her best. 'It was brown fabric fit for a winter coat. Tweed, with a nap. She got it from her cousin.'

The man in glasses translated in a whisper. 'It must have happened while we were hearing the news in the dining hall. Everyone was downstairs.'

Ann-Marie Arvidsson put down her pen. 'There's never been a theft in this hospital before. I really don't know what to do,' she said.

'I do!' announced the stern, blond man from the Red Cross, striking the table. 'We'll find it and return it to the owner.'

~

When my father arrived back in Avesta he reported to the office, then walked across to the barracks to change. It was midday; everyone would be in the canteen.

Miklós caught sight of him immediately and backed away. The booted feet formed an arc above the middle row of beds. The suitcase slipped out of Miklós's hand. He took off his glasses and wiped the good lens. When he put his glasses back on, it was clear that he hadn't imagined it. From where he was standing one of the metal cupboards blocked his view of the upper part of the barracks. But when he moved forward he saw the torso too: the grey trousers and the belt around the waist.

It was Tibor Hirsch. He had hung himself. From a hook—a thick, bent nail near the overhead light. A letter lay on the ground beneath his body. Miklós's legs and hands began to tremble, he had to sit down. Minutes passed. He had an irresistible urge to read the letter. He had to overcome this trembling, this feeling of revulsion. He could see that the letter had an official stamp at the bottom. He knew what it would say even before he forced himself to stand up and shuffle over to the hanging body.

He was right, of course. He didn't need to pick it up; he could tell that the last letter in the life of the electronic radio technician and photographer's aide was a death notice. The death certificate of Mrs Tibor Hirsch, née Irma Klein.

It flashed through Miklós's mind that he had written to Lili about reports that Hirsch's wife had been shot in Belsen. That was when the triumphant conga line had taken over the barracks. What had made him suppress his misgivings? Why had he not hurried over to Hirsch and shaken him to wake him up to the truth? But when? When would he have had the chance?

Was it when Hirsch sat up in bed, waving the letter above his head? Or when he yelled out, 'She's alive! My wife's alive!'? Should he have rushed over and shaken him, shouting, 'No, she isn't alive, she's dead—three people saw her shot down like a rabid dog'?

Or could it have waited? Until when? When Hirsch set out between the beds holding up the message like a flag, turning the single word into a proclamation? Then? Or when Harry joined him, grasping his shoulders from behind, and together they began to chant their marching song?

What could he have done when their fears were transformed into a glorious eruption of words? Alive, alive, alive, alive, alive! How could he have stopped this volcano?

Should he have got up on the table and shouted above the chorus? What would he have shouted? *Come to your senses! Come to your senses, you idiots. You are alone now, they've died, they've gone. All those you loved have turned into smoke. I saw it happen. I know. She's not alive, not alive, not alive, not alive, not alive!*

But instead he had joined the line and become part of the snake, a part of the whole creature that wanted to abandon its common sense, to believe that nothing had changed.

And now, here was Hirsch's lifeless body hanging from the hook.

~

That evening, when the effect of the sedative had worn off, Lili walked down to the office with Sára and made a formal complaint. Two days later, when she got a letter from Miklós—who, within a couple of hours of learning of the theft, had found out what the usual Swedish procedures were in such a case—the investigation was already underway. But both of them knew very well that Lili wouldn't be wearing a decent overcoat that winter.

> My one and only darling Lili!
>
> You must report the theft to the police saying that the culprit is unknown. You must write a letter in German in triplicate (one copy for the hospital, one for the foreigners' office and one for the police) giving exact details of the loss—three and a half metres of brown material for a winter coat, etc.

More important things were taking place. On Tuesday morning, nine girls who were convalescing at the Eksjö hospital, including the three Hungarians, were transported by bus to Smålandsstenar railway station. It was chaos at the station, and all the while it snowed.

Most of the Smålandsstenar patients were already on the train. The arrivals from Eksjö hurried along the muddy platform carrying bundles and suitcases. Dr Svensson and the nurses in their black cloaks rushed up and down beside the train, like a benevolent military brigade, trying to calm everyone down. There was an abundance of tears, kisses and mud, all accompanied by rousing music played through a loudspeaker.

Lili, Sára and Judit Gold managed to find the carriage where their friends from Smålandsstenar, whom they hadn't seen for three months, were sitting. Screams of joy and much hugging followed. Then they pulled down the windows, leaned out and blew kisses to Dr Svensson. A nurse arrived on a bicycle with a bulky leather bag on her shoulder containing that day's post—a nice touch of organisation. She had tucked her cloak up above her knees so it wouldn't get caught in the spokes. People jumped aside when she rang her bell.

'Post! Post!' she called, getting off the bike in the middle of the platform, and letting it crash to the ground. She took a batch of envelopes from the bag and read out the names. She had to shout to be heard above the music.

'Scwarz, Vári, Benedek, Reich, Tormos, Lehmann, Szabó, Beck...'

Madame Ann-Marie Arvidsson, who was also fussing about on the platform and had a slight feeling of remorse about her treatment of Lili, pricked up her ears at 'Reich'. She took the envelope from the nurse and set out to find Lili in the crowd. She ran along beside the train, thinking it must be a letter from Miklós. She was calling Lili's name, but her chirpy voice was lost in the cacophony. Her coat was muddy up to the knees. Flushed and breathless, she held the letter above her head and shouted 'Reich, Reich'.

Then she spotted Lili hanging out of the window of a compartment a few metres away.

Lili saw her, too. 'Ann-Marie! Ann-Marie!' she yelled.

Madame Arvidsson was touched that Lili had called her by her first name. She held out the envelope and caught Lili's hand, giving it a squeeze.

'I expect it's your friend!' she said with a laugh, showing that she was on love's side.

But Lili glanced at the letter and blanched. The envelope had a Hungarian stamp and the address was written in a spidery hand. There was no mistaking it. Lili fell backwards into the compartment. Sára had to catch her to stop her falling to the floor.

'It's Mama's writing,' she whispered, clutching the letter and pressing it to her.

'It'll get terribly creased, let go!' demanded Sára, trying to prise the envelope from her hand. But Lili wouldn't let go.

Judit stuck her head out of the window and shouted to Svensson, who happened to be going past the carriage, 'Reich's got a letter from her mother!'

Dr Svensson stopped, along with his escort. The cloaked nurses surrounded him like a flock of crows, and they all clambered aboard.

There must have been at least fifteen people crammed into the tiny compartment. Lili still hadn't dared open the letter; she kept kissing and stroking it.

'Go on, open it, Lili!' urged Svensson.

'I don't dare,' she sobbed. She handed the letter to Sára. 'You open it.'

Sára didn't hesitate. She tore the envelope open and took out several densely filled pages, which she tried to give to Lili.

But Lili shook her head. 'You read it. Please!'

Svensson, who was now sitting next to Lili, held her hand between both of his. Somehow, news had got round about the letter from Budapest. More people had gathered in the corridor and on the platform. If Sára wanted to live up to the occasion she'd have to declaim the letter as if this were a theatre performance. She was aware of the singularity of the moment, but her voice let her down. She, who could easily get through Schumann's most difficult aria, now began to read in a scratchy, faltering tone.

'"My darling, one and only Lili! I saw your notice in *Világosság* under the headline, Three Hungarian Girls in Sweden Are Looking for Their Relatives."'

Lili could see their building with its long balconies in Hernád Street, their dark-green front door and Mama's shabby dressing-gown. The bell rings. Mama opens the door wide. Her neighbour Bözsi is there, waving that day's *Világosság* above her head and shouting. Lili wasn't sure what she was shouting, but it didn't matter. There was no doubt, though, about the shouting—the muscles in her neck were tensed, and she was tapping the newspaper on the last page where the framed notice had been set in bold letters. Mama snatched the newspaper out of her hands, took a quick look at the notice, saw the name, her name, and fainted.

Lili distinctly heard what she said either before her collapse or after she came round. 'I always knew our little Lili was a clever girl!'

After her initial nervousness, Sára got her voice back.

'"Your miraculous news arrived after a dreadful year! I can't possibly describe to you what it means to me. I can only thank the Lord that I lived to see this day."'

Svensson was still holding Lili's hand.

Bözsi dashed into the larder muttering to herself. 'Vinegar, vinegar, vinegar.'

She found it on the second shelf, drew the cork out with her teeth and sniffed it. Then she rushed back to Mama, who was still lying in the doorway, and splashed some vinegar on her face. Whereupon Mama sneezed and opened her eyes. She looked at Bözsi, but she was whispering to Lili.

"'I'm afraid your dear, good papa isn't home yet. After he was freed he was taken to hospital in Wels in Austria with enteritis. Since May I've heard nothing. I hope that with God's help he will come home soon so that we can live our lives together in happiness again.'"

Lili wasn't sure which bits Sára was reading, and which bits she was hearing in her mother's own voice, as if Mama was sitting in the stuffy compartment and taking over at the most important parts.

"'Since 8 June, when the husband of our dear cousin Relli came home from Auschwitz, I've been living with them, and I'll stay here until one of you returns. God willing, I hope it won't be too long now!'"

The penetrating smell of vinegar filled the flat. Mama wiped her face and got to her feet with Bözsi's help, then staggered over to the kitchen tap and washed her face. After that she sat on a stool, spread the newspaper on her knees and read the notice seven times running, until she was sure she'd remember its words as long as she lived.

"'I don't even know where to begin. What do you do all day? What do you get to eat? What do you look like? Are you very thin? Have you got enough underwear? I'm afraid we were robbed of everything. We got back nothing of what we sent to the country—no bed linen, no material, no winter coat, no clothes, nothing. But don't you worry about that, my girl.'"

Lili heard that last torrent of words in her mother's voice. Mama said 'my girl' in such an unmistakable way. My girl, my girl, my girl. God Almighty, how good that sounded!

Svensson didn't understand a syllable of the letter, but his face shone with as much happiness and pride as the faces of all the Hungarian girls in the compartment. Sára looked around, swallowed and went on reading.

"'Now for some good news. The new piano that you got from your dear father on your eighteenth birthday is safe and sound! I know you'll be very pleased about that, Lili.'"

Mama sat on the stool. She smoothed out the copy of *Világosság*, already composing the letter, smiling to herself. She started writing it down straightaway. In fact she had composed it in her head every night for the past ten months, so it was no effort now to put it on paper. She knew every comma and had checked the spelling over and over—she wasn't going to make mistakes in such an important document. She muttered and hummed while she wrote.

"'If you get the chance, my darling, use a sunray lamp on your hands and feet, even your head, because I suspect some of your beautiful wavy hair might have fallen out from lack of vitamins. You might even have had typhoid. So don't forget about that, sweetheart. When, with God's help, you come home, I want you to be just as radiant as you were before.'"

Someone, probably one of the nurses from Svensson's team,

rushed over to the stationmaster warning him not to let the train depart while the doctor was still aboard. Svensson himself didn't move. He was squeezing Lili's hand. The girls' bodies were pressed against each other in the compartment, their eyes shining. Sára's voice floated out through the open window onto the platform.

"'We've had no news of poor Gyúri, but all four of the Kárpátis are fine. Bandi Horn is apparently a prisoner of war in Russia. Zsuzsi isn't mentioned in your notice. What do you know about her, darling girl? You all set out together, after all.'"

The lump in Lili's throat began to swell. She and her cousin Zsuzsi were lying in each other's arms on the floor of the putrid barracks when Zsuzsi passed away—on butterfly wings, with a smile on her lips and a body scarred by millions of lice. When did she actually die? Lili would never speak to anyone about that.

In her kitchen smelling of vinegar, Mama seemed to sense that she had touched a raw patch. She became quiet: a drop of water fell from the tap. She looked at Bözsi and sobbed. Bözsi hugged her, and they cried together.

Lili could hear clearly what Mama said through her tears and with her head buried in Bözsi's neck.

"'If only I could hug you both. I've no other wish in life, but to live for that day. I'm longing for you and send you a million kisses, your adoring mama.'"

Lili was almost in a trance. She didn't notice Svensson and the nurses leave. Apparently they all hugged her and kissed her before they climbed down from the train. Later, Dr Svensson and his flock stood in the snow like statues on Eksjö platform until the train disappeared.

> My one and only darling Lili!
>
> I can't tell you how utterly happy your news made me! I told you so, didn't I? I knew you'd get a letter from your mother this week. I love you more and more every minute. You're such a sweet girl, and so good. And I'm such an uncouth boy. You'll make me better, won't you?

Twelve

TWO DAYS later, Miklós disappeared. No one noticed his absence until midday. The first to miss him were Harry and Frida, who were used to him slinking into the caretaker's office before lunch to buy his two cigarettes for the afternoon. When he didn't turn up, Harry asked Jakobovits when and where he'd last seen him.

By one o'clock, Dr Lindholm, too, had been informed that his favourite patient had evaporated like camphor. They counted the bicycles, but none was missing. When Miklós didn't show up for lunch, they started to worry.

Dr Lindholm despatched a car to town in case Miklós had

gone to the post office and been taken ill on the road. In the meantime he phoned all the possible places Miklós could have been—the post office, the café, the railway station. No one had seen him. In the late afternoon he notified the police and ordered a curfew.

Everyone linked Miklós's disappearance to Tibor Hirsch's suicide. Miklós had discovered the body, and he was there when they cut Hirsch down from the rope. In the days following he had sat silently on his bed. No one could cheer him up. Later, Harry suggested that he might have wandered off to escape Christmas, which was approaching fast. There was much talk about the festivities, though many of the patients, being Jews, had never observed Christmas. On the other hand, Jenö Grieger claimed Miklós was a socialist and couldn't care less about Christmas—there was no way a man like him would be undone by a religious holiday.

Márta came into the barracks and questioned everyone individually. She spent a long time in Miklós's corner, trying to decide whether she should sift through his correspondence. He kept all his letters in a cardboard box. There were about three hundred envelopes in it, in perfect order, including Lili's letters, which were bound separately with a yellow ribbon. Márta picked up the box, then resisted the temptation. She decided it was too soon. She would give him until the next morning.

At that moment, my father was wandering in the pine forest, lost in thought, seven kilometres away. He couldn't explain to himself why feelings of anxiety and depression had overwhelmed him that morning. It was no different from any other morning. He took his temperature at dawn, and then had breakfast. He wrote a letter to Lili. He played a game of chess with Litzman and then walked to Dr Lindholm's office for a quick check-up and to pester him about Lili visiting at Christmas.

Maybe that was it. The offhand glance with which Lindholm sent him on his way. The doctor listened to his lungs and shrugged. Shrugged!

Miklós stopped in the forest. There was a gentle breeze. Yes, it was Dr Lindholm's thoughtless response, like the first domino falling, that had set the whole thing off. He had come out of the doctor's office with a sinking heart. He had never believed in this stupid diagnosis. He'd always brushed it off as a mistake. Let the clever guys talk—he knew better!

But that morning, Lindholm's casual gesture had been like a blow to the stomach. It took his breath away. He was going to die! He was going to disappear like Tibor Hirsch. His cupboard would be emptied, his bed stripped. And that would be it.

So he left. He trudged through the gate and walked to the crossroads where, instead of turning left to go to town, he turned right towards the forest. He'd hardly ever walked that way before. The paved road soon gave way to a track, which narrowed into a path that had probably been made by deer. After a while it widened out into a large snow-covered meadow. By this time Miklós was completely lost. Not that it worried him. It felt good to walk, and he rather enjoyed keeping company with death. The Grim Reaper. So what if he was going to snuff it? He had lived and loved, and this was it. He'd fade away like the deer tracks. He repeated poems to himself, silently at first, then aloud and then at the top of his voice. He walked on between pine trees that reached towards the sky, reciting poetry the whole way—Attila József, Baudelaire, Heine.

By late afternoon, after a coughing attack, he began to feel sorry for himself. He was cold, his boots were wet through, and he was so tired that he had to sit down on a fallen tree trunk. He might have been reconciled to his fate, but he had no desire to freeze to death. So he set out north, imagining the barracks was in that direction, but not at all sure he was right.

~

At eight in the evening Lindholm phoned his colleague Svensson in Eksjö. He didn't know that the Smålandsstenar patients had been moved to Berga two days earlier. Svensson was surprised to hear of Miklós's disappearance; he couldn't imagine the reason for it but he, of course, gave Dr Lindholm the telephone number at Berga. Lindholm waited until 11 p.m. to call the Hungarian girl, who probably knew more about Miklós than anyone else. For some reason he phoned from the caretaker's office, perhaps because it allowed him to keep an eye on the road, down which he hoped Miklós would come any minute.

~

It was the girls' second day in the Berga rehab hospital. They were housed in a long, stark barracks like the one at Avesta. They were already in bed when a messenger came to summon Lili to the telephone in the main building. Lili got up, found a spare coat, and set out. Sára called after her. She had her misgivings, so she put on her boots and followed.

At the exact moment that Lindholm heard Lili's thin voice issue a hesitant 'hello', he caught sight of Miklós dragging himself towards the gate.

'Is that you, Lili? I have Miklós here on the line for you,' he yelled into the phone, though he reckoned it would take my father at least five minutes to shuffle up to the caretaker's lodge. 'Hold on. He'll be here in a moment.'

~

My father didn't think he would ever get back. He was trying to retrace his steps but it felt like he was going in circles. The imprint of his boots in the snow had faded; then his footprints seemed to double up. For a terrifying period he could have sworn he was following the tracks of a bear, but then he somehow found his own boot prints again.

He was completely flummoxed when the tracks he was following came to an end in the middle of the path. They were there one moment and gone the next, as if the track-maker had taken flight.

The sun had set and it was unbearably cold. Miklós was

suffering. His feet were blistered; his head throbbed. He kept coughing. The thin sickle of a moon barely lit the forest. He often fell, sinking to his knees in the powdery snow. He lost all hope. But he knew he mustn't stop. Gathering up his remaining strength, he concentrated on nothing but walking—one-two, one-two, one-two. But it felt hopeless. He could hear the call of an animal—a hoot, he imagined—but were there owls in Sweden in winter? 'The owl screeched death'—that was a good line, a good first line, but when would he get it down on paper? Never. Never more.

And then Miklós saw the caretaker's lodge, the fence and, behind the bars on the window, Lindholm holding the telephone. Perhaps he was dreaming.

It took him a good ten minutes to make the last fifty metres. He stumbled into the lodge. Lindholm looked at him and pressed the receiver into his hand. 'Lili Reich. You want talk to her, no, Miklós?'

Lili had no idea what to make of the long delay. Since the unknown man from Avesta kept reassuring her that he was about to connect Miklós, she assumed there must be some problem with the line. The receiver hissed and crackled in her ear.

After an eternity, she heard my father's faint voice: 'Yes?'

'Are you all right?'

'Fine. Great.' What could he say?

Lili was relieved. 'We've made a little corner for ourselves in the new place at Berga.'

'And?'

'You can't imagine. It's ghastly! I don't even want to write to you about it. Do you mind me complaining?'

Miklós's facial muscles were frozen. He had no breath. He could hardly form the words. 'Don't worry.'

He was playing for time. He tried to massage his face with stiff fingers. Dr Lindholm was suffocating him too, standing so close that Miklós had to hunch over in order not to touch him.

'What's it like? Tell me,' he asked.

'Wooden barracks, bumpy paths, awful…I can't sleep at night, it is so cold, I wake up with a sore throat and a temperature.'

'I see.'

'There isn't even anywhere in the barracks where we can sit. No chairs, no table! All day we just wander around the place like stray dogs.'

'I see.'

My father went blank. He felt empty. All he wanted to do was lie down and close his eyes.

Lili realised that Miklós wasn't himself. Most of the time she could hardly get a word in. Now there was a heavy silence. 'I've been in a bad mood and terribly uptight the whole day,' she tried again. 'All I want to do is cry. I don't know where I should be. I'm so homesick.'

'I see.'

That didn't sound like Miklós's voice. The tone was icy. Almost hostile. They both fell silent.

Yesterday's call—it was dreadful. I couldn't speak

> properly. I wanted to say how I love you beyond measure and feel for you. Forgive me if I didn't say that. Only a few days now and I'll be seeing you!

'Well, then,' Lili whispered.

'I see. I see.'

'Are you all right?'

'Yeah.'

Lili turned pale. 'I'd like you to write to my mother an airmail letter, now that we've got her address, and tell her everything about us,' she mumbled.

Lindholm could see that all my father wanted to do was sleep.

'Right. I'll do that.'

Silence.

> Yesterday when I put down the receiver I was overcome with a strange sensation…it was as if someone had thrown cold water on me! Your voice sounded so alien and icy that I couldn't help feeling that perhaps you don't love me any more.

Click. The line was cut. Lili was white as a sheet. Sára put her arm round her.

'His voice was so different. Something has happened.'

'His friend who committed suicide,' Sára said. 'That's what's behind it. He's got so much on his mind, poor thing.'

They walked back to the barracks arm in arm. Lili didn't sleep at all that night.

Thirteen

A DANCE was scheduled for the next day at Berga to celebrate the arrival of the new patients. A band was to play in the cavernous hall, which they jokingly called the snack bar. A three-piece playing Swedish tunes: a pianist, a drummer and a guy on the saxophone.

Some girls danced. It didn't seem to bother them that the musicians were the only men in the hall. Most of them, though, stared into space at the wooden tables that had been specially laid out for the occasion. Beer, scones and sausage were on offer.

Lili, Sára and Judit were sitting at a table on their own when two men came into the dining room and, after making enquiries, headed straight for them.

'Are you Lili Reich?' one asked in Swedish, taking off his hat.

Lili remained seated. 'Yes, that's me,' she replied in German.

The man pulled a thin strip of fabric out of his pocket. 'Do you recognise this?' he asked, switching to German.

Lili stood up and took the piece of material from him. 'Yes, I do!' She ran her hand over it, feeling the nap with her fingertips. 'Look,' she said, handing it to Sára, 'it's my coat material, isn't it?'

The other man took off his hat. 'Let me introduce myself, ladies. My name is Svynka, I'm the district representative from Eksjö. And this is the hospital caretaker, Mr Berg.'

Mr Berg nodded, and took over. 'During the investigation at the Eksjö hospital, we found three and a half metres of the cloth that you reported missing at the bottom of a cabinet in one of the corridors. Do you follow me, Miss?'

'Yes.'

'Good. The cloth had been cut into strips.'

He asked for the piece of fabric and held it up. Lili was stunned. The band was playing a slow number, and several girls were swaying around each other on the parquet floor.

Lili wanted to make sure she had understood. She turned to Sára. 'Did I hear right? It was cut into strips?'

Sára nodded, mystified.

'It seems the thief wasn't intending to keep the material, just to destroy it,' Svynka added.

The music had changed. A lively polka started up. Only a few girls were left on the floor, but they danced with gusto. Lili stared at the single strip of cloth dangling from the burly caretaker's fingers.

'It will be difficult to find the culprit at this stage. But, if you wish'—Berg made a sweeping gesture towards the other tables—'we'll question everyone.'

'It won't be easy, but if that's what you want,' Svynka continued.

Lili shook her head. She couldn't speak or take her eyes off the remnant of the never-to-be winter coat between the caretaker's thumb and index finger.

Without a word, the three girls tramped the paths between the barracks in the dark, their hands in the pockets of their quilted uniform jackets. It was freezing and the wind howled.

Lili stopped. 'Who can hate me that much?'

'Someone who envies you your luck,' said Sára, with a sympathetic smile.

Judit was angry. 'I wouldn't let it go if I were you. Make them investigate to find out which girl did it. I'd like to look her in the eye!'

'How could they find out?' asked Sára.

'How should I know? Question all the girls. Search their belongings.'

'Should they look for a pair of scissors? Or a knife?' asked Lili wryly.

Judit was adamant. 'Who knows? Scissors, knife, something!

Maybe a scrap of tweed!'

They walked on.

'Of course, the girl would have it on her! Next to her heart!' said Sára. 'Really, Judit, you're incredibly naïve.'

'All I'm saying is that this kind of thing should be sorted out. It shouldn't be left to fade away. That's my opinion.'

Lili was looking at the muddy, icy path. 'I have no wish to know. What would I say to her?'

'What it calls for. You'd spit on her,' Judit hissed.

'Me? Come off it! I'd feel sorry for her,' claimed Lili, even if she wasn't sure she would be so kind-hearted.

~

Dr Lindholm didn't ask Miklós where he'd gone on that desperately long day, or why. He prescribed a hot bath and something to bring his temperature down. Three days later, however, he felt it his duty to inform him, in person, of his final decision. They were sitting on the couch like old friends.

'I know this will be upsetting you, Miklós,' the doctor said, 'but I am forbidding your cousin to visit you at Christmas.'

'Why?'

'Is no room for her. Everywhere is full. But this only one reason.'

'And the other?'

'Last time I tell you, say goodbye to her, remember? But even if you were healthy, and you are not, I don't allow female visitor to male hospital. As a reading man you must understand that.'

'What should I understand?'

'You once mentioned *The Magic Mountain*? Sensuality is…how I put it…unsettling. Is dangerous.'

Miklós stood up and went to the door. Dr Lindholm's decision seemed irrevocable. What had changed in the last few days? How could Miklós have lost the doctor's sympathy? He urgently needed to do something different, something that would break Lindholm's resolve.

Gripping the doorhandle, he turned back. 'I'd like that in writing, please, Dr Lindholm.'

'Come on, Miklós, our relationship—'

'I don't care about our relationship,' said my father. 'I want your decision in writing, please. Three copies. I want to send your letter to a superior authority.'

Lindholm got to his feet. He lost his cool. 'Go to hell!' he yelled.

'I'm not going to hell; I'm going to the Hungarian embassy. You are restricting my rights. You are obliged to permit family visits. I'd like your opinion in writing.'

No one had ever spoken like this to Lindholm. He was stunned. He stared at my father. 'Get out!' he said.

Miklós slammed the door and set off down the long corridor. He had surprised himself with his quick thinking. A doctor was restricting his freedom of movement. This was a good argument, effective and true too, more or less. On the other hand, this country had taken him in. And was treating him. Dr Lindholm had every right to claim that restricting his freedom was in his medical interest. In reply, Miklós could point out that the International Red Cross was picking up the bill, not the Swedish state. In other words, he owed his thanks and accountability ultimately to the Red Cross. If he wanted, say, to spend Christmas in a nightclub in Stockholm, who could stop him?

But what, in fact, was his status here? It was confusing. Was he a patient, a refugee, a dissident or a temporary visitor? His status, yes, his status should be determined somehow. But who should determine it? The Swedish government? The Hungarian embassy? The hospital? Dr Lindholm?

Behind him, in the distance, a door opened and the doctor dashed out. 'Miklós! Come back. We talk it over,' Lindholm shouted down the corridor.

But my father had no intention of arguing his point.

> My darling, my one and only Lili,
>
> I'm furious and depressed. But I won't give up. I'll think of something.

~

In the afternoons the canteen practically yawned with boredom. It was the only communal area in Berga. The girls didn't have much choice: they could stretch out on their beds in the barracks, go for walks in the biting wind or sit around in this hall crammed with tables and wait for supper.

That afternoon, Lili decided she would have a go at August Bebel's *Woman and Socialism*. Miklós had written to her about it a few times and it was now two months since he had sent her the paperback. Lili had stored it in different places to keep it out of sight. The cover wasn't very inviting: a woman with dilated pupils and bulging eyes, as if she were suffering from goitre, stared out at the reader, her long hair ruffled by the wind.

Lili read for ten minutes, and became more and more angry. By the fourth page, she was incensed. 'This is unreadable!' she said, banging the book shut and hurling it into the furthest corner of the hall.

Sára was knitting a pullover out of Miklós's ugly mud-grey wool, which she had brought with her from Eksjö. 'What's wrong with it?'

'Even the title irritates me. How can a book have a title like that? *Woman and Socialism*. Inside it's even worse.'

Sára put down her knitting and walked over to pick up the book. She dusted it off, returned to the table and handed it to Lili. 'It's a bit dry, I agree. But if you keep going—'

'No chance of that. I'm sick of it! I'd rather read nothing. Sick of it, you hear?'

'It could teach you a thing or two. How Miklós thinks, for example, if nothing else.'

Lili shoved the book away from her as if it were contagious. 'I know how he thinks. This book is unreadable.'

Sára gave up and went back to her knitting.

> Darling Miklós,
>
> I'll be sending the Bebel book back shortly. Unfortunately the circumstances here—and my nerves—aren't conducive to my having the patience for a book like that.

Grey light filtered through the big, dusty windows of the canteen. Judit Gold peeped through to see whether Lili and Sára were in there together. Even like this, when they were having an argument, they clearly belonged together. Judit felt superfluous beside them, but her loneliness had never tugged at her heart as keenly as it did now. Would it always be like this? Would she never have anyone for herself? There'd be no men. Fair enough, she'd given up on them, but would she never have a girlfriend, a true, lifelong girlfriend? Would she always have to accommodate herself to other people? Humiliate herself for a caress? Be grateful for a kind word, a piece of advice, a hug? Who was this Lili Reich anyway?

Judit turned away from the window and hurried towards the barracks. Their dormitory was furnished with twelve iron beds. There were metal lockers in an anteroom. Judit walked over and unlocked one. She took out the yellow suitcase with its brass buckle that her cousin from Boston—her only surviving relative—had sent her in August, stuffed with tins of fish. All the sprats, mackerel and herrings had already been eaten or shared with the other girls, but now and then Judit took out the suitcase and ran her hands over it, imagining that one day she would carry it triumphantly down the main street of Debrecen. But perhaps she wouldn't return to Debrecen. Who of her friends and relatives there had survived? She might settle here in Sweden. She would find work, a husband, a home. Yes, a husband! Who knew? Fate is sometimes kind to the determined.

Judit was alone in the barracks. She took a purse out of one of the side pockets of the yellow suitcase where she had hidden it. And now she took the remnant out and clasped it in her hand. Why she had hidden it? Or kept it at all for that matter? It could have been discovered at any time. But she wasn't really worried about that. Who would dare search her suitcase? Unless! Unless those two unpleasant-looking guys from Eksjö were bent on getting to the bottom of the mystery. Better to get rid of it.

The fabric almost burned her palm—this expensive cloth she'd taken such delight in cutting up into strips. She had good reason for doing so. No one on earth could condemn her for that. No one!

Judit ran to the bathroom and locked the door. She took a last sniff of the material and threw it in the toilet, sighing as she pulled the chain. The rushing water hissed and frothed.

Fourteen

DR LINDHOLM had a few sleepless nights before he made up his mind to phone Lili. He shared his anxieties with Márta. Miklós's wandering off into the forest had disturbed her. She, too, felt that everything had got confused and a talk to clarify things wouldn't do any harm. Dr Lindholm asked Márta to be present as an impartial observer when he called Lili and to warn him, with a sign, if he went too far.

After the formalities, he began to make a little speech. 'Miklós's walk in the forest was part about wanting to escape, and part…'

Lili pressed the receiver to her ear in the caretaker's office at

Berga. She had hoped it was Miklós calling her and had sprinted for the phone. She waited for her heartbeat to slow after hearing Lindholm's voice. She wished he would get to the point.

'Part?'

'Part about facing facts. For five months have I now am treating him, dear Lili. Never, not once, has he faced up to how sick he really is. I mean it. I am going to say something cruel, Lili. Are you ready for it?'

'I'm ready for anything—and nothing, doctor. But, anyway, go ahead.'

Dr Lindholm was sitting in his comfortable armchair. He took a deep breath. 'Miklós must look death in the eyes. Four times we have to drain his lungs. We can treat his illness but we cannot cure it. Out of misconceived heroism he has ignored the diagnosis. As we doctors say, he is denying it. Are you there, Lili?'

'Yes, I am.'

'Now, when he went into the forest, is the first time for five months that he allowed reality to climb up the ivory tower he builds around himself. We have come to a turning place, Lili. Are you still there?'

'Yes, I am.'

'Unpredictable traumatic effects are normal. Can you help me in this, dear Lili? The answer is not to let Miklós cook his absurd pies in the sky. Are you still there, Lili?'

'Yes, I am.'

'This marriage that he is planning with you is not just absurd and sheer madness. At this stage it could even be damaging.

Miklós is no longer able to tell difference between reality and his imaginary world. You realise how symbolic this rambling was?'

'Symbolic? In what way?'

'A signal of alarm. A warning for me, his doctor, and for you who love him.'

'What do you expect from me?'

'You must end this foolishness. With sincerity. With love. With feeling.'

Lili was leaning against the wall in the caretaker's office, cradling the receiver. Now she pushed herself away from the wall. 'Look, doctor, I respect your exceptional expertise, your rich experience. The sensational achievements of medical research. The pills you prescribe, your X-rays, your cough mixtures, your syringes…I respect everything. But I implore you to leave us in peace. Leave us to dream. And not worry about science. I beg you on my knees. I pray and beseech you, doctor, let us get better! Are you still there?'

Lindholm had beckoned Márta to come over to him so she could hear Lili's passionate plea too. All he could manage now was a sorrowful 'Yes, I am'.

~

Two days before Christmas 1945, Miklós made a desperate decision. He persuaded Harry to go to Berga with him without permission or money.

He had weighed up his options. He would not seek official

approval—that would probably mean labyrinthine battles in an unfamiliar legal system. He knew he should stick to the straight and narrow, but his instincts were telling him otherwise.

To get to Berga, they would have to change trains three times. Three trains, three ticket collectors. Both Miklós and Harry were good at talking their way out of things. They were skinny, badly dressed, unwell. No official could help taking pity on them. They would ride their luck.

On Monday afternoon they walked to Avesta station and boarded a train.

> Dear Lili,
>
> What do you think of this? We could place an announcement in the next issue of *Via Svecia* saying, 'We're engaged to be married'. Just that and our names.

> Dear Miklós,
>
> Do write and tell Mama too. How will you get the money? Have you written to your acquaintance the bishop yet?

They were disqualified at the first hurdle. The ticket collector looked at them in surprise and asked them twice for their tickets.

Miklós smiled kindly at him. 'We don't have any. We don't have enough money. We're Hungarian patients from the Avesta rehabilitation centre.'

The ticket collector wasn't the slightest bit impressed. He put them off the train at the next station and reported them to the stationmaster.

They had travelled exactly seventeen kilometres. Someone arranged for a bus to transport the two fugitives back to Avesta. On this bus there would be no need for tickets.

In the meantime, a committee was convened to discuss the punishment for my father's wayward behaviour.

> My darling, one and only Lili,
>
> Half an hour ago we were transported back here into the midst of a whopping hoo-ha. I can't describe the fuss they made.

~

Dr Lindholm X-rayed Miklós once again. The next day he sent for him to give him his assessment. Miklós sat down and, shutting his eyes, leaned back, balancing on the back two legs of his chair. Now all he had to do was concentrate, keep his balance, and he would find his centre of gravity. If he could keep the front two legs in the air for five seconds then he would be cured. Totally.

Dr Lindholm wanted to talk about his escape attempt. He was gentle today, understanding. 'You bungle that, Miklós. The director and governor of the centre are furious.'

Miklós got himself higher and further back on the chair. 'What can they do?'

'Transfer you.'

'Where?'

'To Högbo, probably. Is a village in the north. My medical opinion counts for nothing.'

'Why? Because I tried to go and see my cousin?'

'For breaking rules. Absence without leave. Don't forget, Miklós, you went missing twice recently. But please know I have nothing against you. Frankly, I understand you. You are thinking what difference it makes anyway?'

Miklós was nearing the tipping point. Was he going to topple over or not? That was the real question. 'What did you see on my lungs yesterday?' he asked.

'I wish I could give you good news but I can't. This X-ray confirms that—'

Crash. In anger Miklós let the front legs of the chair hit the floor. He looked up at the doctor. 'I'm going to get better!'

Lindholm winced at the thud. He avoided my father's gaze.

Lindholm got up and held out his hand. 'You are an odd chap, Miklós. Naïve and compulsive at the same time. Stubborn and a likeable fool. I am fond of you. Is pity we have to part.'

~

My father wasn't the least put out by his expulsion from Avesta, but was rattled to discover, when he looked up Högbo on the map, that it was forty-five kilometres further away from Berga. He walked over to the nurses' room. 'Could I borrow your suitcase again, please?'

Márta went up to my father without a word, stood on tiptoe and kissed his cheek.

'Don't forget to take your pills every morning,' she warned him. 'And give up smoking. Promise me. Let's shake on it.'

They shook hands.

In the afternoon, Miklós started packing. He decided to throw out everything that wasn't necessary, so he could cram his entire life into the battered suitcase. His clothes wouldn't take up much room, but he had a lot of books, notes and newspapers. And then there were all the letters, still in their envelopes, in the huge cardboard box.

Being kicked out of the barracks had created a symbolic opportunity. Now, at last, Miklós could jettison everything he had wanted to get rid of for ages. He took from the cardboard box a thick sheaf of letters tied up with silk ribbon. These were from Lili. He gathered up every other letter from the last five months—from Klára Köves, from a naïve sixteen-year-old girl from the north-east of Hungary, the floods of complaints from two divorced Transylvanian women—and set out with them to the shower room. The fact is, even after he came back from Eksjö in early December, after his three days with Lili, he was still writing to eight girls. He told them all that he was madly in love and soon to be married. Two wrote back to congratulate him.

Miklós took this distinguished bundle of letters out to the shower room and set fire to them. He watched all those words burn, and noted with satisfaction that he was also destroying the smooth-talking charmer who had written so many letters.

That was when he heard the sound of a violin. He waited until everything had turned to ashes and then walked back to the barracks. Harry was standing on a table in the centre of the dormitory playing the 'Internationale'. The men appeared from everywhere, from under beds, from behind cupboards, from behind the door. Ten of them lined up as if they were on a stage.

Arise, you prisoners of starvation!
Arise, you wretched of the earth!
For justice thunders condemnation:
A better world's in birth!

All my father's friends were singing: Laci, Jóska, Adi, Farkas, Jakobovits and Litzman. Harry's face was the picture of innocence as he played his violin.

> I'm being transferred to Högbo because I'm an undisciplined, subversive, disobedient trouble-maker. Ten of my friends announced right away that they wouldn't stay here for a moment without me. So Laci, Harry, Jakobovits and others are coming too.

The men marched out, taking Miklós with them. They paraded through the main building singing. Harry was in the lead with his violin, and the team followed him.

It is the final conflict
Let each stand in his place
The International Union
Shall be the human race.

Dozens of doctors, nurses and office workers poured out into the corridor. Only now were the men aware of the considerable army of people who were looking after them. There were a number of faces that Miklós didn't know. Most of them had never before heard this rousing, powerful song, especially not in Hungarian. But as the ten spirited young men marched and sang, arm in arm, it was victory itself.

My dear Miklós,

I'm devastated that our wanting to see each other again could be the cause of so much fuss.

Darling Lili,

Every minute we've spent together was a life for me. I love you so very much! You know, if I think that we've still got months and months to wait before we can be together forever, it puts me in the worst mood.

My one and only Miklós,

I'll try to get permission here in Berga to come and visit you.

~

The director of the Berga rehabilitation centre offered Lili a seat in her austerely furnished office. She was a thin, severe woman in glasses. Lili wondered if she'd ever smiled in her life. A cardboard box sat on her desk.

'Good to see you, Lili. I've just been speaking to Mr Björkman,' she said, indicating the telephone. 'He asked me to call him as soon as the parcel arrived.' She pushed the box across to Lili. 'It's yours. Go ahead and open it.'

Lili undid the string and tore the box open. She laid the contents out on the table. Two bars of chocolate, a few apples and pears, a pair of nylon stockings and a Bible.

The woman leaned back in her chair with satisfaction. 'Mr Björkman asked me to find a family for you here in Berga.'

Lili leafed through the Bible and saw to her disappointment that it was in Swedish—she wouldn't be able to read a word.

'I see you're wearing the present the Björkmans gave you.'

Lili put her hand on the silver cross. 'Yes.'

'Mr Björkman asked me to give you their love and tell you they remember you in their prayers. They are happy that you've been able to contact your mother. How would you feel if I were to let you spend the weekend with an excellent Catholic family?'

The right moment had come. Lili had planned not to beat around the bush or complicate things—she'd sweep the woman off her feet in a cavalry charge. 'I'm in love!' she declared.

The director was astonished. 'What has that got to do with it?'

'I need help, please! I've fallen in love with a man who is

about to be transferred from Avesta to Högbo. I'd like to visit him. I must!' At last it was out. She put on her most imploring expression.

The woman removed her glasses and, squinting fiercely, wiped them with a handkerchief. She must have been very short-sighted. 'One of the two men who went missing from Avesta last week?'

That sounded rather hostile.

'Yes, but they had reason—' Lili began.

'I disapprove of such behaviour,' the director said. She put her glasses back on and looked at Lili.

'I love him. And he loves me,' said Lili doggedly. 'We want to get married.'

The woman was taken aback. This new information required thought. 'How did you get acquainted?'

'Through letters! We've been writing to each other since September.'

'Have you ever met?'

'He came to visit me a few weeks ago in Eksjö. We spent three days together. I'm going to be his wife.'

The woman drew the Bible towards her and started to leaf through it. She was playing for time. When she looked up, there was so much sorrow in her expression that Lili almost felt pity for her.

'This must be a joke. After four months of letter-writing you want to tie your life to a stranger? I would expect more sense from you.'

Lili realised with dismay that she wouldn't be able to convince this woman. She made one last attempt. 'Are you married?'

'That's totally irrelevant.' The director shut the Bible, took off her glasses and looked down at her spindly fingers. 'I had a fiancé once. He was a great disappointment. An enlightening experience, but a great disappointment.'

Fifteen

RABBI EMIL Kronheim's home in Stockholm could hardly have been described as comfortable. But its dark, heavy furniture had served the rabbi's great-grandfather, grandfather and his father, too. The fraying and faded brocade curtains that hung from the massive windows might have been more than a hundred years old. The rabbi felt safe here. It never occurred to him to get the place painted or to move elsewhere.

There always seemed to be unwashed dishes piled up in the kitchen. Mrs Kronheim was no longer bothered by the smell of herring that hit visitors like an attack of mustard gas. But the rabbi always took a new, clean plate for his herring, and that was the source of frequent quarrels.

Mrs Kronheim was sitting in the kitchen staring at the dozens of oily plates scattered around the place.

'Listen to this,' the rabbi shouted to her from the dining-room table. '"Lili even wants to renounce her Jewishness. She and the man who has ensnared her with his letters are planning to convert. The man has a serious case of TB. On top of that he claims to know a bishop in Stockholm—which I'm sure is a lie. I beg you, Reb, please do something!'

The rabbi was reading out bits of the letter, while picking up and devouring pieces of herring without so much as a glance at his plate.

'Who wrote that?' Mrs Kronheim called from the kitchen.

The rabbi noticed, to his surprise, that stains from the salty liquid in which the herring was pickled were forming strange shapes on the tablecloth.

'A moon-faced girl with a moustache, by the name of'—he looked at the envelope on which oily traces of herring were already visible—'by the name of Judit Gold.'

Mrs Kronheim knew that sooner or later she would have to wash up and the thought gave her no pleasure. 'Do you know her?'

'Yes. I visited her in Eksjö months ago. We talked about flies.'

'One of your cautionary tales, no doubt.'

The rabbi demolished another herring. He smacked his lips. 'She is well meaning and emotional. Not afraid to cry.'

'Who is?' sighed Mrs Kronheim.

'This girl, Judit Gold. But deep inside, at the bottom of her heart, do you know what she's like?'

His wife got to her feet and began to gather up the plates, putting them disconsolately into a bowl.

'No, you tell me. You're such a clever man.'

'She's sad and disturbed,' he said, holding up the letter. 'That's what's she's like inside. This is her third letter. She keeps telling tales on her friend—and maybe not just to me.'

~

Miklós and his loyal friends were moved to a two-storey boarding house in Högbo, a couple of hundred kilometres north of Stockholm. They were greeted by Erik, a hefty man in a suit, who introduced himself as the superintendent and read out the house rules. Apart from being strict about meal times, he didn't really require anything of them. Once a week they would have to go to Sandviken for a check-up. My father had the distinct feeling that the whole thing was a waste of time.

He was even more dejected when they went upstairs to their rooms. Twenty men were housed in three dormitories, which meant that seven beds were crammed into rooms more suitable for a family weekend than a long-term stay. The cupboards had been moved out into the hallway. Erik watched from the doorway as they glumly selected their beds and sat with their suitcases on their laps. None of them was in a hurry to unpack.

Erik warned them that smoking in the rooms was forbidden and then disappeared.

> Seven of us live in a cubbyhole: Laci, Harry, Jóska, Litzman, Jakobovits, Farkas and me. So far we don't have a cupboard or a table. Luckily there's central heating. As for the beds! Straw mattresses and the kind of pillow I had in prison.

Miklós picked the bed under the window for himself. He tried not to let the pervasive gloom get a grip. He whistled as he unpacked the photo of Lili and himself from Eksjö. He put it on the sill, propping it up against the windowpane. When he woke up the next morning the first thing he'd see would be Lili's smile.

~

That afternoon Harry and Miklós took a bus into town to visit the jeweller. Harry had brought his violin with him in its case. Erik had warned them that the jeweller was a quibbling old man. Above the door of the shop hung a bronze bell that rang whenever someone entered.

The jeweller, contrary to expectations, was a kindly grey-haired gentleman who wore a purple bowtie.

My father had prepared his strategy. 'I would like to buy two gold wedding rings.'

The jeweller smiled. 'Do you know the sizes?'

Miklós fished a metal ring out of his pocket. He had taken it from a curtain rail in Eksjö. It fitted Lili's finger perfectly.

'This is my fiancée's size. The other one's for me.'

The old man took the ring, estimated its size, and pulled out a drawer in the cupboard behind him. He rummaged around a little.

'Here you are!' he said, holding up a gold ring. He took a gauge from under the counter, compared the two rings to his satisfaction, and slipped the gold ring into his pocket.

'Can I have your finger?' he asked.

He grasped my father's ring finger, pondered a moment, opened a different drawer and chose another ring. 'Try this one on,' he said holding it out to him.

Miklós slipped it on. It was an exact fit.

> I don't like gold; it always makes me think of all the alien, vulgar and wicked emotions associated with it. But I like these two rings; after all they connect your blood with mine.

Miklós and Harry exchanged glances. They'd arrived at the critical moment.

'How much do I owe you?' My father asked.

The old man deliberated. As if he too were brooding over the wicked emotions associated with such a trifle. 'Two hundred and forty kronor, the pair,' he announced.

Miklós didn't flinch. 'I'm living in a boarding house in Högbo—it's a rehabilitation centre.'

The old man straightened his bowtie. 'I've heard something about it.'

'I'd like to take you into my confidence. You see, I've been given an important job there.'

'Oh, a job. Excellent!' The jeweller gave him a friendly smile.

'Yes, and I'll get paid for it. Monthly. I reckon I can save 240 kronor in four months.'

Miklós wasn't making this up. That morning, after the small Hungarian colony, their suitcases on their laps, assessed their wretched situation, the men appointed my father their representative. He promised to stand up for them. And all of them, including the Poles and the Greeks, agreed to set aside a small part of their pocket money each month to pay Miklós for his efforts.

The old man seemed impressed. But he didn't want to be cheated. 'First of all, I congratulate you, young man. This could be the start of a fine career. But, for my part, I made a solemn vow to my mother. I was young at the time and perhaps it was a little rash of me. You know, our family has been in this business for two hundred years. I promised my mother that I would never on any account give credit to anyone. It might seem hard-hearted, but you must agree that a vow made to a mother is binding.'

Miklós, who had planned a two-pronged attack from the outset, nodded earnestly. 'I'm a Hungarian. I'd like you to look me in the eye. You don't think I'm a swindler, do you?'

The jeweller took a step back. 'Certainly not. I can smell swindlers a mile off. I can safely say that you are not the swindling type.'

The moment had come. Miklós gave Harry a kick. Harry sighed, laid his violin case on the counter and opened it. He picked up the violin tenderly and held it out to the old man.

'Well, I was pretty sure you wouldn't give credit to a stranger,' Miklós said, speaking with slow eloquence for heightened effect. 'What I had in mind was to leave this violin here as a pledge until I had saved enough money. It is worth at least four hundred kronor. I hope you'll accept it as security.'

The old man took out a magnifying glass and inspected the violin. It had been given to Harry by the Swedish Philharmonic Orchestra last summer, after a newspaper reported that a young violinist, a concentration camp survivor, was convalescing on the island of Gotland. It was worth a lot more than four hundred kronor. Even the old man's mother would have approved of this.

~

Rabbi Emil Kronheim stumbled off the bus. His legs were stiff from the long journey; it was beastly cold and now it had started to snow again. The rabbi asked where he could find the women's rehab hospital, drew his coat around him and set out.

~

Within a few days Miklós had the opportunity to prove how qualified he was for his elected post.

They were all sitting in the shabby dining room. The ten Hungarians, the Greeks, the Poles and the Romanians. The only sound was the angry beating of spoons as they struck the table in perfect time until Erik, the hefty superintendent, bustled in.

'What's the trouble, gentlemen?' he asked, afraid he wouldn't be heard above the din. Everybody stopped clanging. My father picked up a fork and rose to his feet.

> Just imagine, darling Lili, how grand I've become!
> I've been elected representative of our group. It's not
> much work, but I get paid 75 kronor a month.

Miklós pierced a piece of potato on the prong of his fork and held it up. 'This potato is rotten.'

Erik looked around in embarrassment. Then, since everyone was staring at him and he wanted to live up to his role as superintendent, he sauntered over to my father and put his nose to the potato. 'It smells of fish. What's the problem?' he said, trying not to make a face.

Miklós held the potato aloft as if it were an item of evidence.

'It's rotten. We had our suspicions about the potatoes yesterday, but today they are definitely off.'

A Greek kid, who kept his knitted hat on, even at night, stood up. 'I'll write to the International Red Cross!' he shouted in Greek.

'Pipe down, Theo,' Miklós admonished him. 'I'll deal with this.' He looked at Erik and politely pointed to a chair beside him. 'Sit with us.'

Erik hesitated.

'I'd like you to taste it,' said Miklós, drawing the chair back for him.

Erik sat down tentatively on the edge of the chair. Harry was already bringing him a plate and a knife and fork. My father eased the potato from his fork into the middle of the empty plate.

'Bon appétit,' Miklós said.

Erik looked around in dismay. There was no mercy. He bit into the potato. Miklós sat down beside him, studying him as he chewed and swallowed.

The superintendent tried to make a joke of it. 'It tastes a bit like shark. But I like shark. It's really quite nice.'

'Is that so? Well, if it's quite nice, have some more,' said Miklós with a deadpan expression as he stabbed another potato and put it on Erik's plate.

Erik knew he had to tackle this potato too. It was more difficult to get down, but somehow he managed it.

'Believe me, there's nothing wrong with it. Nothing on earth.'

'Nothing? Well, go on, have some more.'

Miklós sped up. He kept stabbing potatoes and piling them onto Erik's plate. The men were on their feet by this time, crowding around him.

> My darling one and only Lili, just imagine, the superintendent turned pale, but he led from the front and right to the end he heroically maintained they were edible.

Erik reckoned his best bet would be to get through this circus as quickly as possible. So he wolfed the potatoes down. 'Quite edible. Not bad at all. Good, in fact.'

But now he was feeling sick. Drinking between every mouthful, he bravely finished off the mound of potatoes. Then he lurched to his feet, clutching the edge of the table to stop himself falling.

Miklós grabbed his shoulders and tried to support him. 'As you very well know, every last potato peel is paid for by the United Nations. I would be obliged if you did not treat us inmates as beggars, expecting us to show our gratitude for every last boiled potato.'

The men started clapping. This is what they were expecting of my father, this tone. This was what he was being paid for.

Erik belched, clutching his stomach. 'You misunderstand the situation,' he spluttered, and then collapsed with stomach pains so severe he had to dig his nails into the floor to stop himself crying out.

Sixteen

ONE HUNDRED and sixty girls ate lunch together in the Berga canteen, where all the tables had been pushed together to form three long rows. Two kitchen maids served the food, along with three patients elected each week to help. It took an hour and a half to serve everyone.

Emil Kronheim was escorted into the canteen by the unsmiling woman in charge—the director. The rabbi had grown accustomed to the bleak, military atmosphere of these places, but they still disheartened him. He had requested a room adjacent to the canteen be made available for him.

Judit Gold was sitting with Lili and Sára a long way from the door, but it was as if she sensed a change in the atmosphere. She couldn't say why she did it, but she glanced at the door just as it opened—and there was the rabbi. Judit turned pale and started to sweat. She willed herself to focus on her spoon as it dipped into the red soup.

The director came over and stopped right beside them. Judit almost buried her head in her soup bowl.

'You've got a visitor,' she whispered in a confidential tone.

Judit looked up. She found it strange that no one could hear her heart beating.

'Me?' asked Lili, getting to her feet.

'Rabbi Kronheim from Stockholm. He'd like to speak to you.'

'A rabbi? From Stockholm? Now?'

'He's in a hurry. He's got to catch the two o'clock train.'

Lili looked over the heads to the doorway where Emil Kronheim was standing. He gave her a friendly nod.

There was a small room next to the canteen, linked to it by a serving window. If Judit sat up straight, she could see into this room, and she couldn't resist peeking from time to time. She saw the two of them introduce themselves and sit at a table. Judit was trembling. She put her spoon down. She was sure the rabbi wouldn't betray her, but her remorse gnawed at her.

The rabbi had put his pocket watch on the table in the small room. He was relying on its quiet tick to create the right atmosphere. They had been listening to it for a while now—Lili had no intention of breaking the silence.

When Rabbi Kronheim felt that the tick-tock effect had been achieved, he leaned forward and looked into Lili's eyes. 'You have lost God.'

The pocket watch ticked away. Lili didn't ask how this stranger had the ability to see into her mind, but his powers of intuition didn't surprise her. 'No, God has lost me.'

'It's beneath you to split hairs on such a question.'

Lili was fiddling with the crocheted tablecloth. 'But what makes you think that about me?'

'It's not important at the moment. I just know.' The rabbi shifted his weight, making the chair creak. 'Have you got a cross, too?'

Lili blushed. How did he know? She felt in her pocket for the envelope where she kept the cross. Since she had come to Berga she had worn it only once, when she went to the director to beg for the visit. It hadn't helped. 'Yes. Yes, I do. It was a gift. Do you object?'

'Well, I'm not exactly thrilled,' he said sadly.

The pocket watch continued to tick.

'Look here, Lili, we are all filled with doubts. Big ones and lesser ones. But that doesn't mean we have to turn our backs.'

Lili thumped the table. The watch bounced like a rubber ball. 'Were you there? Did you come with us?' Lili was whispering, but her fist was clenched and her body was rigid. 'Were you there with us in the cattle wagon?'

The rabbi pointed to the others in the canteen beyond the window. 'I won't insult you by saying it was a test. I wouldn't dare tell you that, after all you've been through. God has lost you—all right. Or rather, it's not all right—I too have an issue with him about that. I'm angry. I don't forgive, either. How could he have done this to us? To you! To them!'

He put his watch away. It had served its purpose. He got to his feet and knocked his chair over. Taking no notice, he started pacing. It was four steps from wall to wall. He strode up and down, passionately waving his arms around.

'No, there can be no forgiveness for that. I, Rabbi Emil Kronheim, am telling you this. But...but! Millions of your brethren perished. Millions were murdered, like animals in a slaughterhouse. No, even animals are treated better than our fellow Jews were. But, for crying out loud, those millions aren't even cold in their graves yet! We haven't even finished the prayers for them. And you would leave us already? You would turn your back? Don't be fair to God; he doesn't deserve it. Be fair to the millions. You have no right to abandon them.'

From the canteen, Judit Gold could see Kronheim storming around the room and shouting. She felt lucky to be where she was. Here, she had only to put up with the hum of the dining room, the clatter of spoons, the quiet chatter of the girls. She had, however, lost her appetite. She was nauseated even by the thought of the risotto growing cold in her bowl.

~

> Darling Miklós,
>
> Today a rabbi came from Stockholm and gave me a little moral sermon about our conversion. How on earth did he hear about that? Could your bishop have told him?

This part of the letter prodded my father into urgent action. He decided to take a short cut with regard to the complicated matter of their conversion. He looked up the phone number of the nearest parish. The less significant the parish, he reckoned, the less fuss there would be. A country priest would surely be easier to convince than a bishop from the capital.

He discussed everything on the telephone and a few days later caught a bus from Högbo to the nearby village of Gävle.

In Gävle he found the friendly, simple wooden church that he was secretly hoping for. The light flooded in through the windows above the gallery. The priest was over eighty and his head shook constantly. Miklós had gone to the public library in Högbo the day before and buried himself in canon law in preparation for the meeting. It was well worth the effort. When he brought up the term *Congregationes religiosae* and explained how he and Lili were Jews who wanted to be married in his church, the old man's eyes shone with tears.

'How do you know about things like that?'

Miklós didn't respond; he went on in a rather self-important way. 'The main thing is that, instead of taking a solemn vow, my fiancée and I would only take a simple vow to bind us to the Catholic faith.'

The priest's hands were shaking too. He took out a handkerchief and wiped his eyes. 'I'm very touched by your fervour.'

Miklós was in full swing, and he began to quote, line by line, the relevant passages from the ecclesiastical literature. 'Do correct me if I'm wrong, Father, but as I understand it the simple vow is one-sided. It binds the party that takes the vow—that is, me and my fiancée—to the Church, but it doesn't bind the Church to us. On the other hand the solemn vow would be mutual, meaning that it couldn't be broken by either party.'

'How do you know all this?'

'We are serious about conversion, Father.'

The old man gathered his strength, got to his feet and began striding towards the sacristy. Miklós could hardly keep up with him. The priest took out an enormous leather-bound book and dipped his pen in the ink. Miklós was fascinated that the ink was green.

'You've convinced me. I have no doubts regarding the seriousness of your intentions. I'd like to write down your particulars. You should let me know when your fiancée can travel here from Berga. Once we have the date I will arrange for your baptism right away. I'll say one thing, Miklós, in all my time as a priest I've never come across such touching enthusiasm.'

~

Miklós and Lili now wrote to each other even more often. Sometimes they sent two letters in one day. On New Year's Eve, Miklós went up to his room. He didn't want to get drunk with the men in the boarding-house dining room downstairs. He lay on his bed, put Lili's photo on his chest and swore he would stay alive. He kept repeating this until he fell asleep. Towards dawn Harry and the others staggered in. They found my father lying on his back fully dressed, with tears trickling down his cheeks in his sleep and Lili's photo peeping out from under his hand.

> Darling Lili,
>
> Damn the *Via Svecia*! I ordered the notice, sending in the exact wording, and they go and publish it with a shocking mistake. They mixed up the names! According to the notice, you asked for my hand! I hardly feel like sending it to you.

~

New Year's Eve in Berga began with Lili playing the piano and Sára singing. They had practised some songs from operettas—'Péter Hajmási' from *The Csárdás Queen* was such a success they had to perform three encores. The rest of the evening was less cheerful. The three-piece band played, a lot of girls danced, and a lot cried, too. They had each been given a litre of red wine with supper.

> I thought of you today at lunchtime because we had tomato sauce, and I know you love that! Oh, how I love you, my little sweetie-pie!

~

On New Year's Day the men made resolutions. Ever since he'd been allowed to get out of bed, in July, Pál Jakobovits had been secreting a slice of bread into his pocket at every meal. He was aware of the stupidity of this; after all, there would always be bread here. But force of habit was stronger. On 1 January 1946, he resolved not to stuff his pocket with bread from that day on. Harry swore not to chat girls up unless he felt there was love involved. Litzman decided to emigrate to Israel. Miklós resolved to start learning Russian as soon as he got back to Hungary.

> When we daydream together, we think of everything, not only a self-serving love. We imagine a future together, working, following our vocations, in the service of mankind and society.

On the morning of New Year's Day in Berga the Hungarian girls sang the national anthem.

> My one and only darling Miklós,
>
> When are you going to the dentist in Stockholm?

~

A week later Miklós caught the bus to Sandviken, about half an hour away. He sat alone. It was one of the coldest winters for years—this day it was minus twenty-one degrees Centigrade. Thick ice coated the windows. The bus looked as if it had been wrapped in tin foil. It jolted along in its silver splendour.

> At home I only want to work for a left-wing newspaper and, if I can't find anything, I'll look around for some other occupation. I'm sick of the bourgeoisie.

On the same morning, in Berga, Lili refused to get out of bed. At about midday Sára and Judit pulled her up by force. They even dressed her, like a doll. They had found a sled somewhere, and they put Lili on it and took turns pulling her up and down the main pathway.

> My darling Miklós,
> I've never ever felt as homesick as I do now. I'd give ten years of my life to be able to fly home.

My father sat on the bus like a forgotten chocolate in a box wrapped in silver paper. He could forget the outside world. The engine hummed. It was warm inside, the lighting was magical, and the springs rocked him. He put his hand in his pocket and felt something slim and pointed.

> I reached into my pocket and found a Mitzi Six carmine lipstick. I bought it the other day and forgot

> to send it to you. I'll be able to give it to you in person soon. First of all we'll check out whether it's kiss-proof. All right?

Lili was flying along on the sled. This time Sára and Judit were pulling it together. They were determined to cheer Lili up, and hoped that whizzing around in this clear, cold weather would have the desired effect.

> Your letter's in front of me and I've read it about twenty times. Every time, I discover something new in it, and every moment I am madder and madder with happiness.
>
> How I love you!!!
>
> Last night I had a dream that I can't get out of my mind. It was so clear. We had arrived home. Mama and Papa were at the train station to meet me. You weren't with me. I was alone.

In her dream Lili arrived at Keleti station in Budapest. Crowds of people were waiting but there was no pushing or shoving. People stood stiffly, staring straight ahead. The only movement in the dream was the train ceremoniously puffing its way alongside the covered platform. The smoke enveloped the crowd. Then it cleared, and in the grey light of dawn passengers began to step down from the train, carrying heavy suitcases. Those who were meeting them, several hundred, maybe several thousand, were waiting, transfixed.

Lili was wearing a red polka-dot dress and a wide-brimmed hat. She caught sight of her mother and father in the motionless crowd. She started running, but didn't get a step nearer to them. She was trying so hard to run that her mouth became dry and she could barely breathe. But she couldn't bridge the distance between them. It couldn't have been more than ten metres. Lili could see her mother's sad, lustreless eyes. Luckily, her father was laughing. He held his arms out wide to hug his little girl, but Lili couldn't reach him.

~

The X-ray room in Sandviken was very small; there was space only for the apparatus. By this time Miklós considered X-rays his personal enemy. He had pressed his narrow shoulders so many times against the cold pane of glass that he felt acute loathing if he even glanced at an X-ray machine.

He closed his eyes and tried to stifle his feeling of disgust.

It wasn't possible for Miklós to cultivate a close relationship with his new doctor, Irene Hammarström, as he had with Lindholm—though Irene was compassionate, softly spoken and delicately pretty. She always gave my father a searching look, as if she were trying to fathom his secret.

Now, she stood by the window and held the X-ray up to the light. Miklós played his usual game. He put his weight on the two back legs of the chair and pushed off. He didn't look at her; he was steering the chair into an increasingly precarious position.

'I can't believe my eyes,' gasped the doctor.

Miklós was at the point where a fraction of a millimetre mattered. If he miscalculated, he would crash down like a bowling pin.

Irene Hammarström didn't waste time. She walked over to the table and picked out an older X-ray from the file. She went back to the window and compared the two. 'Look, this is June. The patch is the size of a thumbnail,' she said to Miklós, who had eased himself back a smidgeon.

My father's act had reached its climax. The chair was balancing and his feet were dangling in the air.

'This is today. It's hardly visible. Miraculous! What did Dr Lindholm tell you?'

Miklós had reached his zenith. After all his practice he could balance on the chair between heaven and earth like a motionless falcon about to swoop.

'He said I had six months to live.'

'Somewhat brutal, but the truth. I wouldn't have been able to say anything different.'

My father's one-man show was still running. 'What do you mean by that?'

'Now I'm not quite sure, looking at this latest X-ray.'

'What do you mean?'

'Now, I'd probably encourage you. Tell you to keep up the good work. What about your high temperature? Your dawn fever?'

The show was over, but those five seconds would live on, in

the land of miracles. Miklós crashed backwards onto the floor.

'Good Lord!' Irene dropped the X-rays and rushed over to him.

My father had hit the back of his head pretty hard, but he was smiling. 'It's nothing, nothing. I made a bet with myself, that's all.'

Seeing Miklós's ghastly metal dentures, the doctor decided to refer her grinning patient to the district centre in the hope that they could sort out this amicable young Hungarian's teeth for a reduced price, or even for no fee.

~

It was a memorable day. When Miklós returned to the boarding house he found the men waiting for him upstairs, standing to attention. He couldn't imagine how they knew he was on the road to recovery. But as their faces were shining with pride and joy, he reckoned it must be the reason for this performance. He sat down on his bed and waited.

Then the men began to hum Beethoven's 'Ode to Joy'.

When the mystery of the ceremony became unbearable, when the humming chorus of the *Ninth Symphony* had reached its hymnal climax, when my father leaned back on his bed and with eyes shut started to soar, Harry brought out the newspaper. Without a word he held it up in front of Miklós.

There was the poem, in black and white. On page three of *Via Svecia*. In Swedish. In italics. *'Till en liten svensk gosse'* ('To a Little Swedish Boy'). Above it was the name of the poet: my father.

~

Miklós composed all his poems in his head. Days and weeks later, when he felt the poem was ready, all he had to do was write it out.

He had finished this poem, however, in about ten minutes. He was sitting in a deck chair on the ship, munching biscuits, savouring the taste of raspberry and vanilla. The ship's horn bellowed, and they drew away from the shore. The women on their bicycles were watching; not one of them stirred. There, an arm's length away, was the country that would take him in, for who knew how long. Miklós felt this sweet gift should be reciprocated. He would write a poem for Swedish children. Advice about life, a warning that would draw its power from his infernal experiences.

He turned the crumbly biscuit in his mouth and set out the first two lines in his head. 'You have yet to learn, little brother, of the deep furrows ploughed across the forehead of a continent.' And now he could see the blond six-year-old child to whom his poem was addressed, who stood staring at him, hugging his teddy. The little Swedish boy.

The lines poured out; it was almost more difficult to remember them than to create them. By the time the ship had turned round and reached the open sea, the poem was finished.

You have yet to learn, little brother,
of the deep furrows ploughed across the forehead of a continent.
Here, in the north, you saw an aeroplane
dipped in starlight on a moonlit night.

You didn't know what air-raid warnings or bombs were,
or what it is to survive what's on the film—
the troubles of the world weren't washed
by evil waves onto the children, making them suffer.

Here you had points for clothes, meat rations and bread tickets;
you could play sometimes, though, little brother!
But your skinny playmates were burnt in the flames,
and death grinned at its meagre bread.

By the time you grow up and become a man,
a kind, smiling blond giant,
all these falling tears will be clouds,
this age will be history, a hazy vision.

If you muse on this bloody age,
remember a pale little boy—
his plaything was a scrap of grenade,
his minders murderous weapons.

If you have a son, little brother, teach him
that the truth is never a gun or revolver;
and it's not the long range of the rocket
that relieves the suffering of the world.

And in the toyshop, little brother, don't buy
soldiers for your son; on the white toy shelf
let there be wooden blocks, so that in his childhood
he'll learn to build and not to kill.

Harry gave Miklós a pat on the shoulder. 'I took your career in hand. I sent your poem to a Swedish newspaper, anticipating your approval. I asked them to translate it, telling them not to commission any old translator with the task because this was the work of a great Hungarian poet. You. That was three months ago. And this morning it appeared in print. I had the translation checked. It's good.'

The others were still standing up straight, humming 'Ode to Joy'. Miklós got to his feet and gave Harry a hug, concentrating on holding back his tears. Crying wouldn't befit a great Hungarian poet.

~

This really was a fateful day—as Miklós was to discover.

It wasn't yet midnight. Someone was hammering on the door, calling my father's name—there was a man on the phone for him. Miklós woke up. For a moment he had no idea where he was. He found his way downstairs to reception in his pyjamas, his heart thumping.

'Did I wake you?' The voice on the line was unfamiliar.

'It doesn't matter.'

'I apologise. I'm Rabbi Kronheim from Stockholm. I want to speak to you on a matter of importance.'

Miklós's feet were cold; he pressed one sole against his calf. 'I'm listening.'

'Not over the phone! What are you thinking?'

'Sorry.'

'Listen, Miklós, I'm catching the train from Stockholm to Sandviken in the morning. I've got two hours before I have to catch the train back. Let's meet halfway.'

'I can meet you in Sandviken if you like.'

'No, no, I insist on halfway. Will Östanbyn be all right?'

Östanbyn was the first stop after Högbo on the bus to Sandviken. Miklós had passed through it many times.

'Where in Östanbyn?'

'Get off the bus and walk towards Sandviken. Take the first right and keep going until you come to a wooden bridge. I'll be waiting for you there. Got it?'

'Okay.' Miklós was in a daze. 'Could you tell me your name again, please?'

'Emil Kronheim. So, 10 a.m. at the wooden bridge. Don't be late.'

The rabbi hung up. It was all so fast that Miklós realised, with the receiver buzzing in his hand, that he had forgotten to ask what the rabbi wanted to discuss.

~

Miklós followed the rabbi's directions and got off the bus in Östanbyn. He took the first right. He must have been walking briskly for about twenty minutes before he saw the wooden bridge. At the far end a man in a black ankle-length coat was resting on a big stone. Miklós was amazed that anyone could sit still in this frozen world. In fact, he looked as if he were enjoying a summer picnic beside a lake.

'What's the news?' the rabbi yelled across the bridge in a cheerful tone.

Miklós stopped. Not only was the news good, it was positively splendid. But who knew what that grotesque figure over there was talking about?

'Rabbi Kronheim?'

'Who else? Who is this Catholic bishop? The one you promised to Lili? If it is the bishop of Stockholm, I know him well. He's a charming man.'

Lili's letter about a rabbi who lectured her on morality flashed into Miklós's mind. Of course, this was Emil Kronheim! Miklós understood everything! The rabbi had come to chastise him. To hell with it! To think he had made a pilgrimage to Östanbyn for that.

'We don't need the bishop any more.'

'I'll wager you've found someone else.'

The wooden bridge was at least thirty metres long. In the valley below, ancient pine trees were standing guard, silence frozen in the light on their snow-covered branches. There wasn't a breath of wind, no birdsong. The sublime beauty of the countryside was disturbed only by their shouting.

'Well guessed, Rabbi. An excellent old man in Gävle. He will baptise us.'

On the other side of the bridge, Kronheim ran his fingers through his wiry hair. 'Lili isn't so keen now on that silly idea.'

Miklós decided it was time to look the man in the eye. He walked across the bridge and held out his hand. 'She wrote just the opposite to me.'

'What did she write?'

'That a rabbi from Stockholm had preached her a sermon. Somehow or other he had sniffed out our intentions. Something like that.'

'Your lovely fiancée would never have used such a cynical expression. Sniffed out, indeed! I'm not a bloodhound.'

'Seriously, Rabbi, how did you find out? We haven't spoken to a soul about it.'

Kronheim took my father's arm and walked with him to the middle of the bridge. He leaned against the railing and gazed at the scene below.

'Have you ever seen anything as magnificent? It's looked like this for a hundred years. Even a thousand.'

The valley was eerily impressive. Dense pines as far as the eye could see, sprinkled all over with icing sugar.

Miklós decided it was time to leap the last hurdle. 'Look here, before the war I'd have considered this a way to escape. But now it's a clear and independent decision.'

Kronheim didn't look at my father. He had surrendered to

the wonder of nature. 'This landscape is utterly unspoilt.'

'I'm thinking of the fate of our unborn children,' said my father, determined to continue. 'In any case, I've never been a believer. I'm an atheist, and you can despise me for that. But I'd like you to know that our conversion has nothing to do with cowardice.'

The rabbi appeared not to have heard a word. 'It's been here from time immemorial. This bridge, for instance, was designed for people to admire the view. But they made sure to build it out of wood. Can you see any alien material here? Iron, glass or brass? You can't, can you, son?'

'Is this what you wanted to talk to me about, Reb, the wooden bridge at Östanbyn?'

'Among other things.'

Miklós was fed up with all this riddling talk. Just when he was getting the better of his misgivings, this little wiry-haired man turns up and preaches to him about the pristine countryside. He understood him, of course he understood him. Several thousand years—you bet! But if Lili wanted to convert, he would sweep away every worry or hesitation that lay in her path.

He bowed. 'I'm glad to have met you, Rabbi Kronheim. Our decision is final. No one can dissuade us. Goodbye.'

And he strode off in the direction he had come from. At the end of the bridge he turned round. It was as if Emil Kronheim had been waiting for him to do that. The rabbi pulled a letter out of his coat pocket and waved it.

'I hate myself for this,' he shouted. 'But as the scripture

says…or maybe it doesn't. Anyway, the main thing is I want to strike a dirty deal with you, son.'

Miklós stared at him, baffled.

'Come and see what I've got.' The rabbi was still holding the letter in the air.

Miklós reluctantly retraced his steps.

'I've written this request; it's so heartfelt that no eye will remain dry. You sign it and I'll take it to Stockholm today. They'll agree, have no worries about that. On one condition: I'd like to be the one who joins you in marriage at the synagogue in Stockholm. Naturally under a *chuppah*. I'll foot the bill for clothes, the ceremony and a reception for your friends. After that the Red Cross will be obliged to offer you, as newlyweds, a room of your own, say, in Berga.'

My father took the letter. It was written in Swedish. As far as he could make out it was addressed to the Stockholm headquarters of the Red Cross.

'They don't deal with cases like this.'

'Yes, they do. They'll be proud to. They'll pull out all the stops. Make good use of it. Get the story into the newspapers. After all, two young people under their patronage, struggling to live again after all but dying, have forged a commitment to a new life together. By the way, what does your doctor say?'

'About what?'

'Your TB.'

'So you know about that, too?'

'It's my duty to find out. That's what I'm paid for.'

'I'm getting better. The cavity is calcifying.'

'Thank God!' Kronheim gave my father a hug. 'Do we have a deal?' he whispered.

Miklós softened. He was already composing the letter to Lili in which he would explain that a grown-up person—especially if he's a socialist—doesn't quibble over trifling religious questions.

Seventeen

EVERYTHING HAPPENED quickly. The rabbi, as promised, procured the relevant permits. Within two months Lili and my father found themselves in the synagogue in Stockholm under the *chuppah*. Kronheim paid for the rental of a white taffeta dress for Lili and a dinner jacket for my father, and organised a reception after the wedding. The King of Sweden, Gustav V, sent a congratulatory telegram to the young couple who, having barely survived the concentration camp, were now about to swear their undying love.

In February 1946, before the wedding, my father suffered for weeks in a dentist's chair. Kronheim had insisted he swap his alloy teeth for porcelain.

'It can't be much fun kissing you, son,' he said one day. 'I've been talking to my congregation and they unanimously decided to raise the funds for the dental work. They collected six hundred kronor in three days. I've been in touch with a first-class man for the job. Here's his address.'

~

Emil Kronheim could have rubbed his hands. He really had pulled this whole thing off. But before the wedding, at the beginning of March, a visitor arrived to dampen his happiness.

It began with two long impatient rings of the doorbell. The rabbi was eating herring, as usual, and chuckling to himself as he read an American comic. His wife let the visitor into the flat and was so shocked by the stranger's distracted appearance that she led her into the main room without taking her coat, fur cap and snow-covered galoshes. The rabbi didn't even notice her as he lifted a bit of herring out of the brine.

Mrs Kronheim restrained herself from slapping his hand. 'You've got a visitor,' she hissed.

The rabbi stood up in embarrassment, wiping his hands on his trousers. Mrs Kronheim made a distressed sound. 'Your trousers! Dear God!'

There were snowflakes on the young woman's upper lip. She looked like a female Santa Claus.

'Ah, my conscientious letter writer! Sit down,' Kronheim

said, offering her a seat.

Judit sat, not even unbuttoning her coat. Mrs Kronheim left discreetly and went into the kitchen.

'I saw you in Berga, Rabbi. Thank you for not giving me away.'

'How about a little salted herring?' he asked, pushing the plate of fish towards her.

'No, thanks. I don't like it.'

'What is there not to like about salted herring? It's full of vitamins. Full of life. Now why would I have given you away, dear Judit? I'm grateful to you for the last-minute warning.'

The snow on Judit's galoshes was melting.

'No, the last minute is now!'

'Good God, did you come all the way to Stockholm to tell me that?'

Judit grabbed the rabbi's hand. 'We have to save Lili.'

'Save her? From whom? From what?'

'From marriage! I can't believe it. My friend wants to get married.'

Kronheim would have liked to withdraw his hand, but her grip was tight. 'Love is a wonderful thing,' he said. 'Marriage is its seal.'

'But the man who wants to marry her is a scoundrel. A marriage con man.'

'My gosh, that's no joke. What makes you think that, Judit?'

Mrs Kronheim came in with homemade vanilla biscuits and tea.

The rabbi hated anything sweet. 'Help yourself to tea. Relax. I'll stick to herring if you don't mind.'

Judit took no notice of the biscuits or the tea. Nor did she notice that the tile stove was pouring warmth into the room of imposing furniture. She didn't even loosen her scarf. 'Listen to me, Rabbi. You don't know everything, so just listen. Imagine a man who gets hold of the names and addresses of all the Hungarian girls convalescing in rehab hospitals in Sweden.'

'I can imagine him.'

'Now imagine that he sits down and writes a letter to each of them. Do you follow? To every single one of them.'

'I see a determined man before me,' said the rabbi, picking up another piece of herring.

'The letters are identical. The same sickly sweet wording. As if he'd made carbon copies. He then walks to the post office and posts the lot. Can you picture it?'

'Oh, that can't be true. Where did you hear that?'

Judit Gold gave the rabbi a triumphant look. Her moment had come. She took a crumpled letter out of her bag. 'Look at this. I got one too. In September last year. Of course I had no intention of replying. I saw through his tricks. What do you say to that? Lili received an identical letter. I saw it and read it. The only difference was the name. You can check it for yourself.'

Kronheim smoothed out the letter and studied it.

> Dear Judit,
>
> You are probably used to strangers chatting you

> up when you speak Hungarian, for no better reason than they are Hungarian too. We men can be so bad-mannered. For example, I addressed you by your first name on the pretext that we grew up in the same town. I don't know whether you already know me from Debrecen. Until my homeland ordered me to 'volunteer' for forced labour, I worked for the *Independent* newspaper, and my father owned a bookstore in Gambrinus Court.

'Very odd,' remarked the rabbi, shaking his head.

Judit was on the verge of tears. 'And Lili wants to tie the boat of her life to this crook.'

Kronheim put another herring dreamily into his mouth. 'The boat of her life. How lyrical. Tie the boat of her life to him.'

~

More than fifty years later, when I questioned Lili, my mother, about the moment she decided to reply to Miklós's letter, she searched for a long time among her buried memories.

'I don't remember exactly. You know, in September, after the ambulance took me from Smålandsstenar to Eksjö, during my second week of being confined to bed, Sára and Judit turned up in the ward. They brought some of my personal things from Smålandsstenar—including your father's letter. Judit sat on my bed and tried to persuade me to write back, prattling on about how much that poor ill boy from Debrecen must be hoping for a reply. Then the girls left and I was stuck in bed. I wasn't even allowed to go out to the bathroom. I lay there bored, with your father's letter beside me. Two or three days later I asked the nurses for pencil and paper.'

~

Lili and Miklós were assigned to the second transport of Hungarian returnees, in June 1946. They flew from Stockholm to Prague and caught a train to Budapest the same day.

They held hands in the crowded compartment. After they crossed the border into Hungary my father got up, with an apologetic smile, and made his way to the tiny, filthy toilet and locked the door. As usual his thermometer was in his pocket in its elegant metal case. The train rattled along on the newly repaired track. Miklós stuck the thermometer in his mouth, shut his eyes and clung to the doorhandle. He tried to count to 130 in time to the clattering of the wheels. When he got to ninety-seven he glanced up, and in the cracked mirror above the basin he saw a thin, unshaven man in glasses and an oversized jacket with a thermometer pressed between his lips. He peered closely at the mirror image. Was this what he'd see for the rest of his life? This cowardly looking fellow hooked on his thermometer?

He came to a decision. Without looking at the level of the quicksilver, he yanked the thermometer out of his mouth and chucked it down the toilet. He threw the metal case in as well. Then, determined and angry, he flushed twice.

By nine o'clock on that June evening in 1946 a huge crowd was gathered at Keleti station, even though this was a special train and its arrival hadn't been announced on the radio. But the word had got round. Lili's mother, for instance, heard about the train on the number six tram. A woman in a headscarf had yelled the news down the tramcar during the afternoon rush hour. She also had a daughter coming home after nineteen months away.

Lili was wearing a red polka-dotted dress; during the spring she had begun to put on weight and was now seventy kilos. Miklós's trousers still hung off him; he left Sweden weighing fifty-three kilos. They travelled in the last carriage.

My father stepped onto the platform first, carrying the two suitcases. Mama rushed over to Lili and they hugged each other without speaking. Then she hugged Miklós, who had no family to meet him.

Lili's mother hoped that her husband would make it back. The truth was, however, that Sándor Reich, suitcase salesman, returning home from Mauthausen concentration camp, found his way into a storeroom filled with food. He ate smoked sausage and bacon and was taken to hospital that same night. Two days later he died from a ruptured bowel.

It was a dusty, humid evening. Lili, her mother and Miklós wandered through the excited crowd. They couldn't stop looking at each other. They were at home together.

For the next two years I was in the making, silent and yearning.

Epilogue

MY PARENTS, Miklós and Lili, wrote to each other for six months, between September 1945 and February 1946, before they were married in Stockholm.

Until my father died in 1998, I had no idea the letters still existed. Then, with hope and uncertainty in her eyes, my mother gave me two neat bundles of envelopes bound in silk ribbon, one cornflower blue, the other scarlet.

I was familiar with the story of how they met. 'Your father swept me off my feet with his letters,' my mother would say, and make that charming wry face of hers. She might mention Sweden, that misty, icy enigmatic world at the edge of the map.

But for fifty years I did not know that their letters still existed. In the midst of political upheaval and the chaos of moving to new apartments, my parents had carted them around without ever talking about them. They were preserved by being invisible. The past was locked up in an elegant box it was forbidden to open.

Now I could no longer ask my father about what happened. My mother answered most of my questions with a shrug. *It was a long time ago. You know how shy your father was. We wanted to forget.*

Why? How could they forget a love so wonderfully uninhibited and so splendidly gauche that it still shines? If there were difficult moments in my parents' marriage—and every marriage has its share of them—why didn't they ever untie the ribbons to remind themselves of how they found each other? Or can we allow ourselves a more sentimental line of questioning? In their fifty-two-year relationship wasn't there a moment when time stood still? When the angels passed through the room? When one of them, out of pure nostalgia, longed to dig out the bundles hidden at the back of the bookcase, the testimony of how they met and fell in love?

Of course, I know the answer: there was no moment like that.

~

In one of his letters my father writes that he is planning a novel. He wanted to describe the collective horror of being transported to a German concentration camp—a book (*The Long Voyage*) Jorge Semprún later wrote instead of him.

Why didn't he ever get down to writing it?

I can guess the answer. My father arrived home in June 1946. His younger sister was his only living relative, and his parents' house had been bombed. His past had evaporated. His future, however, was taking shape. He became a journalist and started writing for a left-wing paper. Then, one day early in the 1950s, he found his desk had been moved outside the editorial office.

When exactly did my father lose his faith in communism? I don't know. But by the time of the show trial of László Rajk in 1949 it must have been shattered. And during the revolution in 1956 my parents were concerned primarily with the possibility of emigrating.

I remember my father standing in desperation in our kitchen, which was reeking as usual with the smell of boiling sheets. 'Do you want me to wash dishes for the rest of my life? Is that what you want?' he hissed at my mother.

They stayed.

During the Kádár era, between 1956 and 1988, my father became a respected foreign-affairs journalist. He was founder and deputy editor of *Magyarország*, a quality weekly newspaper. He never wrote the novel about the journey in the railway wagon, and he stopped writing poetry.

This leads me to record the sad fact that in my father's hands neither his own experiences nor those of his companions in distress became a literary work.

I'm convinced that the idea of a new future, the belief that grew into a religion at the beginning, was later cancelled out by his resigned submission to the political circumstances that undermined his aspirations as a writer too. This proves that talent alone is not enough. It doesn't hurt to have luck in life as well.

But my parents took great care of the letters. That's what matters. They kept them safe, until my mother's decision and my father's approving wave from the next world allowed them to reach me.

About the Author

Péter Gárdos is an award-winning Hungarian film director. *Fever at Dawn* is his first novel and is based on the true story of his parents. It has been made into a film in Hungary, and is being published in thirty territories around the world.

Fever at Dawn
Reading Group Questions

1. Discuss the author's decision to narrate the novel from Miklós's son's perspective. Why does the son narrate from his father's perspective? At what point do you know who the narrator's mother is? What kind of narrative distance does this create and how did it affect your reading?

2. The events of the novel are based on a true story. Did you know this before you started reading? How did it affect your reading of the story? Why do you think the author chose to write this as a novel instead of as nonfiction?

3. Did you learn anything new historically in reading this novel? What surprised you?

4. Why did Miklós persist in writing his letters? What did they mean to him?

5. The opening chapter depicts 'an army of women' on bicycles delivering freshly baked biscuits for the survivors arriving in Sweden. What other random acts of kindness are described in the novel? How do these contribute to the novel as a whole?

6. The author, Péter Gárdos, is also a filmmaker. Where could you see evidence of this in the writing?

7. The doctor gives Miklós very specific measures to guide him toward health: weight, temperature, X-ray results. How does this contrast with Miklós's nature as a poet? What does his temperature

each morning come to mean to him – i.e. why is the novel called 'Fever at Dawn'?

8. What are Miklós's politics before and after the war? Does Lili share these views? Do his fellow Hungarians, or the Swedes? (Does it matter?)

9. Talk about the idea of hope. What does it do for Miklós and Lili? How does hope help (or harm) us as humans in such extreme situations? Are there any other stories of hope that this story reminded you of?

10. After Lili and Miklós finally meet, the author writes, 'But they never spoke about certain important things. Neither then, nor later.' Why do you think they both silently, but mutually, agreed to do this? What do you think avoiding these topics meant for them and their relationship?

11. Lili and Miklós each have their own group of friends that they confide in about the letters. How did these friendships affect their letter-writing and relationship? And how were Lili and Miklós's friends influenced by their love story?

12. Why do you think Judit betrayed Lili to the Rabbi? Why didn't she want Lili and Miklós to get together? Were you sympathetic to her at all? How do you think the traumatic events she's suffered affect her choices here? How did their experiences of the war change – or not – all of these characters?

13. What role do you think humour plays in Lili and Miklós's relationship?

The Mistress of My Fate

Hallie Rubenhold

THE CONFESSIONS OF HENRIETTA LIGHTFOOT
There is much to be learned from a woman of her sort . . .

England, 1789. The Bastille has fallen, King George is mad, and Henrietta Lightfoot flees her home at Melmouth Park after a suspicious death, for which she is blamed. She has no life experience, little money and only her true love, Lord Allenham, to whom she can turn . . .

When he suddenly goes missing, Henrietta embarks on a journey through London's debauched and glittering underworld in the hope of finding him, but discovers more about herself and her mysterious past than she imagined. With the assistance of a sisterhood of courtesans, her skills at the card table and on the stage, the unstoppable Henrietta is ready to become mistress of her fate.

'A remarkable picture of a fascinating age'
DAILY EXPRESS

'A full-blooded historical romp'
INDEPENDENT

'Ricochets with energy, witty observation and rollicking pace'
EASY LIVING

The Ballroom

Anna Hope

1911: Inside an asylum at the edge of the Yorkshire moors, where men and women are kept apart by high walls and barred windows, there is a ballroom, vast and beautiful. For one bright evening every week, they come together and dance.

When John and Ella meet, it is a dance that will change two lives for ever.

'Moving, fascinating'
The Times

'A tender and absorbing love story'
Daily Mail

'Heartbreaking and insightful'
Sunday Express

'Fiction at its finest . . . the reader is utterly transported'
Irish Independent

Longbourn

Jo Baker

'If Elizabeth Bennet had the washing of her own petticoats,' Sarah thought, 'she would be more careful not to tramp through muddy fields.'

It is wash-day for the housemaids at Longbourn House, and Sarah's hands are chapped and raw. Domestic life below stairs, ruled with a tender heart and an iron will by Mrs Hill the housekeeper, is about to be disturbed by the arrival of a new footman, bearing secrets and the scent of the sea.

'A triumph: a splendid tribute to Austen's original, but, more importantly, a joy in its own right'
GUARDIAN

'A fascinating insight into the harsh working conditions of life in a grand house two hundred years ago'
GOOD HOUSEKEEPING

'Superb . . . The lightest of touches by a highly accomplished young writer of whom more, surely, will be heard'
MAIL ON SUNDAY

The Finding of Martha Lost

Caroline Wallace

Martha is lost.

She's been lost since she was a baby, abandoned in a suitcase on the train from Paris to Liverpool. Ever since, she's waited at the station lost property office for someone to claim her. It's been sixteen years, but she's still hopeful.

In the meantime, there are lost property mysteries to solve: a suitcase that may have belonged to the Beatles, for one. And that stuffed monkey that keeps appearing. But there is one mystery Martha has never been able to solve – until anonymous letters start to arrive, offering clues to the past she longs to know.

Time is running out, though. The authorities have found out about the girl in lost property, and if Martha can't discover who she really is, she will lose everything . . .

'Charming, magical and beautifully imagined'
CARYS BRAY

'A charming, quirky tale'
WOMAN & HOME

'If you love the films *Amelie* or *Hugo*, you will adore this magical modern fairytale'
ESSENTIALS MAGAZINE

Five Rivers Met on a Wooded Plain

Barney Norris

'There exists in all of us a song waiting to be sung which is as heart-stopping and vertiginous as the peak of the cathedral. That is the meaning of this quiet city, where the spire soars into the blue, where rivers and stories weave into one another, where lives intertwine.'

One quiet evening in Salisbury, the peace is shattered by a serious car crash. At that moment, the lives of five people collide – a flower-seller, a schoolboy, an army wife, a security guard, a widower – all facing their own personal disasters. As one of those lives hangs in the balance, Norris draws the extraordinary voices of these seemingly ordinary people together into a web of love, grief, disenchantment and hope that is startlingly perceptive about the human heart.

'Wonderful . . . I was hooked from the first page. It's the real stuff'
MICHAEL FRAYN

'Remember the name Barney Norris. He's a new writer in his mid-twenties, but already outstanding'
THE TIMES

The Book Thief

Markus Zusak

1939. Nazi Germany. The country is holding its breath. Death has never been busier.

Liesel, a nine-year-old girl, is living with a foster family on Himmel Street. Her parents have been taken away to a concentration camp. Liesel steals books.

This is her story and the story of the inhabitants of her street when the bombs begin to fall.

Features special bonus content, including manuscript pages, original sketches and pages from the author's notebook.

'Extraordinary'
SUNDAY TELEGRAPH

'Brilliant and hugely ambitious'
NEW YORK TIMES

'This is a novel of breathtaking scope, masterfully told'
GUARDIAN

The Boy in the Striped Pyjamas

John Boyne

What happens when innocence is confronted by monstrous evil?

Nine-year-old Bruno knows nothing of the Final Solution and the Holocaust. He is oblivious to the appalling cruelties being inflicted on the people of Europe by his country. All he knows is that he has been moved from a comfortable home in Berlin to a house in a desolate area where there is nothing to do and no one to play with. Until he meets Shmuel, a boy who lives a strange parallel existence on the other side of the adjoining wire fence and who, like the other people there, wears a uniform of striped pyjamas.

Bruno's friendship with Shmuel will take him from innocence to revelation. And in exploring what he is unwittingly a part of, he will inevitably become subsumed by the terrible process.

'An extraordinary tale of friendship and the horrors of war seen through the eyes of two young boys . . . raw literary talent at its best'
IRISH INDEPENDENT

'Overwhelmingly powerful . . . This is a story so exceptional and vivid that it cannot be erased from the mind'
CAROUSEL